A WAY WITH MURDER

A WAY WITH MURDER

R.J. JAGGER

PEGASUS CRIME

NEW YORK LONDON

A WAY WITH MURDER

Pegasus Books LLC
80 Broad Street, 5th Floor
New York, NY 10004

First Pegasus Books cloth edition August 2012

Interior design by Maria Fernandez

Library of Congress Cataloging-in-Publication Data is available.

ISBN: 978-1-60598-363-9

10 9 8 7 6 5 4 3 2 1

Printed in the United States of America
Distributed by W. W. Norton & Company

For Eileen

A WAY WITH MURDER

1

MONDAY MORNING EVERYTHING IN BRYSON Wilde's life changed. It happened when he was in his office, pacing next to the windows with coffee in one hand and a smoke in the other. It happened when the door opened and a woman walked in.

She wasn't dressed to impress.

Down below were sandals and up top was a baseball cap, slightly tilted to the side, with a dishwater blond ponytail hanging out the back. Between the two was an uneventful pair of loose cotton pants and a plain white blouse.

She looked to be about twenty-three or twenty-four.

Her eyes were lagoon blue.

Her face was mysteriously hypnotic.

Her body was curvy.

"I'm in trouble," she said. "I was hoping you could help me."

Wilde tapped a smoke out of the pack and handed it to her.

She took it and said, "Thanks."

He lit her up from his.

"What's your name?"

"Secret," she said. "Secret St. Rain."

"I've never seen you around town."

"I'm not from here."

"Too bad. So what kind of trouble are you in, Secret St. Rain?"

She blew smoke.

It was the sexiest thing Wilde had ever seen.

"I guess I should rephrase it," she said. "I'm not sure if I'm in trouble or not. I guess that's what I want you to find out—whether I am or not."

WILDE TOOK ONE LAST DRAG on the Camel, which brought the fire as close to his fingertips as the law allowed, then flicked the butt out the window.

Damn it.

That was a bad habit.

Alabama had told him a hundred times to not do that.

He leaned out to be sure it hadn't landed on anyone down at street level.

To his disbelief, there it was smack dab on the top of a gray Fedora, moving down the street compliments of a man who didn't have a clue.

"Hey, you!"

The man looked around but not up.

"Your hat's on fire."

Wilde ducked out of sight as the man looked up.

"Sorry about that," he told Secret. "Tell me what's going on."

SECRET PULLED A PAPER OUT of her purse, unfolded it, and handed it to Wilde. It was a page out of the *Rocky Mountain News*, Saturday edition. She tapped her finger on an article titled "Woman Falls to Death."

"Did you hear about this?"

No.

He hadn't.

"Read it," she said.

He did.

It was a short piece about a woman in a red dress who was found horribly smashed at the base of a building on Curtis Street, the victim of a fall, on Friday night. Police were investigating the incident as a possible homicide.

When Wilde looked up, Secret said, "I was there when it happened, down below on the sidewalk."

"Really?"

She nodded.

"Interesting."

"Isn't it?"

"So what happened? Did she jump, or what?"

"She didn't jump," Secret said. "Someone was dangling her over the edge, holding her by the hands, then he let her go."

"Ouch."

"She almost landed on me," Secret said. "Here's the problem. It was murder. The guy who dropped her was just a black silhouette to me. There were no lights shining up there. I have no idea who he was."

"Okay."

"The opposite isn't true, though," she said. "I was under a pretty strong streetlight."

Wilde tapped two more sticks out of the pack, lit them both, and handed one to Secret.

She took it, mashed her old one in the ashtray, and said, "Thanks."

"So you're a witness to a murder," Wilde said. "That's what it comes down to."

She nodded.

"I want to know if the guy saw my face good enough to recognize me," she said.

Wilde frowned.

"How am I supposed to figure that out?"

"I've been thinking about it," she said. "First figure out who he is. Then we'll arrange a situation where I walk past him or get in his vicinity; what I'm talking about is a situation where he looks at me."

"All right."

"You'll be there off to the side," she said. "When he looks at me, you look at him and see if there's a reaction. See if he recognizes me."

Wilde shrugged.

"There will be a reaction," he said. "I can already tell you that."

She blew smoke.

"You're too kind. What we do is see if he tries to follow me. We see if he tries to kill me. If he does, that means he's the killer. At that point we can tell the police."

"So you're looking to trap him?"

"He'll trap himself is a better way to put it."

Wilde took a sip of coffee.

"Why me? Why not just do this with the police?"

She shook her head.

"This can't get screwed up." She pulled an envelope out of her purse and handed it to him. "That's a retainer."

Wilde felt the weight.

It was solid.

2

DAY ONE
JULY 21, 1952
MONDAY MORNING

WAVERLY PAIGE WOKE UP MONDAY morning slightly numbed from too much wine and too many wee hours last night. She popped two aspirin, got the coffee pot going, and studied her face in the mirror while the shower warmed up.

It was a train wreck.

Her apartment was too.

It was a hole in the wall in the low-rent district on the north edge of the city where the buses hardly went. Her particular unit was a fourth-floor walkup with one window that looked directly into the wall of another apartment building thirty feet away. Outside her window was the only good thing about the place, namely a fire escape that was twenty degrees cooler than her couch.

That's where she drank the wine last night.

That's where she woke up this morning, on an air mattress next to the only living thing she ever owned, a potted geranium.

She got herself into as good as shape as she could and headed for the bus stop.

She was a reporter with *The Metro Beat*, which in turn was the third dog in a pack of three, slightly behind the *Rocky Mountain News* and

a long way behind *The Denver Post*. It had an excuse for being last, namely that it was only two years old. Unfortunately there was only enough local food to keep two dogs alive. One of the three would have to die, probably within the next year.

Waverly didn't worry about it too much.

She had a few good things going for her.

She was young, only twenty-one.

She was healthy and well proportioned, not too tall, not too short, not too heavy, not too thin. Her thighs and ass were tight and strong. She could run the hundred-yard dash in eleven seconds, faster than most boys.

Her face would never be on the cover of a magazine, but it was pretty enough for daily life in Denver.

SHE GOT TO THE MORNING status conference ten minutes late, which was a big no-no. Fifteen faces looked at her, then almost as one turned to see what Shelby Tilt—the owner—would do. The man scrunched his fifty-year-old face into a wad and blew cigar smoke.

"Okay guys, that's it," he said. Then to Waverly, "Step into my office for a minute."

She recognized the tone.

This wouldn't be pretty.

3

DAY ONE
JULY 21, 1952
MONDAY MORNING

DAYTON RIVER LIVED ON A 22-acre railroad spur at the west edge of Denver that he had bought from BNSF two years ago. The property had no buildings. It consisted solely of dilapidated excess track that had been unused and unneeded for some time given the

movement of industry to the north. Three decommissioned boxcars sat on a track. Three others sat on a parallel track, thirty feet
distant. A canvas canopy, something in the nature of a circus tent,
was strung across the middle boxcars.

The interiors of the boxcars had been converted to living quarters,
to the point of even torching out holes to install windows.

One was a bedroom.

One was a bathroom.

One was a kitchen.

One was a living room.

One was storage.

One had nothing inside and was kept locked.

Down the track, active BNSF switching took place. Hundred-foot sec-
tions of track had been removed to prevent unintended travel into River's
property. Stoppers had also been placed at the end of the active tracks.

The setup fit River's six-three, Tarzan-like frame nicely.

The clanging of switching operations woke him at dawn Monday
morning. He took a long heaven-sent piss, splashed water on his face, drank
two larges glasses of water, then headed outside shirtless for a run.

He normally went five miles.

The distance didn't change that often.

What did change was the speed, depending on how he felt.

Today he was strong.

His hair swung back and forth. It was pitch-black and thick and
hung halfway down his back.

He headed down the track and got into a steady rhythm, letting his
legs stretch and his lungs burn. The pace was good, five-minute miles
or better.

Every so often he stopped for a warrior routine.

Three sets of a hundred pushups.

Five sets of twenty pull-ups.

One set of three hundred sit-ups.

WHEN HE GOT BACK HE spotted an envelope on the ground under
the boxcar. The edges had tape. It must have been taped on his door
at one point and fallen off. He opened it. Inside was a piece of paper

with typewriting. It came from the same machine as always, with the
S slightly higher than it should be.

> Alexa Blank
> 937 Clarkson, Denver, CO
> 21, strawberry hair, medium height
> Waitress at the Down Towner
> Standard commission
> Take her by Monday night. Store her someplace safe and
> wait for further instructions. Do not kill her until and unless
> you are told. Timing is crucial.

He didn't know when it initially got delivered but did know one
thing—the deadline was tonight. He burned the paper, showered,
hopped on the Indian, and headed for the Down Towner. It was time
to have a look at his target, Alexa Blank.

He'd take her tonight after dark.

Before then, he needed to find a place to stash her.

4

DAY ONE
JULY 21, 1952
MONDAY MORNING

WILDE'S OFFICE WAS IN THE 1500 block of Larimer Street, once the
heart of Denver, now an unhealthy conspiracy of liquor stores, bars,
gambling houses, brothels, and flophouses. He was thirty-one and
wore his hair combed straight back. It was blond, thick, longer than
most and played well against his green eyes and Colorado tan. He wore
his usual attire, namely a gray suit, a white long-sleeve shirt rolled up
at the cuffs, a loose blue tie, and spit-shined wingtips.

His hat, ashen-gray, was over on the rack.

When he went out it would go on, dipped over his left eye.

With a strong body topping out at six-two, he had no problem making women stare.

He pulled a book of matches out of the desk drawer, lit one, and set the pack on fire. He held the fire in front of his face and watched Secret through the flames as she headed up the street and disappeared around the corner.

Lightning was in his veins.

It was a feeling he hadn't had in a while.

He now realized how much he missed it.

The door opened and Alabama Winger walked in wearing a pre-caffeine face. She was twenty-three or twenty-four. Wilde had hired her as a Girl Friday last month after she didn't kill him—a separate story in and of itself. She was the only Girl Friday in Denver who couldn't type. To be fair, she disclosed it right after Wilde hired her.

She was slightly on the smaller side and scrubbed up pretty good when she got the urge. Temporarily, she was staying with Wilde at his place.

She headed for the coffee pot, poured a cup, and studied Wilde's face as she took a slurp.

"You're already up to no good," she said.

"How can you tell?"

"I don't know, I just can."

He blew smoke.

"A woman got dropped off a roof this weekend," he said. "She was wearing a short red dress. Have you heard about her?"

No.

She hadn't.

"So what?"

"So, we're going to find out who did it."

"Why?"

"Because it's our new case."

"Someone actually hired you?"

"Funny," he said. "What I want you to do this morning is go out and buy a sexy short dress. Get one of those French garter belts too, and a pair of nylons with a seam up the back."

"A sexy short dress?"

Wilde inhaled, held the smoke then blew a ring.

"It's not for you. Take that look off your face."

"What do you mean, not for me? It's too late for take-backs, Wilde. I already pictured myself wearing it. You can't just yank it off me."

Wilde pictured it and smiled.

"It's for our new client," he said. "Her name's Secret St. Rain."

Alabama tilted her head.

"It sounds like it's more for you than her."

"There's probably some truth in there," he said. "Make the dress black. Be sure it shows lots of cleavage and lots of leg. Get a bra too, something lacy. Deliver everything to Room 318 at the Clemont, that's where she's staying. If she answers, tell her I'll be picking her up at 7:30. If she doesn't answer, leave a note to that effect."

"Does she have a size, this woman?"

She did.

Wilde described her.

"Oh, get some black high-heels too," he said. "I almost forgot."

"What do you want me to get for myself?"

"Nothing."

Alabama shook her head.

"It can't be done, then," she said. "I can't be that close to new clothes without getting something. It's physically impossible."

Wilde frowned.

He could argue but he'd lose.

"All right, get one thing for yourself. Only one thing, though."

"A dress."

"Fine," he said. "Not the same one though."

"You'll have yanking rights on it," she said.

"You're bad."

"Yes, I am."

SHE WAS ALMOST OUT THE door when she turned and said, "The woman who got dropped off the roof, you said she was wearing a short red dress, right?"

He nodded.

"Are you setting our new client up as bait?"

"No."

"Are you sure?"

"Positive," he said.

"Maybe subconsciously?"

"No, neither," he said. "The more I think about it, don't make your dress red. I don't want to find out later that that's what triggers this guy."

She shrugged.

"I don't mind," she said. "I'll be bait if you want."

He put a look on his face.

"Don't even talk like that."

"Fine."

"I'm serious."

She studied his face and then smiled. "You never said anything about panties. Do you want me to get panties for her or not?"

He did.

"What color?"

He pictured it.

"Black."

"You're so evil," she said. "By the way, no one's named Secret."

"She is."

"Trust me, no one is," Alabama said. "Not me, not you, not her. It's a fake name. My advice is to find out why before you get in too deep with her."

5

DAY ONE

JULY 21, 1952

MONDAY MORNING

THE *BEAT* WAS HOUSED IN a three-story, 62-year-old brick building on Curtis Street that was an affront to every building code known to man. It was still standing, but not by much. Everything was there—the offices, the printing presses, the distribution hub, the vans, everything. Except for the areas where the ink permeated the air, the place smelled like a bad cigar. Most of that could be attributed to Shelby Tilt, the owner, who was everywhere all the time and never without his nasty little habit in his nasty little mouth.

His office was on the second floor, cantilevered over the presses. The wall on the press side wasn't actually a wall, it was a opening where a wall had once stood, together with a guardrail to keep dumb asses from falling off.

The noise of the presses, when they ran, was deafening.

Tilt liked it that way.

They were the sound of money.

Right now they weren't running.

The space wasn't big. What it lacked in volume was made up for in clutter. Tilt's desk probably had a surface but no one had ever seen it.

Waverly sat in a worn chair in front of the desk.

Tilt mashed the stub of a cigar in the ashtray and lit another. His forehead—the gateway to a bald top—wrinkled up.

"I'm going to pose a situation to you that you can either accept or decline," he said. "Whatever you decide, there are no repercussions. I want you to be clear on that, there are absolutely no repercussions whatsoever. That means you can say no, you're not interested, and nothing is going to happen to you. Do you understand?"

"Okay, then, *no*," she said and headed for the door.

Then she smiled and came back.

"Had you going."

He took a deep puff and blew a ring.

"Keep this on the down-low, but we're in serious financial trouble around here," he said.

"I thought we were doing good."

"We are, for the time we've been at it," he said. "The problem is we're running out of time. The paper's been losing money since it started. At the rate our circulation is growing, we'll be profitable in six months. The problem is that I can't keep making up the difference for that long. We need to get our circulation numbers up and get 'em up now, otherwise we're a done dog."

"Ouch."

Right.

Ouch.

"Keep it confidential," he said.

Sure.

No problem.

"I don't get why you're telling me this," she said.

"Here's the reason," he said. "Before I propose what I'm about to propose, remember that you can say no."

She tilted her head.

"You're like a vibrator on slow speed," she said.

HE GOT UP, WALKED TO the railing, and looked at the presses. "I love that junk down there," he said. "I really do. We need some big stories. That's how we can get our circulation up."

Waverly nodded.

"Like what?"

"Like getting out in front of the news instead of just reporting it," he said. "There was a woman who ended up taking a dive off a building Friday night, just two blocks up the street. The word is that she was wearing a short red dress. Did you hear about her?"

Waverly nodded.

She had.

"The police don't know if it was a suicide or she got pushed off or what," he said. "I have reason to believe she was dangled over the side and then dropped."

Waverly wrinkled her face.

"Why do you say that?"

Tilt lowered his voice.

"I'm going to tell you something, but I don't want you to repeat it. Before I came to Denver and started the *Beat*, I worked for a paper in San Francisco."

Right.

Waverly knew that.

"About three years ago, I got assigned to cover a small matter," he said. "It was a woman in a short red dress who ended up taking a dive off a building, same as we have here."

He stopped talking and waited for Waverly to process the information.

The implications hit her.

"So what are you saying, that this is some kind of a serial thing?"

He nodded.

"Exactly. That's why it will be such a big story if we can break it."

"Wow."

Right.

Wow.

"Now," he said, "my offer to you is to find out who's doing it. That's your assignment if you want it. Be clear, though, it's risky. If you start snooping around and closing in on the guy, and he finds out, well, you do the math. That's why you can say no and there won't be any repercussions. In fact, my advice to you is to say no. My advice is to say, *Screw you, Tilt. Are you crazy?*"

She exhaled.

"Can I think about it until tomorrow?"

"Of course."

She smiled.

"Just kidding," she said. "Of course I want it."

He studied her.

"Okay," he said. "But don't go and get yourself killed. I don't want to spend the rest of my life hating myself."

"Why not? Everyone else does."

"Not funny," he said.

Then he laughed.

6

DAY ONE
JULY 21, 1952
MONDAY MORNING

RIVER PARKED THE INDIAN TWO blocks from the Down Towner and swung over on foot to see what his little target Alexa Blank looked like. No waitresses matching her description came into view after two passes. A third pass would be risky. Going inside was out of the question. He headed back to the Indian and drove south out of the city.

He needed a place to keep her.

It needed to be secluded.

The miles clicked off.

The city gave way to less city which gave way to no city.

An abandoned barn or structure would work. Sunshine was everywhere, pure and uncompromised. Yellow-winged butterflies dotted the sides of the road. The air was warm.

A narrow dirt road appeared up ahead.

River stopped at the base and gave it a look.

It was choked with weeds.

Whatever it had been used for, it wasn't used for it anymore.

The world had abandoned it.

He turned in and drove far enough to get the Indian out of sight. Then he shut it down and continued on foot. If it turned out to be useful, he didn't want to fill it up with motorcycle tracks.

The topography rolled, a prelude to the foothills three miles to the west.

In typical Colorado prairie style, trees were almost non-existent except for the occasional scraggly pinion pine. Tall grasses and rabbit brush ruled, dotted with sharp-pointed yucca and small hidden cactuses. Rattlesnakes were at home here.

River loved the city.

He loved the noise and smoke and buzz, the danger, the anxiety and desperation, the beauty and opportunity, the night neon and the early-morning shadows.

He was equally at home out here.

This is where the real men met the world.

It was raw and unforgiving, there for the taming.

Back in the day, River could have been one of those tamers. He could have been one of the persons who boarded a wooden ship and headed for the horizon, not knowing if anything was out there except a slow descent into starvation.

It was in his genes.

THE PRESENT ASSIGNMENT WAS GOING to be tricky. River was supposed to take the target—Alexa Blank—but not kill or harm her until and unless given orders. That conceivably meant that he might be told to release her at some point. He couldn't do that if she saw his face. That was the tricky part, staying anonymous.

He could wear a mask but that would only partially solve the problem.

There was still the issue of his body, both the warrior physique and the height.

Baggy clothes, he'd need those for sure.

Also, there was his voice. How could he disguise that? The only positive way to do it would be to never speak. That would be impossible. He'd need to give the woman orders.

Complicated, that's what it was.

Too complicated.

Too complicated for the standard commission at any rate.

He'd renegotiate at the first chance.

UP AHEAD SOMETHING APPEARED ON the horizon that wasn't part of the landscape. It looked like a rusty metal remnant of some type.

Another appeared.

Then another.

There were dozens of them.

It was some kind of machinery graveyard, mostly old farm machinery and truck hulks from the looks of it.

Interesting.

He picked up the pace.

As he walked a thought came to him. If the woman did end up seeing his face, he could have her die by a rattlesnake bite. He could say it wasn't his fault, just nature at work.

7

DAY ONE
JULY 21, 1952
MONDAY MORNING

THE DEAD WOMAN IN THE red dress was someone named Charley-Anna Blackridge. The phone book had her listed at 1331 Clayton in near-east Denver. Wilde headed over in the MG, parked two blocks away, and doubled back on foot, intending to break in and find out who was in her life before the night in question. The house was a small brick bungalow with no driveway or garage, jammed in the middle of an endless sea of the same. Wilde knocked on the front door to be sure no one was home before heading around back.

Something happened he hadn't expected.

The door opened.

A woman in her early twenties appeared. The knock had woken her up. Her hair was tossed. Sleep was thick in her eyes. She wore a pink T-shirt that covered her ass but not by much.

"Sorry to wake you," Wilde said.

She studied him.

"Are you a cop?"

"No, a PI."

"Are you here about Charley-Anna?"

He was.

"Come on in but don't expect much," she said. "I don't know anything. You got a cigarette?"

He did.

He did indeed.

THE WOMAN TURNED OUT TO be 22-year-old Alley Bender, the dead woman's roommate who was, in fact, wearing something under the T, namely white panties that flashed with regularity. She reminded Wilde a little of Night Neveraux, his high school squeeze.

"We were out dancing Friday night at a couple of clubs," she said. "The last one we were at was a place called the El Ray Club. I met a guy a little after midnight and we ended up leaving. Charley-Anna had her eye on a guy and said she was going to stick around. That was the last I saw of her."

"Who was the guy?"

"That I left with?"

"No, the one Charley-Anna had her eye on."

The woman shrugged.

"I didn't know him," she said.

"Did she point him out?"

"Yeah, but he wasn't anyone I knew."

"Describe him."

Her eyes faded to the distance, then back.

"He reminded me of Robert Mitchum. He had that same dimple in the chin and those same bedroom eyes."

"Robert Mitchum, huh?"

Right.

Robert Mitchum.

"He was nice looking," she said. "Too nice looking. He had more than his fair share of women gawking at him. There was no danger he was going to end up going home alone, that's for sure."

"Did he talk to Charley-Anna?"

She shrugged.

"Not while I was there," she said. "What happened after I left, I don't know. Do you want to hear something strange?"

Yes.

He did.

"When they found her she was wearing a short red dress," she said. "That's not what she had on that night, though. She was wearing a black dress, a longer one with a slit up the side."

"Well, that's interesting."

"Isn't it?"

She brightened.

"Actually, I think I have a picture of her wearing the dress she had on that night. Do you want me to see if I can find it?"

"That would be great."

She drained the last of the coffee and stood up.

"I like your eyes," she said. "I've always been a sucker for green eyes."

WILDE WATCHED THE WOMAN WITH a half-eye as she dug through a metal cookie tin jammed with photos. Her knees were slightly open and her panties peeked out.

It wasn't an accident.

She knew exactly what she was doing.

Wilde pictured the two of them in bed.

The picture didn't last long though. It got squeezed out by Secret St. Rain.

8

DAY ONE
JULY 21, 1952
MONDAY MORNING

SHELBY TILT DIDN'T REMEMBER MUCH about the San Francisco case other than the red dress. He didn't even remember the dead woman's name. His file, if you could even call it that, was long gone.

"If you're serious about breaking this story," Waverly said, "then I'm going to say something that you're not going to want to hear."

"Like what?"

"Like I think I need to go to San Francisco."

Tilt frowned.

"Go there?"

"Right."

"That costs money," he said.

"I'll take the bus," she said.

Tilt shook his head.

"Stay here and work the Denver angle," he said. "The Denver stuff's fresh."

"Let the cops work the Denver angle," she said. "I'll get Johnnie Pants to feed it to me."

Tilt knew the name.

Pants was one of the homicide detectives.

"How are you going to get him to do that?"

"I'll give him a blowjob or something," Waverly said. "The point I'm trying to make is that if we're going to find a common denominator, we need to run down the San Francisco case. There's no way to do that except to go there."

Tilt puffed the cigar and blew a ring.

"If I get totally stupid and say okay, you'd need to do it on a shoe-string," he said. "You'd need to stay at the cheapest flophouse in town and not even think about eating anything more fancy than peanut butter and jelly. No cabs when you get there either. Take the trolley or the bus. Or better yet, walk." A pause, then: "There's a Chinese girl I know there named Su-Moon. Maybe you could stay with her. I'll give her a call."

"Who is she, an old girlfriend?"

"Sort of," he said. "She gives massages."

"She's a massage girl?"

"Don't say it like that," he said. "It's a legitimate profession."

"Does she give happy endings?"

He smiled.

"I'm taking the fifth on that." He got serious and added, "I'm going to go ahead with your plan partly because you're right that we need to run down the San Francisco connection and we can't do that from Denver. That's only ten percent of it though. The other ninety is because you'll be safer there. I'm still deciding whether I really have the right to put you at risk."

"The world's a risky place," she said. "We should be glad. Otherwise there wouldn't be anything to report."

TWO HOURS LATER, WAVERLY WAS sitting in the window seat of a shaky airliner as it left Denver in the rearview mirror and headed west over the mountains.

A small hastily packed suitcase was in the overhead bin.

In her purse was all the money Tilt could spare, a banana, and the phone number of a Chinese woman who gave happy endings.

9

DAY ONE
JULY 21, 1952
MONDAY MORNING

THE GRAVEYARD OF RUSTY HULKS had an eerie patina even in the daylight. Everything was ancient—thirty, forty, maybe even fifty years old. There was no evidence that anyone had visited the place in a long time. There were no pop cans or cigarette butts or empty rifle shells. It would be a great place for target practice or bonfires or to scare the high school girls after dark with ghost stories. If anything like that had happened in the last decade, there was no evidence of it.

There were a couple of good options.

One was an old combine.

River almost decided on it until something farther back caught his eye.

It turned out to be an old wrecked truck of some kind. The hood was gone and the engine compartment was gutted all the way to the firewall. The wheels and tires were gone; the undercarriage sat squat on the ground. The interesting part was the cargo box, about half the size of an eighteen-wheeler, with closed double doors at the back.

The handle was rusted in place.

River worked at it with a rock and a rusty metal bar for fifteen minutes before it got enough motion to open. The door hinges were tight but not enough to keep the door from opening.

The inside was empty.

Eight or ten drainage holes in the floor would allow enough air for breathing. There might be a better place somewhere in the universe to hold a person captive but River couldn't imagine where.

FROM THE GRAVEYARD HE HEADED to the target's house on Clarkson, parking three blocks away and walking past it on foot, then down the dirt alley that ran behind it.

That's where the cars got parked.

A few houses had small garages.

Some had overhangs.

Alexa Blank's house had neither.

A dirt path was beaten through scraggly brown grass between the rear door and the alley.

This is how he'd enter, from the back, right up that path.

The house had two stories.

The bedroom would be upstairs.

He didn't spend any time.

All he did was walk past, barely glancing at it. Two doors down he spotted an extension ladder on the ground near the house. Three houses farther down was a German shepherd on a ten-foot rope.

It barked as River walked past.

Damn dogs.

The world didn't need them.

Every one of them should be dead.

He'd take the woman tonight, sometime between one and two. That would give him plenty of time to get her to the graveyard in the thick of the night.

He'd be home before dawn.

HE HEADED HOME, OPENED THE padlock on the storage boxcar, and stepped inside. From the inventory he assembled the goodies he needed—three lengths of chain, an ankle iron, handcuffs, rope, padlocks, a blindfold, two flashlights, and an assortment of miscellaneous items.

Everything went into an army backpack.

He relocked the boxcar with the backpack inside, then headed down to the grocery store. There he purchased enough non-perishable food to keep someone alive for a week—beans, tuna, spaghetti, cookies, crackers, bread, peanut butter, jelly, toilet paper, toothpaste, aspirin, soap, hairbrush, water, pop, and the like.

Back home, all the grocery items went into the backpack.

Then he headed back to the graveyard, using the car this time. He parked on the shoulder two hundred yards down from the old abandoned road.

Wearing the backpack, he walked straight into the terrain until he was out of sight, then cut left until he intersected the dirt road.

The graveyard was just as he had left it.

He got everything situated, then sat down in the shade and went through tonight in his mind, playing out everything that could go wrong and outlining the best responses.

10

DAY ONE
JULY 21, 1952
MONDAY MORNING

CHARLEY-ANNA WASN'T SHORT IN the looks department. She'd have a chance at any guy she took a run at, including a Robert Mitchum type, especially in that black dress. Wilde headed over to the El Ray Club to see if anyone knew who Mitchum was. The front door was locked and the place was dark, but he headed around back just in case. A beer truck was parked behind the club and the back door was open. Inside, two men were in the basement stacking cases.

One had the barrel body and the tanned left arm of a truck driver.

The other was a scraggly guy.

A memory of sneaking down there one drunken Saturday night and screwing the socks off Mary Browning flashed briefly in Wilde's brain. He let it play for a few moments, then focused on the ratty looking guy.

"You work here?" Wilde asked.

Yes.

He did.

"I'm trying to find a guy who looks like Robert Mitchum," he said. "He was here Friday night."

"Don't know him."

"You never saw anyone like that?"

"I only work days."

"Okay," Wilde said. "Thanks."

He was almost to the steps when a voice came from behind him. "There's a night bartender who might know. Her name's Michelle Day. She lives over on Delaware just past Colfax."

"Thanks."

"If you wake her up, tell her Joey sent you," he said.

"I take it you're not too fond of her."

"No, not really." The man walked over and held his hand out. "That'll be a dollar."

Fair enough.

Wilde paid and headed upstairs for a phone book.

She was there—1732 Delaware.

HE DROVE A 1947 MG/TC named Blondie, British Racing Green over tan leather, a two-seat roadster only made from 1946 to 1949. The English steering wheel was on the wrong side and the vehicle didn't have bumpers or a heater or a radio or hardly any other amenities, but it did have a drop top and a Moss Magnacharger engine.

It also tended to make the women spread their legs ever so slightly when they sat in the passenger seat.

He took the top down.

The sunshine spilled in.

The drive to Michelle Day's house took hardly any time. He found a slot on the street for Blondie two doors down and headed back on foot.

The door was shut and the house was quiet.

If he knocked, he'd wake her.

That would be the second one today.

"One more reason I'm going to hell," he told himself.

Then he knocked.

No one answered.

No sounds or vibrations came from inside.

He knocked again, harder.

No answer.

He turned the knob just for grins and found it unlocked. He opened the door far enough to get his voice through and said, "Anyone home?"

No answer.

Louder, "Michelle, are you here?"

No answer.

He stepped inside, leaving the door open.

The place was trashed.

It wasn't the kind of trashed that came from sloppy house-keeping, it was the kind that came from someone tearing the place apart.

His pulse raced.

A quick search of the first floor turned up more disorder but no humans.

He headed upstairs two at a time.

11

THE GREEN DRAGON ORIENTAL MASSAGE TURNED out to be in the heart of Chinatown on the Street of Painted Balconies, which was an alley between Stockton and Grant. Waverly opened a metal mesh screen door and stepped into a dim red room with lots of plants, a koi pond and soft abstract music. Herbs scented the air. An Asian woman entered from the back through a barrier of hanging beads.

She was striking, exotic, about thirty, with a tiny waist and long black hair styled with bangs that hung a little too far over her eyes. Her body was wrapped in a full-length kimono. Her glance dropped to Waverly's suitcase then back up.

She walked over, pecked a kiss onto Waverly's lips and said, "You're prettier than I expected."

"You're Su-Moon?"

"I'm Su-Moon, Su-Sun, whoever you want me to be. Tilt says he's a big-shot owner of a paper now, is that true?"

"Mostly."

"That's because of me," Su-Moon said. "I wished him good karma. It always comes true."

"Why did you wish him good karma?"

"He was a good tipper," Su-Moon said.

"Tilt?"

Su-Moon nodded.

"Shelby Tilt?"

Right.

Him.

"There must be two guys with the same name."

SU-MOON LAUGHED, THEN HELD WAVERLY'S hands and looked her up and down. "Later I'll give you acupuncture—very, very sensual.

There's a deep part of you inside that you don't know about yet. You'll never be the same. I'll bring it out for you. No charge." She picked up Waverly's suitcase and said, "Follow me."

Through the beaded barrier was a long black hallway with doors painted cartoon colors. All were open except three. The moaning of a male voice came from behind one of the closed ones.

"I assume that's a happy ending," Waverly asked.

"A very happy ending," Su-Moon said. "Happy for us too. More money that way."

"What about the cops?"

"What about them?"

"They don't, you know, interfere?"

Su-Moon smiled.

"All the massage parlors are controlled by an organization," she said. "That organization puts money in the right hands to make sure things operate smoothly."

"What kind of organization? Like the mafia?"

"Basically yes," Su-Moon said. "Except all Asian, no outsiders. I don't own this place. The organization does. I only manage it. Right now we have three girls working. Tonight we'll have ten."

At the end of the hall was a door.

Su-Moon unlocked it, then relocked it after they passed through.

On the other side of it was a wooden stairway.

On the second floor was an apartment.

"This is where I live," Su-Moon said. "And now you."

The place was a throwback to another land and time, filled with all things Eastern, knickknacks and treasures, large and small.

"There's only one bed," Su-Moon said.

"I can sleep on the floor."

"It's big enough for two," Su-Moon said. "I don't mind sharing if you don't mind."

"Okay. Thanks again."

THEY HAD TEA.

Then Waverly got directions to the San Francisco Public Library and headed out.

Time was ticking.

12

DAY ONE

JULY 21, 1952

MONDAY AFTERNOON

RIVER GOT THE CHAINS AND ropes and supplies situated at the grave-yard and headed back across the topography under a warm Colorado sun. As his car came into sight something was wrong. The passenger door was open and some scumbag was inside ripping him off.

He broke into a sprint, a silent sprint, not shouting, not giving a warning.

There was nothing worth stealing.

That wasn't the issue.

The issue was respect.

Someone didn't respect him enough to leave his stuff alone.

That was a mistake.

If someone wanted to screw with him, fine, but do it to his face.

At least be a man about it.

Don't be a rat-faced sneak.

Rat-faced sneaks ended up dead.

Two choppers with narrow grips came into view at a standstill on the other side of the car. There were three figures total, a woman and two men, heavily tattooed, wearing leather vests and bandannas. The men looked strong even at a distance; the woman too, for that matter.

One would be no problem.

Two would be tricky but doable.

Three was pressing his luck.

If he was smart he'd just hang back and not give them the chance to screw up his life.

Let them go.

Concentrate on tonight.

It made sense but he couldn't get his feet to stop. He couldn't control the fire in his brain. He slowed a little so he wouldn't be totally winded when he got there, but he kept going.

Someone was about to get hurt.

THEY SPOTTED HIM CHARGING.

One of the men grabbed a six-foot length of chain from the back of a bike and whipped it through the air.

The man in the car pulled a knife and stepped out.

He was already in a warrior position.

The woman had something in her hand, too small to make out. River sensed a box-cutter. She picked a rock off the ground with her other hand.

"Come on, asshole!"

River stopped ten steps away.

The men were stronger than he thought.

They were dangerous.

He'd seen eyes like that before.

The man whipped the chain on the ground. Dirt exploded. They were already spreading out trying to box him in.

He backed up.

"Come on, asshole," the woman said. "Don't chicken out now."

13

DAY ONE
JULY 21, 1952
MONDAY MORNING

UPSTAIRS WILDE FOUND A NAKED woman laying face down in bed on the top of the sheets. She was flipped the wrong way with her head at the bottom and her feet by the pillow. Her arms were sprawled out, her right knee was up and her legs were spread. He approached slowly, trying to figure out if she was sleeping or dead. Her body had no movement and no sounds of breathing came from her mouth.

He was pretty sure she was dead even though he saw no blood or bruises.

Who did it?

Robert Mitchum?

Suddenly she moved.

Her head came up and flipped to the other side.

There was nothing wrong with her face.

It hadn't been stabbed or punched.

She hadn't been suffocated.

Her legs twisted around for a more comfortable position and then all movement stopped.

She was already back asleep.

Wilde stood coffin-quiet, breathing with an open mouth, letting her drift into an even deeper unconsciousness before he took a step. Just as he was about to tiptoe out, something bad happened. The woman rolled onto her back, raised her arms above her head and stretched. Her eyes opened but were faced the other way.

Four steps.

That's how far Wilde was in the room.

There was no way he'd get out without making a sound. The floor was wood, his shoes were leather, his body was heavy.

He didn't move, not a muscle.

Go back to sleep.

Go back to sleep.

Go back to sleep.

Suddenly the woman put a hand between her legs and massaged herself in a slow, steady motion. She closed her eyes and spread her knees.

It felt good.

Wilde was six feet away, directly behind the woman's head. If she turned her face even a bit, or looked up at the ceiling, she'd probably pick him up in her peripheral vision.

The tempo of her motion increased.

Her legs stiffened and spread even farther.

Wilde was just about to take a step back when the woman's eyes opened and pointed at the ceiling.

He didn't dare move.

Any movement would be detected.

The woman moaned.

14

DAY ONE
JULY 21, 1952
MONDAY AFTERNOON

THE SAN FRANCISCO PUBLIC LIBRARY had all the past ghosts of the *Chronicle* on microfiche in a musty old basement corner that was three times quieter than a tomb. If Waverly died there, no one would find her for a week. It took some time and eyestrain, but she eventually found a June 12, 1949 article titled *Woman Falls to Death,* reporting about a woman found at the base of a building in the downtown area early Saturday morning.

The cause of the fall was unknown.

The woman was 24-year-old Kava Every, an architect who worked at Bristol Design Group. She was an attractive blond with a white smile and a Haight Street address.

There was no mention of a red dress.

Shelby Tilt.

That was the reporter's name at the top of the article.

Waverly hunted down a librarian, got a copy of the microfiche printed for five cents, and headed out of the guts of the building into very welcome sunshine.

The air was in the low seventies, a good twenty degrees cooler than Denver, and had a salty hang to it.

It felt more like spring than summer.

From the library in the Civic Center, she hopped on a red Cal Cable trolley that took her into the downtown area on the east side of the city.

The buildings were taller than Denver.

The buzz was louder.

The traffic was faster.

SHE FOUND THE ADDRESS SHE was looking for, took the elevator to the third floor and got dumped in a vestibule. To the left was a copper door set in a glass cinderblock wall. Lights and movement on the other side distorted through the rounded glass bricks.

The place was hopping.

Above the door was red lettering.

Bristol Design Group.

She took a deep breath, opened the door and stepped in. The reception desk was cluttered with papers but had no human inhabitant in the chair. Waverly stood in front of it and waited.

A minute passed, then another.

Lots of men scurried around plus an occasional woman, but no one paid her any attention.

Then a man appeared from her left and handed her a ten-dollar bill. "Do me a favor," he said. "Run down to Murphy's and get me an Italian sausage with everything, plus an RC and a bag of chips."

He was in his mid-thirties and wore it well, in a rough, manly way.

His eyes were wolfen-blue.

He reminded her of a Marlboro billboard.

She looked down to see if he was wearing a ring. He wasn't, but his pinky finger was missing. She had a strange urge to touch the stub.

He must have seen the expression on her face because he said, "It got shot off. If you're temping for more than just today, I'll tell you about it some time. Are you?"

"Am I what?"

"Temping tomorrow too?"

She shrugged.

"I'm not sure yet."

Then she noticed something.

His shirt was buttoned wrong.

She unbuttoned the top button, re-buttoned it in the proper hole, and said, "Just follow my lead the rest of the way down."

He smiled.

"I can't believe nobody told me."

SHE SHOVED THE TEN IN her purse and headed for the elevator. Over her shoulder she heard, "Hey, what's your name?"

"Waverly Paige."
He was Sean.
Sean Waterfield.
He was happy to meet her.

15

DAY ONE
JULY 21, 1952
MONDAY AFTERNOON

RIVER DIDN'T WANT TO KILL the bikers, but that changed when the first knife swished past his head. They tried to surround him but he darted this way and that, forever elusive, leading them deeper and deeper into the terrain. They got more desperate, trying to get him in the middle. River bided his time and waited for his move.

Then it came.

One of the guys tripped over a rock and went down. River kicked him in the face, wrestled the knife away and stabbed it with full force into the side of the asshole's head.

The woman screamed and charged.

River backed up as if escaping then suddenly closed the gap with a leap forward and punched her in the face.

She went down, bloody, and curled into a ball.

Now there was one, the one with the chain, the big one.

"You're going to die, asshole," he said.

River pointed his index finger at the man and then moved it in a come-here motion.

"Come on and do it," he said.

The man charged and swung the chain with so much strength that River didn't dare grab it. He skirted it and got his footing.

The woman was getting to her feet.

"Stay down!" River said.

Her face was covered in blood.

The only clean part was the whites of her eyes.

She didn't stay down.

She couldn't.

She was insane with rage and charged.

River grabbed her, wrapped his arm around her neck and held her in front of him—a human shield. "Put the chain down and I'll let her go," he said. "We'll finish it fist to fist."

The chain didn't drop.

The man didn't move.

"Do it!" River said. "Do it or I'll snap her neck!"

"Screw you and screw her!"

He charged and swung the chain.

River dropped and forced the woman with him. The chain passed over their heads. Before the man could get it cocked again River got a hand on his arm and swung him to the ground.

A punch landed on his face with the force of a rock.

He tried to shake it off before another one came.

It didn't work.

A second one landed, so hard that the inside of River's head exploded in colors.

Then a third landed.

He was dying.

A few more and he'd be dead.

He made a desperate move to close the gap and get the man in a bear hug.

It worked.

The fists kept pounding but they were more on his back than his head and weren't full force. River kept the man locked in position until the explosions in his head softened, then he wrapped his arm around the man's neck.

At that second, they locked eyes.

The man made a desperate move, trying to twist.

It partially worked but not enough to get away.

River rolled and jerked with all his might.

The man's neck snapped, then he twitched for a few seconds and stopped moving.

RIVER ROLLED ONTO HIS STOMACH and closed his eyes.

The darkness felt like water.

Cool, cool water.

Blood was in his mouth.

The taste was strange but not necessarily bad.

He didn't mind it.

He'd earned it.

HE SAT UP TO SEE how far away from the road they were, which he guessed to be fifty or sixty or seventy steps, it was hard to tell. It was close enough that someone driving past could have seen the fight if they'd looked in this direction. They might have been able to tell that one of the fighters had long hair.

He didn't remember hearing any cars during the fight.

That was good but not conclusive.

Obviously he wasn't focused on the road.

Right now, in any event, there were no cars around. If someone had looked over, they hadn't bothered to hang around.

The biker woman was still on the ground, watching him with fearful eyes.

River walked over, extended his hand and helped her up.

"I'm not going to hurt you," he said, and headed for the road.

She fell into step.

Then she stopped and said, "Wait a minute."

She went back to the closest man, pulled a wallet out of his pants pocket and stuck it in hers. Then she did the same with the other one, the one with the chain. She hovered over him for a second, narrowed her eyes and then dropped a mouthful of spit onto his face.

"Okay," she said.

16

WILDE SILENTLY BACKED OUT OF the woman's bedroom when her thrashing and moaning got sufficiently loud, then he tiptoed down the stairs, ducked out the door and was gone.

Back at his office, he drank coffee and had a smoke.

He still needed to talk to her.

Should he head over now and knock on the door?

He pictured it.

No, she was too fresh in his mind.

He wouldn't be able to look her in the eyes.

So now what?

He struck a match and watched the smoke snake up. The sulfur smelled like sex and was just as addicting. He lit the whole book on fire and stared at the flames. They were always the same. They were predictable.

Secret St. Rain.

Who was she behind those haunting eyes?

Suddenly the door opened and a woman walked in.

It wasn't Secret.

It wasn't Alabama.

It was someone Wilde didn't know.

Their eyes locked, and in that brief moment Wilde's life got complicated.

IF SECRET WAS YIN, THIS woman was yang. She was just as hypnotic but in a contrasting way. Her hair was black, her skin was sun-kissed gold, her eyes were mysterious, and her lips were made for one thing and one thing only. She was older than Secret, somewhere around the twenty-seven mark, four years younger than Wilde.

A perfect age, actually.

She was conservatively dressed in a crisp white blouse and a black skirt that was tight but ended slightly below her knees. Her hair was up. She wore a simple gold necklace. An image flashed in Wilde's brain of him ripping it off and licking her neck.

"I'm London Marshall," she said. "I'm in trouble and I'm hoping you can help."

Wilde tapped a Camel out of the pack and held it toward her.

"No, thanks," she said.

"You don't smoke?"

"I do, but only when I'm on fire."

Wilde smiled, lit the stick, and blew smoke.

"So what kind of trouble are you in exactly, London?"

The woman exhaled, pulled an envelope out of her purse, and handed it to him.

It was too light to be money.

"This is what has me in trouble," she said.

"This?"

"Right. Open it up and look inside."

17

DAY ONE

JULY 21, 1952

MONDAY AFTERNOON

THE MAN FIXING SANDWICHES AT Murphy's Deli looked sideways at Waverly when she ordered an Italian sausage and said, "Is this for Sean Waterfield?"

Yes.

It was.

"Tell him he's lucky, this is the last one left. Tell him I could have sold it ten times but was saving it for him," the man said.

"I will."

"I'm Murphy," the man said. "Sean always gives me a two-bit tip, four bits when I save him the last one. Did he tell you about that?"

Waverly wrinkled her forehead.

"No."

"He'll confirm it when you get back," Murphy said.

"Okay."

"You look like you're not so sure."

"No, it's okay, I trust you," Waverly said.

BACK AT THE OFFICE, WATERFIELD was nowhere to be seen so Waverly walked into the guts of the place like she owned it. He turned out to be in a corner cubicle with windows on both sides, hovering over a drafting table and marking a drawing in red pencil.

"Got your food," Waverly said.

He took the bag, set it down and said, "There's something wrong with this. What is it?"

This referred to the drawing, which was the size of a poster board and depicted the front view of a stately columned building reminiscent of ancient Rome or Athens. At the top in perfect letters were the words, New York Museum of Modern Art.

Waterfield was right, there was something wrong.

What it was, though, eluded her.

Waterfield broke the silence. "I'm thinking that maybe the windows are maybe just a tad too small. Another possibility is that it might be better if the front stairs had a broader footprint, extending another ten feet to each side. This area up here on the upper corner might be a bit too plain, but I'm not sure how to jazz it up without making it too busy."

He pulled the sausage out, took a bite, and chewed as he watched her face.

Waverly looked for what was wrong.

It wasn't coming to her.

She pulled the change out of her pocket and handed it over. "Murphy said that was the last Italian he had and he saved it for you. He said you give him a fifty-cent tip when he does that."

Sean wrinkled his face as if bitten.

"Got me," he said.

"What do you mean?"

"Murphy, he got me," Waterfield said. "We have a little bet going. He's winning."

"So he was leading me on?"

Waterfield smiled.

"Yeah, but don't worry about it," he said. "Tell me what's wrong with this design."

Waverly refocused on it.

Then she said, "I guess the thing I don't understand is that if it's a museum of modern art, why does it look like something ancient instead of something modern?"

Waterfield hesitated.

Then he said, "It's in the same era as the other art buildings on the same grounds. It's meant to match."

"There's no law that says it has to, right?"

"If you mean zoning laws the answer is *no*, but the general rule is that you try to blend in new architecture with the existing architecture."

Waverly shrugged.

"In that case you're asking the wrong person," she said. "I would have made it modern."

WATERFIELD POPPED THE CAP OFF the RC, took a long noisy swallow, and looked out the window as if staring at everything and nothing.

The window was open.

A pigeon landed on the ledge and strutted with an eye on Waterfield's sandwich. He broke off a piece of bread and held it in his hand.

The bird hesitated.

Then it darted in, bagged the prize and flew off.

The corner of Waterfield's mouth turned up ever so slightly.

"You're a dangerous woman," he said.

The words took Waverly by surprise.

"How am I dangerous?"

"You're dangerous because you've only been here five minutes and you've already set this project back two months."

"I did?"

"Yes, you did. And thank you for that." He kissed her on the cheek. "I want to take you to supper tonight."

She smiled.

"We could go to Murphy's and stiff him on the tip," she said. "Get even."

"Do you see what I mean about you being a dangerous woman?"

She shrugged.

"I won't deny it."

18

DAY ONE
JULY 21, 1952
MONDAY AFTERNOON

THE TWO DEAD BIKERS POSED a problem, and so did the third one—the live one—for that matter. River didn't want to be a person of interest in the killings even though everything he did was in self-defense. He didn't want the cops snooping around in one part of his life where they might accidentally stumble on another part. Equally important, he didn't want to be associated with that particular corner of the universe. He still wanted to use the graveyard tonight and needed to keep his name a hundred miles away from it.

The biker woman could ruin everything.

She could go to the cops.

Ordinarily he wouldn't be too concerned about it, but he'd punched her in the face and killed her boyfriend. She might seek revenge any way she could.

More to the point, she might bring a gang back to hunt him down.

He could eliminate that problem by killing her.

Instead he decided to keep her close until he could get a better read.

As they walked back to the road he said, "You got a name?"

She did.

"Tatt."

"I'm not talking about that," River said. "I'm talking about a real name."

"That is a real name," she said.

River shook his head.

"I'm not calling you Tatt," he said. "From now on until you answer my question, your name's Susan."

"What's it matter? You're going to kill me anyway."

"I'll be honest," River said. "That's going to be up to you."

THE NEXT HOUR WAS BUSY. They drove the choppers three miles down the road and into the terrain on the opposite side of the road where they couldn't be seen from the asphalt in a hundred years.

No one saw them.

They walked back.

A few cars passed and a few startled heads turned at the sight of people out in the middle of nowhere on foot, but no one stopped.

Now they needed to bury the bodies.

That was a problem.

River opened the trunk and found nothing even remotely capable of digging except perhaps a tire iron.

He closed the lid, opened the passenger door for the woman and said, "Get in."

"Where we going?"

"To my place."

UNDERWAY, HE LIT TWO CIGARETTES, handed one to the woman, and said, "Thanks for not darting off on the bike."

"It's not like I had a choice."

"Sure you did," he said. "You could have made a break for it."

She flicked ashes out the window.

"You had the faster bike," she said. "We both knew that."

River smiled.

"You're smarter than I thought."

"Tell me something," she said. "If I would have made a break for it, would you have killed me?"

"I don't know," he said. "Maybe."

She nodded.

"Fair enough."

River took a long drag, blew smoke, and said, "The more I think about it, we'll bury them tonight after dark. You never told me which one of them you were with."

"The asshole."

"The one with the chain?"

"Yeah, him." A pause, then she said, "My name's January, if you're still interested."

River looked over to see if she was messing with him.

"January? Like the month?"

Right.

That.

"January James," she said. "You can call me Susan, though, if you want."

"January's fine," River said. "Actually, I like it."

19

DAY ONE

JULY 21, 1952

MONDAY AFTERNOON

WILDE TOOK ANOTHER LOOK AT the mysterious woman and got pulled into her eyes momentarily before he broke away and opened the envelope. Inside was a wrinkled, dirty piece of paper. He unfolded it and found some kind of handwritten picture.

"What is it?"

"It's a map."

"A map to what?"

"To tombs."

"Tombs?"

Right.

Tombs.

"Where'd you get it?"

The woman spotted the coffee pot on the credenza and said, "Can I buy a cup?"

Wilde got her fixed up. She took a noisy sip and said, "What do you know about the pyramids in Mexico?"

"I thought the pyramids were in Egypt."

"They are, but there are some in Mexico too," she said. "There was a civilization that lived in central Mexico, about twenty-five miles from where Mexico City is located today. The best guess is that it began somewhere around 200 B.C. and ended in the seventh or eighth century, meaning it was around for almost a thousand years. Who they were remains one of the biggest archeological mysteries today."

"How do you know all this? Are you an archeologist?"

"Not officially," she said. "Officially I'm a lawyer here in Denver. I work at Colder & Jones."

Wilde nodded.

He'd heard of them.

They were one of the bigger firms in Denver with offices on the upper half of the Daniels & Fisher Tower over on 16th Street.

That meant she had money.

She could afford his services.

"Unofficially," she added, "I dabble with the ruins down in Mexico. I don't have any official archeological training, but I tag along with whoever will have me. I've spent two or three months a year down there for the last four years. The site itself is enormous and largely unexplored, even to this day. There are two large pyramids. One's called the Pyramid of the Sun and the other's called the Pyramid of the Moon. They're located some distance apart. Running between them is a long street, for lack of a better name, that's called the Avenue of the Dead. There are a number of structures on that street and, indeed, structures emanate out in all directions for some distance. It's probably the biggest archeological site in the world and ninety percent of it is still virgin. Most structures have yet to be entered."

"Interesting."

"They call it Teotihuacán. Can I have some more coffee?"

Sure.

No problem.

Wilde liked her voice. Every sentence was a melody, every word a note. The movement of her lips was pure sex.

"I'M GOING TO GO OUT on a limb here and conclude that this map has something to do with that archeological site," Wilde said.

London smiled.

"Good limb climbing," she said. "Like I said before, almost nothing is known about this civilization. The biggest mystery of all is what brought it to an end. We do know that almost every prominent wooden structure was burned to the ground. Some think the city was conquered and burned down by enemies. Others think that the lower class got repressed to the point of revolution and burned down their repressors. Still others think that it was nothing more than an accidental fire that spread from building to building. No one really knows."

Wilde lit a cigarette.

"This is actually sort of interesting," he said.

"When you really get into it, it's absolutely fascinating," London said. "In a very slow kind of a way, but fascinating nonetheless. Last year, they began to work into the interior of one of the pyramids. Not much progress has been made yet, but what they found so far was the remains of humans, together with birds in cages and various other animals in cages. The thinking is that these were all sacrifices that took place during the construction."

"Sacrifices for what?"

"The usual," she said. "To the gods, whoever they were, to make the construction go smooth or whatever. Most civilizations evolving during that time frame did the same thing. The Romans and Egyptians are the best examples."

WILDE BLEW SMOKE.

"Skulls and dead birds," he said. "What a way to go, be sacrificed to some god who doesn't even exist."

London nodded.

"Exactly," she said. "They might have been enemies who were taken prisoner. Some day it will all get figured out. Anyway, over the years I started to come up with a theory."

"What theory is that?"

"A theory that this civilization, although it was advanced enough to flourish and exist for a long time, was still barbaric at heart," she said. "Pyramids don't get built because everyone thinks it would be a nice idea. They take a tremendous amount of labor. That level of labor generally means there is a lower caste of slaves. When you have that kind of social structure, that means that there's someone at the top—a ruler, someone in the nature of a king or queen or pharaoh, one after the other, century after century."

That made sense.

"People like that acquire wealth during their tenure," London said. "The riches rise to the top."

"Right."

"Are you following me?"

He was.

He was indeed.

"When the riches rise to the top, the ruler starts to worry about the afterlife," London said. "They want to be sure they appease the gods that are going to play a role in what happens next. That means temples and gifts and sanctuaries. We've seen that in Egypt in all the pyramids that have been found in the Valley of the Kings."

"Okay."

"Here's the interesting thing," London said. "This entire archeological site has almost no structures of prominence that would indicate a king or queen was buried there."

"What about the two pyramids?"

London nodded.

"Right, we have those, but that would only account for a few, assuming there are tombs inside, which is almost certain. So, where did all the other kings get laid to rest?"

Wilde shrugged.

"I don't know."

"Well, I do," London said. "That's what the map shows."

Wilde looked at it again.

It was modern paper.

It wasn't ancient parchment.

"This isn't old," he said.

"I know."

"How could it be a map, then?"

"That's a good question."

"You say that like you have a good answer."

"I do. Do you want to hear it?"

He did.

He did indeed.

With that, she told him a story so rich and vivid that he felt as if he was actually there.

———

UNDER THE CLOAK OF A moonless Mexican night, the young American lawyer chipped away as quietly as she could at the outside wall of the ancient temple. The structure couldn't be more than two feet thick and she'd already gone almost that far. She wiped sweat off her forehead with the back of her hand.

Her 26-year-old body ached.

If the guards stumbled on her, she'd be weak.

She wore all things black. Her long raven hair was fastened in a ponytail and pulled through the back of a green baseball cap.

Her body was well-conditioned and taut.

Her face—ordinarily sensual and mysterious—was tense and focused.

The temple was located on the Avenue of the Dead, midway between the Pyramid of the Sun and the Pyramid of the Moon, in the middle of the Teotihuacán archeological site twenty-five miles northeast of Mexico City.

No one had ever been inside this particular ruin.

It was nothing special from the outside, just a rectangular stone structure with fifty-foot sides and a ten-foot height. Unremarkable pillars stood upright on the four corners and four midpoints. Hundreds of years ago, they supported a wooden canopy. The structure paled against the mystery and grandeur of dozens of larger and more ornate works, not to mention the pyramids of the Sun and the Moon, where most of the archeological efforts had been directed to date and, even at this time, were still in their infancy.

Legend had it that the temple was cursed.

The reason for the curse had been lost to antiquity.

A HOLE OPENED UP, NOT a big one, but enough to indicate the beginning of the end. She chipped away at the edges with renewed energy and didn't stop until the opening was large enough to crawl through.

She took a look around and saw no one.

Okay.

This was it.

She stuck her head close to the opening and took a sniff followed by several deep breaths. The centuries-old air had no detectable odor. No lightheadedness followed, indicating the oxygen hadn't been eaten away by mold.

She shined a flashlight inside.

The chamber was large and not broken into smaller rooms. As she anticipated, several support pillars for the stone top came into view. There were no snakes, spider webs, or sounds. Whatever dust had been there at one time had settled many hundreds of years ago.

She turned the flashlight off, tied a rope around her backpack, and slithered backwards through the opening until she was inside.

The air was cooler by several degrees but not damp.

She stood up and turned the flashlight on.

Intricate murals ordained all four walls.

In the middle of the room was a stone box the size of a casket, also with ornate sides.

The top was wooden, elegantly carved, and hand-painted.

She pulled the backpack through the opening, took out a hammer and chisel, and carefully pried the top up, managing to keep it in one piece. She maneuvered it to the side, tilted it over the edge, and lowered it carefully to the floor.

Then she shined the flashlight inside.

What she saw, she could hardly believe.

A COLD CHILL RAN UP her spine.

Outside, a bright arc of lightning flashed, so close and violent that the inside of the chamber lit up.

Thunder snapped.

The flashlight dropped out of her hand.

The bulb exploded with a blue flash.

Then everything in the world turned black. The darkness was so absolute that she couldn't even tell where the opening was.

She stood there, breathing deep and heavy, hearing nothing but the sound of air moving in and out of her lungs.

SUDDENLY A NOISE CAME FROM behind her.

It was a heavy breathing not more than a few steps away.

She backed away, tripped over the side of the casket, and fell inside.

20

DAY ONE
JULY 21, 1952
MONDAY AFTERNOON

WHEN SEAN WATERFIELD DISAPPEARED INTO a meeting, Waverly wasn't quite sure what to do. They were supposed to go out to dinner tonight but hadn't discussed the time or place, no doubt because he planned on her being around the rest of the afternoon. She almost headed for the elevator but instead took a seat at the reception desk.

Ten seconds later, the door swung open and an out-of-breath librarian-type walked over.

"I'm Evelyn from the temp agency," she said. "I'm so sorry I'm late."

Waverly's heart sank.

She was busted.

Then she said, "You're late."

"I know. I'm sorry."

"They didn't think you were coming. They got me."

Silence.

"For tomorrow too?"

"For all week, as far as I know."

"What agency are you with?"

"That's not important," Waverly said. "What's important is that they have more than one temp agency in their phonebook. Be on time next time, that's my advice."

The woman left.

The phone rang.

The caller wanted Bobby Baxter.

The phone had transfer buttons marked 1 to 10, but none were labeled.

"Do you know what extension he is?"

No.

He didn't.

"Just give me a minute."

She asked around until she found him, back in a corner with a drafting pad working on some kind of mathematical or engineering calculation. He had a mean, square face and narrow caveman eyes. "Put him through on line 2," he said. His mouth smiled and his voice was calm, but he scared her. There was something behind his eyes that he didn't want anyone to see. She didn't know what it was, but it was definitely something.

An hour passed.

People came and had her do things.

One of the men, a young man named Aaron Gull, sat on the corner of the desk and hit on her for ten minutes. In another time and place she might have been interested.

Another hour passed.

Then Sean Waterfield appeared.

HE LOOKED BATTERED BUT HAPPY, as if he'd been in a fistfight and won.

"I had a meeting with two of the partners and convinced them to throw away the mold and approach the project from a modern perspective," he said. "We had a conference call with the client. At first they were reluctant, but then they came around. They gave us the go-ahead to come up with something fresh and present it to them for consideration. They're going to pay us for all work done, no matter which way they eventually decide to go. Now my job is to come up with something they can't say no to."

"What do you have in mind?"

"I don't have a clue," he said. "All I know is that I'm excited as all hell. Help me think about it. We'll discuss it over dinner."

Okay.

Fine.

He looked at his watch.

"I have to go and I'll be gone the rest of the day," he said. "Why don't we say seven o'clock?"

She nodded.

Perfect.

"Where do I pick you up?"

She hesitated.

Then she told him.

She was staying with a friend in Chinatown. He could pick her up in front of the Green Dragon Oriental Massage. "Have you ever been there?"

He diverted his eyes and was about to deny it. The words that came out of his mouth, though, were "Not recently."

21

UNLESS THERE WAS SOMETHING HE was missing, River didn't see January James, the biker woman, as wanting to kill him. She was more like someone who'd been kicked around for a long time and just didn't want to be kicked anymore. He took her home, showed her where the shower was, and threw her clothes in the washer. Then he drove the Indian over to the department store and did a little shopping.

When he got back, the woman was sitting on a rail with a towel wrapped around her.

Gone was the road grime.

Gone were the tangles in her hair.

Gone was the bandanna.

Soft hair blew over her face and she didn't brush it away.

River handed her two May D&F bags and said, "I got you some things."

The words surprised her.

She looked inside, pulled out a pair of shorts and checked the size, which was right. Next came out a pair of jeans, two tank tops, two T-shirts, and five button-down blouses. Under all that were a half dozen pair of panties and bras.

She checked the bra size—34C.

"I think you gave me a little more credit than I deserve."

"I took my best shot."

She dropped the towel into her lap.

Bouncy breasts came into view, one with the tattoo of a rose on the cleavage side. She paid no attention to River and put the bra on. It was too big but not by much. She tightened the straps.

There.

Good enough.

In the other bag were more feminine clothes—three dresses, nylons, garter belts, and black high heels. She held up the simple short white one and said, "I haven't worn a dress in a hundred years."

River turned his head.

"Try it on."

"Why?"

"Because I pictured you in it," he said. "I want to see if I was right."

He focused on two BNSF workers turning a wrench under a flatbed coupler as the woman rustled behind him. Then she said, "Okay, turn around."

He did.

What he saw, he didn't expect.

Take away the tattoos and she'd be a pinup girl.

"Were you right?" she asked.

He shook his head.

"No, I wasn't even close."

22

DAY ONE
JULY 21, 1952
MONDAY MORNING

LAST MONDAY NIGHT, LONDON BROKE into a temple on the Avenue of the Dead. "No one had ever been inside. It wasn't big or overly remarkable, definitely not the kind of place where you'd expect a king or queen to be entombed. What intrigued me about it was the curse."

Wilde set a book of matches on fire.

"The curse?"

Right.

The curse.

"I don't believe in all that ancient voodoo crap," he said. "There's no such thing as a curse."

"That's what I used to think," London said.

"Used to?"

The flames drew her attention.

"The curse drew me to it because it still exists to this day," she said. "The reason for the curse was long forgotten but not the rumor. Anyway, I felt it was worth going into so I did it."

The fire was down to Wilde's fingertips. He looked out the window, found no one below and dropped it out.

"And?"

"And it was a burial site of someone important," she said. "Live people had been chained to the wall."

"And left to rot?"

London nodded.

Wilde screwed his face in disgust. "That's sick. Why?"

"I don't know," London said. "Maybe they were sacrifices, maybe they were some kind of soul currency, maybe they were virgins he was taking to the next place."

Wilde pictured it.

"What a way to go."

"Here's the important thing," London said. "The person was buried in a stone casket with a wooden top. When I took off the top, there was a painting on the underside. As soon as I saw it, I knew what it was. It was a map of a catacomb system."

She pointed to the map.

"This section here is the entrance," she said. "It's been buried with rock for thirty feet."

"Why?"

"To prevent looting, that's my guess," she said. "These squares most likely denote rooms where past kings and queens were buried. The system was probably guarded as well, possibly for decades and maybe even centuries."

SHE LOWERED HER VOICE.

"When I was inside the tomb, my flashlight dropped and went

out. I was in the blackest blackness you could ever imagine. All of a sudden there was something behind me. Something alive. I could hear it breathing."

Wilde pictured it.

"What was it?"

"I don't know," London said. "I like to think it was just a stray dog that followed me in, or something like that. It only lasted for ten seconds or so and then disappeared as quickly as it came, but it was real, it wasn't my imagination. I made my way to the entrance and got out alive. I almost got the hell out of there, but I was too close to history. The past had a fist around my throat and was pulling me back in. I grabbed my other flashlight and a paper and pencil and went back in. Then I made a sketch of the painting on the underside of the casket lid." She tapped on the map. "That's what this is. Then I scraped the painting off with a rock, all the way down to the wood."

Wilde tilted his head.

"So this is all that's left."

London nodded.

Then she got a distant look before refocusing.

"Something strange happened. That night, starting even before I got out, the sky exploded with lightning bolts, one after another after another after another. The sky literally screamed with thunder."

Wilde wasn't impressed.

"Don't tell me it was the curse."

"Why not?"

"Because there's no such thing. There's only science."

"Maybe you're right," London said. "But this particular science started right over where I was and then set off for Mexico City. It ended up burning down a good portion of it." She exhaled and added, "There was no rain, only lightning."

"That happens sometimes."

"Maybe."

"It was just a coincidence."

"Maybe, maybe not."

"SOMEONE BROKE INTO MY PLACE yesterday," she said. "I didn't notice it until this morning, but things were definitely moved. They were careful, but not careful enough."

"Who was it?"

"I don't know, but they were after the map," she said. "I want you to take possession of it and keep it safe."

Wilde looked at it.

"Sure. Anything else?"

She nodded.

"Actually there is. I want you to find out who's after it," she said. "I want you to persuade them to go away. And most importantly, I want you to protect me in the meantime."

23

DAY ONE
JULY 21, 1952
MONDAY EVENING

SAN FRANCISCO WAS SO EXOTIC and atmospheric that Waverly could live there forever, starting right now. The trolley cars, the hills, the water, the bridges, the diversity, the fog, the harbors, the downtown skyline, it was all conspiring to make her stay.

Sean Waterfield didn't see the need to leave Chinatown for dinner and took her to a place called the Hong Kong Clay Pot at 9th and Grant.

He looked nice.

Better than nice, actually.

"A woman named Kava Every used to work at your firm," Waverly said.

Waterfield raised an eyebrow.

"That's right. Do you know her?"

"She's my cousin. That whole temp thing today, that was sort of unintended," she said. "I came to town to see if I could find out what happened to her. That's why I came to the firm, to see if anyone might know something."

The words sunk in.

Waterfield's face changed.

"So you aren't really a temp?"

"No, but after you wanted me to get you food, well, you seemed nice so I figured, what the hell," she said. "Then one thing led to another . . ."

Waterfield shook his head in amusement.

Then he got serious.

"Kava was a good person," he said. "It was a damn shame, what happened to her."

True.

"Do you have any idea who might have done it?"

Waterfield got a distant look.

"There's one little thing," he said. "I don't know if it's anything or not."

"Tell me."

He hesitated.

"Do you live in San Francisco?"

"No, Denver."

"That's a long ways off."

Right.

It was.

"I'm actually thinking of moving here," she said. "Trade the sun-shine for fog."

"Well, if there's anything I can do to convince you to do it, let me know."

"I will."

HE SPEARED A SHRIMP, CHEWED, and swallowed, washing it down with a sip of tea. "The cops talked to a number of us at Bristol after the fact. The theory was that it was a murder rather than an accident or suicide and that the murder was done by someone who knew her and knew her well, a boyfriend or lover to be precise. None of us at the firm knew anything about a boyfriend or lover."

"So it was a dead end," Waverly said.

"It was. Over the years it's been gnawing at me. She was a vibrant woman. She wasn't the kind of woman to not have a sex life. In hindsight, I think she was seeing someone in the firm. I think they were keeping it quiet to avoid complications."

"Who was it?"

"Two people come to mind," he said. "One is an associate architect named Brian Fernier."

Waverly tried to picture him and drew a blank.

"He wasn't at work today," Waterfield said. "The other is Tom Bristol. Actually, he makes the most sense. If he was having an affair with one of the firm's architects, there'd be cries of favoritism every time she got assigned to a good project or promoted or whatever. They'd have a motive to keep it close to the vest."

"Tom Bristol."

"Right, Tom Bristol."

"Tell me about him," Waverly said.

Waterfield frowned.

"He's a hell of a man, actually. You don't build up a firm like ours and raise it to national recognition without being something of a force."

Waverly took a sip of tea.

"I'm going to come back tomorrow and continue temping," she said. "I need to see him up close and personal."

Waterfield's face tightened.

"Be careful."

24

DAY ONE
JULY 21, 1952
MONDAY EVENING

RIVER HAD NO INTENT TO bring January with him to bury the bikers' bodies, but she insisted and had already learned how to get her way. He wasn't exactly sure how it happened, but it was a fact. It wasn't just a product of her being attractive. He'd had plenty better. There was something else at work, something he couldn't put his finger on.

He pulled to the shoulder, turned off the headlights, and killed the engine a half mile short of the scene.

The sun had already crept behind the mountains.

Twilight was thick.

By the time he got to the bodies, visibility would be down to thirty steps.

He popped the hood and disconnected the positive battery cable.

January would stay with the car. If anyone stopped, she'd tell them it broke down and that her boyfriend had gone to get help.

That would explain the car being there.

River would head into the terrain for fifty steps and then walk parallel to the road until he got to the bodies. He'd bury them deep enough to keep the coyotes out.

He got the shovel out of the trunk.

January stepped out and watched.

The air was quiet except for crickets. A bat zigzagged overhead.

"Be back in a jiffy," River said.

"Wait."

She put her arms around his neck and pressed her stomach to his. It was the first time they had touched. It felt nice. It felt right.

"Don't go. Something's wrong."

"What?"

"I don't know, just something."

He looked around.

Everything was normal.

"It's just the night playing a trick."

She looked around, then raised her lips so close to his that he could feel the warmth of her breath.

"Be careful."

"I will."

"Promise me."

"I promise."

HE HEADED INTO THE DARK with the shovel in hand, counting fifty steps, then turning left. An orange moon lifted off the horizon.

The terrain dipped and the temperature followed.

The road was a strip of black to his left, darker than the surroundings but not by much. It was visible enough to follow and that's all he needed.

In his pocket was a flashlight.

He'd only use it if he couldn't find the bodies.

A whoosh came overhead.

He looked up and saw nothing, but pictured a bat snatching a bug.

"Bad night to be a bug," he muttered.

Somewhere in the distance a coyote barked.

No pack joined in.

It wasn't a hunt.

Maybe it was just a lost soul out there in the world alone, separated from his kind.

Something's wrong.

That's what January said.

Something's wrong.

River suddenly realized she was right.

Something was going to happen.

Something bad.

HE SHOOK IT OFF AND kept going.

He didn't need the flashlight to find the bodies; the rancid smell pulled him in. He shined the light down to find something he didn't expect, namely that both men had been torn apart by coyotes. Their faces and necks were mostly gone, their hands too.

Now the flies were having their turn.

He went through their pockets.

There he found a folded-up newspaper article. It was about the murder of a businessman in Kansas City last week. He shoved it in his wallet and started digging.

The soil was hardly soil at all.

It was mostly rock.

He should have brought a pick.

It took over an hour to dig a hole for the both of them to where they were under a good foot. He filled it in, dispersed the extra dirt, rolled a couple of big rocks on top, and then raked everything down. If anyone wandered out here, it would look suspicious for a couple of days. After that, the wind would make it less and less visible. The first good rain would cloak it completely.

He headed back for the car.

When he got to where it should be, it wasn't there.

He must have passed it or not gone far enough.

He hiked in one direction down the road far enough to know it wasn't that way, then turned around and went the other way.

It wasn't there either.

It was gone.

January James.

He should have never trusted her.

25

DAY ONE
JULY 21, 1952
MONDAY AFTERNOON

WILDE KNOCKED ON MICHELLE DAY'S door, trying with all his might to put the image of this morning out of his head. The harder he tried, the more vivid it got. He could see her hips wiggling with all the clarity of the movie screen down at the Zaza Theatre. He could feel her passion and taste her breath.

Suddenly the door opened.

It was Michelle Day, dressed now and brightly awake, wondering who he was.

She was short, not much more than five feet, built in shades of brown—brown hair, brown eyebrows, brown eyes, and brown skin.

The hair matched up and down, a fact Wilde shouldn't know but did. She wore shorts, brown, and a T, brown.

Her feet were bare.

Wilde pulled the photo of Charley-Anna Blackridge out of his pocket and handed it to her.

After she studied it, he said, "My name's Bryson Wilde. I'm a private investigator. The woman in the photograph was killed Friday night. Before she got killed, she was at the El Ray Club where you were bartending. I'm trying to find out if you saw who she left with."

The woman processed it.

"How'd she die?"

"She fell from a roof."

"Fell from a roof. Was she pushed?"

"The theory is that she was pushed or dropped," he said. "Same landing either way."

The woman nodded.

"Right, I suppose so." She turned and headed for the kitchen. "Come on in. I remember her."

"You do?"

"Yeah, she tipped me."

"Good."

"Not everyone does," she said. "You'd be surprised."

"I probably would."

"There are a lot of cheapies out there. They can rot in hell as far as I'm concerned. Do you ever get stiffed by your clients?"

He did; not often, but on occasion.

"Then you know what I'm talking about," she said.

He did.

He did indeed.

THE KITCHEN WASN'T MUCH MORE than a closet with faded appliances, but it was large enough to hold a newly made pot of coffee that got poured into two cups.

"Sorry, no cream," she said.

"This is fine."

Wilde tapped out a Camel, lit it, and held it out to see if she wanted it, which she did. He fixed a second for himself and they ended up outside on the front steps.

"I remember her, but I didn't see who she left with," the woman said. "When I'm working, my world's pretty much the three feet that's in front of me. Everything else is a blur."

"Understood."

"Sorry."

Wilde blew smoke.

"According to a friend she was with that night, the woman was hanging around to maybe take a run at some guy who looked like Robert Mitchum. Do you remember him?"

Her face brightened.

"I do," she said. "He was one of those cheapskates I was talking about. He came over and flashed his smile and said, *What's your name, baby?* I told him and he shook my hand. He said, *I'm Robert.* He ordered a beer but didn't tip. I guess he thought that telling me his name and flashing me his teeth was going to help me pay the electric bill. Three more times after that, he ordered but didn't tip, not once. He had money, though, you could tell by his clothes."

"Did you ever see him there before?"

She shook her head.

"No, never," she said. "I hope I never see him again, too."

"Who'd he leave with?"

"I don't know. I'm just glad he did."

WILDE ASKED MORE QUESTIONS, BUT the woman didn't have any more answers. He said his thanks, tipped her a five, and was headed down the driveway when the woman called after him and said, "I just remembered one more thing."

He walked back.

"What?"

"He had a tattoo on his left arm, up high," she said. "It was a war plane."

"How big?"

"I don't know, average? It wasn't flying. It was sitting on the ground.

A woman was standing in front of it posing. She was one of those pinup girls with the big smile and the big tits."

TWO MINUTES LATER, HE FIRED up Blondie and headed for Larimer. Halfway there, he remembered something bad. He'd left London's map sitting on the top of his desk.

The window was open.

The fan was blowing.

He wasn't sure he'd locked the door.

Suddenly police lights appeared in his rearview mirror.

He looked at the speedometer to find he was fifteen over.

26

DAY ONE
JULY 21, 1952
MONDAY NIGHT

SU-MOON DIDN'T HAVE A car but did have a 90cc scooter she called Vibrator together with the guts to use it in San Francisco traffic. When Waverly told her about what she'd learned today, Su-Moon said, "Let's go find out if this guy—Tom Bristol—and the girl who got dropped were doing the nasty."

Waverly raised an eyebrow.

"And how do you propose we find that out?"

Su-Moon lit a cigarette and blew smoke.

"When it comes to being a criminal, you're not exactly a natural, are you?"

Under a black night, wearing sweatshirts and long pants, they took Vibrator across the Golden Gate Bridge into Sausalito, which was an upscale community across the bay, given to bigger-than-necessary houses with hundred-dollar views carved into the hillsides and marinas down below jammed with floating houseboats.

The air was moist, salty, and chilly.

According to the phone book, Tom Bristol lived at 22C, Last Lighthouse Marina.

They pulled to a stop a hundred yards short and studied the place through an eerie fog. "The docks must run in order, A, B, C, et cetera. C would be the third dock. I'm guessing that 22 is the 22nd slip down that dock."

"You're getting better," Su-Moon said.

"At what?"

"At being a criminal. Let's walk by and see if anyone's home."

"For the record, this is nuts."

"For the record, duly noted."

A COOL BREEZE PUSHED THE air, strong enough to wrinkle the water and rock the boats. Waverly put the hood of her sweatshirt up.

"It's winter," she said.

"Always."

They walked through a nearly-packed gravel parking lot, past a large land-based building and into the docks, turning right at the third one.

The houseboats were more houses than boats, technically floating but not built for waves or much of anything other than stationary sitting.

Front porches had flowerpots.

One even had a white picket fence.

It was after ten on a Monday night.

Most of the structures were dark.

The shadows on the docks were thick and deep.

They encountered no one.

Some of the boats were numbered—fifteen, nineteen, twenty, twenty-one.

The one they wanted, 22, was dark.

They walked past, keeping an eye on it, then turned at the end of the dock and doubled back.

Waverly's heart beat.

"He might be gone but he might be sleeping," she said. "There's no way to tell."

Su-Moon said nothing.

The boat was a large box with a flat roof and a ladder up the side. Su-Moon stepped onto the front porch, transferring her weight carefully.

Waverly followed.

Su-Moon put a hand on the front door and twisted.

"It's locked," she whispered.

They stepped back onto the dock and then walked down a finger alongside the boat. The windows were down and the shades were drawn.

When they got to the last window, something happened that they didn't expect.

A faint light appeared from inside.

They looked in around the edge of a shade.

This end of the boat was the bedroom. A bed abutted the wall next to the window. The light came from two candles on a dresser. A man was sitting in the bed with his back against the wall and his legs stretched out, facing the opposite way.

A woman was draped across his lap. She wore a dress but it was pulled up past her waist. She had no panties.

The man's hand massaged her exposed flesh.

Suddenly it rose up and spanked down.

The slap was audible.

The woman wiggled.

Then she said something.

It sounded like, "Forty-two."

WAVERLY HELD HER BREATH, WAITING for the next spank. It didn't come for a long time, but when it did it was hard, with two more right behind it.

The woman flinched but made no effort to get off.

Then she wiggled her body seductively.

Her head was to the left where she couldn't see the window even if she turned.

The window was an anonymous portal.

If either of the people inside turned, Waverly and Su-Moon would have plenty of opportunity to duck down. They were invisible. Because of that, they were in no hurry.

The spanks went to a hundred.

Then the woman slid down between the man's legs and worked her mouth.

Waverly tugged on Su-Moon's arm and they tiptoed off.

Twenty steps down the dock Su-Moon said, "Her dress was red, did you notice that?"

"Yes I did," Waverly said. "We need to find out who she is."

"Why?"

"Because we may have to warn her."

27

DAY ONE
JULY 21, 1952
MONDAY NIGHT

RIVER LET OUT A WAR cry that shook the night, so pissed at January for leaving him stranded that every fiber of his body ached. She'd regret it, oh how she'd regret it. She'd learn a lesson about screwing with him. She'd learn a lesson she'd never forget, not in a million years.

The keys to all the boxcars were on same ring as the car key.

She had full access to everything.

Right now she was probably rifling through his stuff, grabbing everything that had even a snippet of value.

He walked north at a brisk pace, trying to remember how far it was to that Sunoco station they'd passed way back.

Ten miles?

Even then, it would be closed.

All he could hope for is that it had an outside phone booth.

Ten miles.

That would take him two and a half hours.

A mile down the road, he wandered into the terrain for fifty steps and threw the shovel away, far enough that it wouldn't be associated with the buried bikers.

The night was black but the road was detectable.

Every so often he turned the flashlight on and shined it around.

The topography was always the same—dirt, rabbit brush, prairie grass, and rocks.

Half an hour farther down the road when he flicked the light on, something unexpected happened. A red reflection came from something off the road.

As he got closer, the reflection took the shape of a taillight, two taillights actually.

He headed that way, shining the light on the ground and keeping a lookout for snakes.

A car came into view.

His car?

It looked like it.

He picked up the pace.

Damn it, it was his car.

What the hell was it doing out here?

HE TROTTED TO IT AND got in.

January wasn't there.

The keys weren't in the ignition.

They weren't on the floor or up in the visor or in the glove box or anywhere else.

He slammed his fist on the dash.

Goddamn it!

Then he heard a muffled sound from somewhere outside. It turned out to be a weak voice coming from inside the trunk.

"Help me . . ."

"January is that you?"

It was.

"River, help me . . ."

The lid was latched solid.

He shined the flashlight on the ground and found no keys, not there or all the way around. The passenger side door and front fender were smashed in.

He grabbed a rock the size of a gorilla's fist and beat on the latch.

Wham.

Wham.

Wham.

It dented in but didn't unlatch.

He beat on it more but still couldn't bust it.

Then suddenly on the last smash something broke and the lid popped.

Inside was January. Her dress was filthy and ripped to shreds. Her panties were gone. Dried blood was on her face and her eyes were raw and wet. As soon as River bent down, the woman wrapped her arms around him and held on with the strength of someone being pulled from the grave.

28

DAY ONE

JULY 21, 1952

MONDAY AFTERNOON

WILDE'S WORST FEAR MATERIALIZED WHEN he got back to the office. The door was wide open, no one was inside and the map was gone. He'd screwed up before but never this badly. This was a new personal best. Suddenly the toilet flushed in the adjoining room and Alabama walked in. She looked at his hat, still in hand, not yet thrown at the rack and said, "What's wrong?"

"There was a map on my desk."

She scouted around.

"Is that it?"

She pointed to a piece of paper on the floor.

Wilde picked it up and smiled.

Then he tossed his hat at the rack, forgetting to aim to the left. It flew out the window, not a corner of the window, either, smack dab center—nothing but air.

"Ringer," Alabama said.

"Can you run down and get it for me?"

"Me?"

"Please."

"I don't type, I don't fetch hats," she said. "We settled that on day one."

Wilde could argue but he'd lose.

He ran down, got it and brushed the dust off on the way up, stopping at the door and taking aim for the rack. This time he threw to the right. It curved left, grabbed the rack by the edge and stuck.

Alabama was sitting on the desk wiping spilled coffee off the map.

"That's better," she said.

WILDE LIT A CAMEL, PUT the map in his top desk drawer and said, "So how'd it go with the clothes?"

"You got me a sexy red dress," she said. "You spent more than I wanted you to, but there was nothing I could do to stop you."

Wilde frowned.

"I'm talking about Secret. Was she in when you got there?"

Alabama nodded.

"She was."

"And?"

"And, wow. I didn't know they built them like that on this planet."

Wilde pictured it.

"What'd she say about the clothes?"

"On that front, I have some good news and some bad news," she said.

Wilde's chest tightened.

Bad news.

Damn it.

Bad news was never good.

"Tell me the good news first," he said.

"Well, the good news is that she absolutely loved the clothes. She changed into them right in front of me. That woman has a body like you can't even believe. The clothes fit perfectly, thanks to my incredible shopping abilities. I told her you wanted to pick her up at 7:30 and she told me to tell you she was looking forward to it."

She stopped to sip coffee.

Wilde wrinkled his forehead.

"So what's the bad news?"

"The bad news is that you're a good looking guy, Wilde, but you're not good looking the way Secret is," she said. "You'll never land her."

"That's the bad news, that I won't be able to land her?"

She nodded.

"We'll see about that."

"I can already tell you, it won't happen."

"We'll see."

"If you had a better personality, that might get you up to a one in ten chance. But you're you and you always will be. Therein lies your problem."

HE SMILED AND BLEW SMOKE, then told Alabama about his conversation with Michelle Day, the bartender at the El Ray Club. "She'd never seen this guy before, the one who looks like Robert Mitchum and even has the same first name. I've never seen him around either."

"It's a big town."

Wilde shook his head.

"It's not that big," he said. "The guy's a player. If he was from here, I would have bumped into him by now."

"What are you saying, that he's from out of town?"

Wilde nodded.

Exactly.

"Here's your next assignment," he said. "Go to every hotel in town and see if he stayed there this past weekend. Get a name and find out where he's from. I doubt that he's still in town. It sounds like he came in specifically to do what he did. Just the same, be careful. If he's still checked in, get a room number but don't do anything stupid. Repeat—don't do anything stupid. Come straight back here."

"Yes, master. Do you want me to model the dress you bought for me? It's in the other room."

Wilde pulled up an image.

Alabama scrubbed up pretty nice when she had a mind to.

Under different circumstances he might take a run at her.

Right now the circumstances were what they were.

They worked together.

"No."

She ran a finger down his chest.

"It's going to happen sooner or later," she said.

"No, it's not."

"Yes, it is." She paused and added, "I want to show you something."

She got a rubber band from the drawer and stretched it out to show it was straight. Then she popped it in her mouth. Ten seconds later she pulled it out.

It was in a knot.

She tossed it to him and left without looking back.

WILDE SET A BOOK OF matches on fire and watched Alabama through the flames as she swaggered down Larimer. Suddenly she turned to see if he was looking.

He tried to duck back but it was too late.

She saw him.

29

SU-MOON CAME UP WITH AN idea back at the scooter, just as the fog turned to a cold drizzle—"Let's hang around and see if the woman leaves. We can get her license plate number." They headed back to the parking lot and took cover in the shadows on the dry side of a van. Waverly couldn't get the spanking out of her head.

"Have you ever been spanked like that?" she said.

"Once. You?"

"No, never. Did you like it?"

"Someone else has control of you," she said. "That makes it dangerous. Danger can be an aphrodisiac. It can also be scary and inhibiting. It depends on the people involved. For me, the night I got it, it got me hornier than hell."

Waverly exhaled.

"I'm not sure if I'd like it or not."

"I'll tell you what. When we get home, I'll give you a few."

"Spanks?"

"Right."

"We'll see."

Ten minutes passed.

The drizzle turned to rain.

Five minutes passed.

The rain turned to a hard rain.

It crept around the van and into their clothes.

SUDDENLY THE SOUNDS OF SPLASHING feet and out-of-breath chatter entered the parking lot from the marina side. Waverly peeked around the edge of the van. It was Bristol and a woman, under an umbrella, walking fast.

"Bingo."

They made their way to a black Mercury where Bristol got the woman into the passenger seat then ran around to the driver's side, collapsing the umbrella and darting in.

The engine fired.

The headlights turned on.

The vehicle took off.

The women couldn't make out the license plate number.

"He's taking her home," Su-Moon said. "This is our chance."

"Our chance for what?"

"What do you think?"

Su-Moon grabbed Waverly's hand and led her at a trot back to C-Dock and down to Bristol's slip. The front door was locked.

The bedroom window was shut but not locked.

It lifted up when Su-Moon tried it.

They looked around and saw no one.

"Boost me up," Su-Moon said.

Waverly shivered.

"This is a bad idea."

"It will be if you keep wasting time," Su-Moon said. "Come on, boost me up—hurry."

Waverly looked around one last time and saw only black rain and lifeless houseboats. Then she cupped her hands for Su-Moon's foot and tried not to buckle under the woman's weight.

Inside, Su-Moon said, "Go around to the front and I'll let you in," then closed the window.

The front door was open by the time Waverly got there.

She entered and shut it behind her.

"What are we looking for?"

"I don't know, but it will be in the bedroom," Su-Moon said. "Maybe he keeps a journal."

"This is crazy."

"You keep a lookout, I'll search."

"I'm dripping water all over the floor."

"Don't worry, if it's still there by the time he gets back he'll think it's from him. Just keep a lookout."

WAVERLY GOT THE FRONT DOOR ajar and kept an eye on the dock. If someone approached, they wouldn't be visible until the last second.

The dock was a dead end.

It was a perfect place to be trapped.

Her heart pounded.

Something bad was going to happen.

They'd pressed their luck one step too far.

30

DAY ONE
JULY 21, 1952
MONDAY NIGHT

JANUARY HAD BEEN THROUGH A lot in her life, but what happened tonight shook her to the core. It took a hundred questions before River got the story out of her as to exactly what happened. Two drunk cowboys in a pickup truck spotted her on the side of the road and stopped.

She told them she had car trouble and her boyfriend had gone for help.

She tried to get rid of them but the one with the big gut—the one the other one called Jackson—ended up popping the hood. He fumbled around for a long time and eventually spotted the problem, one of the battery cables had come off.

He said, "Try it again."

She turned the key.

The engine started.

She said "thanks" and shifted into first but before she could pull away the other drunk—the stringy muscular one called Condor— grabbed the steering and turned the key off.

"You're going to give us a reward, right?"

She nodded.

"Sure."

She reached in her purse.

That's when Condor grabbed her tit and said, "I'm not talking about money, baby. Why don't you get your sweet ass out here and show us how grateful you are."

Her heart raced.

"Sure." She opened the door as far as it would before Condor's body blocked it. "Step back, baby."

When he did, January fired the engine, did a one-eighty and took off. They gave chase and ran her off the road.

Then they raped her, both of them.

They didn't do it nice.

They were mean about it.

THUNDER ROLLED THROUGH RIVER'S BLOOD as he listened.

"What'd they do with the keys?"

"They threw them that way," she said.

River shined the flashlight to where January pointed and said, "Over there?"

She nodded.

"Somewhere in that direction."

It took five minutes and he almost gave up twice, but then he found them, smack dab in the middle of yucca spines.

Yeah, baby.

The tires weren't buried and he was able to get the vehicle back to the road.

"Do you know which way they went?"

She did.

She was in the trunk but the assholes were shouting and honking the horn like some kind of sick victory celebration when they headed up the road.

"That way."

River put it in gear and took off, deeper into the country.

"Tell me about their truck," he said. "What'd it look like?"

"It was old," she said. "It was mostly white but the tailgate was a dark color, red or blue or black, something like that."

"It must have been replaced," River said. "Too bad for them."

31

DAY ONE
JULY 21, 1952
MONDAY NIGHT

IN THE BLACK DRESS, SECRET St. Rain was a sight that brought every single fiber of Wilde's universe to a screeching halt.

"Damn," he said.

"Is that a good damn or a bad damn?"

"I don't know. Did I say it out loud?"

She smiled.

Yes, he did.

"Then it's a good one." He spun her around to get a better look and said, "Bring your license for that body. I don't want to get arrested."

She grabbed her purse.

"Where are you taking me?"

"You'll see."

Twenty minutes later he escorted her through the front door of a smoky club called the Bokaray. Sex, sin, and perfume were already thicker than the law allowed. The bodies were sardine-tight and the bellies were full of alcohol. Speakers dropped whiskey-soaked jazz. That would change in half an hour when Mercedes Rain took the stage.

Everyone knew Wilde.

The men slapped him on the back.

The women planted kisses on his lips and cast sideways daggers at Secret.

"Mister Popular," she said when they got to the bar.

Wilde went to answer but a redhead waitress behind the counter grabbed his tie and pulled him halfway across. "Bryson Wilde, you dog, you're in love."

He put a shocked look on his face.

"Me?"

She shook her head in wonderment. "I thought I'd never see the day." Then to Secret, "He's never brought a woman here before. You're the first. I'm not saying he never left with one. I'm just saying he never brought one."

Secret tilted her head.

"So how many has he left with?"

"In round numbers?"

"Sure."

"Counting me or without me?"

"Either way."

"Tons."

WILDE PUT HIS ARM AROUND Secret's waist and swept her into the crowd saying, "She's just messing around." At the stage he introduced her to a sultry blond who set a glass of white wine down long enough to hug Wilde, then Secret.

She was Mercedes Rain.

"Secret's a blues singer," Wilde said. "I was thinking maybe you'd let her sit in on a song."

The woman looked at Secret.

"Sure, but if she sings anything like she looks, I'm going to need a new job." To Secret, "How about 'Lady Sings the Blues'? Do you know the words to that one?"

"I do, but . . ."

"Okay, we'll open up the second set with you," Mercedes said. To Wilde, "You want to take the drums on that number?"

"Sure."

"Done then," Mercedes said.

"No, not done," Secret said. "I'm not a singer. I've never been on a stage in my life."

"Then this will be your first time," Mercedes said. "Good luck."

WILDE GRABBED HER HAND, PULLED her through the crowd to the bar and ordered a white wine for her and a double Jack for himself.

Secret was confused.

"Why do you think I'm a singer?"

"Because I heard you."

"When?"

"When I went to the bathroom this morning."

She reflected back.

"You were singing to the radio," he said.

Her face focused.

"You heard that?"

He downed the Jack, slammed the jigger on the bar upside down and said, "Apparently I did. Why'd you think I brought you here tonight, to get you drunk and take advantage of you?"

"Well, the thought crossed my mind."

He ordered another Jack and said, "In that case, it looks like you were ten percent wrong."

She brought her mouth close to his.

Dangerously close.

Almost brushing.

Her breath was hot.

Hotter than sin.

"You're an evil man," she said.

32

DAY ONE
JULY 21, 1952
MONDAY NIGHT

WITH EVERY SECOND THAT PASSED, Waverly's throat got tighter and tighter. No menacing silhouettes were coming down the dock, but one could spring out of the cold black thickness at any second.

"Su-Moon, hurry up."

"I am hurrying up."

A moment passed.

Waverly kept her eyes fixed on the wooden planks that disappeared into the eerie weather.

A distant light washed through the darkness, faint and vague, bringing a luminescence to the rain.

It wasn't close but it was something.

Did headlights pull into the parking lot?

"We need to go," she said.

"One more drawer."

"Make it quick, I might have seen headlights."

"Hold on, I found a file."

A moment passed, then another.

"What are you doing?" Waverly said.

"This is weird."

"What's weird?"

"Quiet, let me read."

Waverly's chest tightened.

Breathing got difficult.

Suddenly what she feared would happen did happen.

A DARK SHAPE CAME DOWN the dock, hunched against the weather, walking fast but not so fast as to lose a grip on the slippery wood.

"He's coming!"

There was no time to get off the boat, the figure was that close.

Waverly stepped inside, closed the door and made sure it was locked. Su-Moon already had the candle blown out. Waverly met her there.

"What do we do?"

"Can you swim?"

"No."

The room had a door at the back wall. They opened it to find a narrow swim platform.

They stepped onto it and shut the door behind them.

The rain assaulted them.

It was a billion frozen needles.

The boat rocked, ever so slightly but enough to indicate that someone had stepped onto the front deck. Waverly checked around the edge of the boat, which stuck out ten feet past the edge of the finger. They couldn't reach it, not without getting into the water.

A narrow fixed ladder led to the roof.

They headed up, laid flat on their stomachs and got motionless.

Lightning arced across the sky.

The marina lit up.

The water was choppy.

Waverly suddenly had an image of it swallowing her down and sucking the last breath out of her lungs.

33

DAY ONE
JULY 21, 1952
MONDAY NIGHT

TEN MILES DOWN THE ROAD, a small prairie town popped up. On the main street of that town was a hillbilly-looking bar called the Coyote's Breath. A couple of dozen pickup trucks were parked in the vicinity together with a smattering of cars and a handful of motorcycles. One of those pickup trucks was white with a black tailgate.

River drove by slowly.

The place had no windows, but the door was propped open.

The interior was long and narrow. A bar ran down the right wall. The stools were filled with rough-looking drunks fondling brown bottles.

"Did you see 'em?"

January shook her head.

"No, but I can smell 'em."

River did a one-eighty, circled back, and scoped it a second time before pulling over at the end of the drag three blocks down and killing the engine.

"I'm not sure exactly how to do this," he said.

"Let's forget it."

He grunted.

"That's not an option."

She tugged on his arm.

"If you go in there, you're dead," she said.

He kissed her and said, "Stay here."

"River, no!"

He already had the door open.

"I'll be back."

A LOUDER AND LOUDER THUNDER pounded in his chest as he headed up the street.

He had no gun.

He had no knife.

He had no club.

When he got to the door he took a deep breath, crossed his chest, and stepped in. A jukebox somewhere near the back was spitting a hillbilly twang from crummy speakers. The air was thick with smoke and stale beer. The floor was scuffed linoleum, buried with butts and peanut shells.

River got onto the bar, grabbed a bottle of beer and smashed it on the edge of the counter.

Every face turned.

"Who owns that white pickup truck with the black tailgate?"

Noise broke out.

"Looks like we got ourselves a girl," someone said.

"A fag is more like it."

"Hey, baby, you want to choke on a big one?"

RIVER GAVE THE CLOSEST GUY a warning look.

"I said, who owns that white pickup truck with the black tailgate?"

Eyes turned to two men in the back standing next to the pool table with cues in hand.

One of them said, "Why the hell do you care?"

"Is it yours?"

"That's none of your damn business."

River hopped down and headed for him.

The bodies separated in front and closed in behind.

River got face to face with the man.

Their eyes were the same height.

He was a lot bigger close up.

"Is that your pickup truck?"

"Maybe. What's your problem, girlie?"

"You forgot to do something," River said.

He looked around. The faces were quiet. "I forgot to do something," he told everyone. Back to River, "So what did I forget to do exactly?"

"You forgot to cut your dick off," he said. "That's the proper etiquette after you rape someone. You cut your dick off and give it to 'em for a souvenir." He tossed the broken bottle onto the pool table. "You can use that."

Someone said, "Jesus, Jackson. Did you rape someone?"

"Hell no. He's making it up."

"Do it," River said. "Do it now. Do it now or I'll do it for you."

The man stepped back, slowly with a confused smile on his face, as if pondering the next thing he would say. Then he exploded in a motion that brought the thick end of the cue swinging with full force at River's face.

River jerked.

He was fast.

The stick was faster.

34

BY MOST PEOPLE'S SCORE, WILDE was Denver's best drummer, hands down, end of story, next subject please. He could land a seat with any band in its right mind as well as a few that weren't. He didn't do that though. Instead he filled in at clubs when regular drummers couldn't make it, for pay of course; that, and he did studio work—also for pay, also of course.

He was particularly effective in the studio.

He could keep a constant beat throughout the song.

He didn't speed up.

He didn't slow down.

He didn't get up halfway through to go to the restroom or spit-shine his wingtips.

He'd sat in with Mercedes Rain twice before, once when her regular drummer got arrested for murder, and the second time when her next drummer got arrested for murder.

"This probably means I'll get arrested for murder," he told her.

That was last year.

Now, tonight, he got Secret as composed as he could during the break.

In two minutes, the break would be over.

Wilde worked the drumsticks on his knee, getting the speed up.

"Here's the main thing to remember," he said.

"What?"

He tilted his head and softened his voice.

"Even a lot of established singers don't know what I'm about to tell you," he said. "But if you remember this one thing, you'll always be tops."

"Okay."

"Are you ready?"

"I'm ready."

"Whenever you sing, be sure you sleep with the drummer after the gig."

She punched him on the arm.

"You're awful."

"Thank you."

THEN THEY WERE UP.

Mercedes introduced them.

Secret took the microphone.

She was shy, uncertain, looking down.

Wilde got his frame comfortable on the throne.

Then the band broke into the greatest Lady Day song ever. Wilde altered his eyes from Secret's backside to the crowd.

Just as Secret was about to let the first word loose, something happened that Wilde didn't expect.

A familiar face appeared by the bar.

It was Alabama.

She wasn't work-Alabama, not at the moment, she was sexy-little-thing Alabama, wearing a short red dress that was strong on color but short on coverage.

She looked into Wilde's eyes, saw she had his attention and pointed discretely to her left.

He looked that way.

About four steps down, leaning against the bar, was a tall, good-looking man in a white suit and a matching hat.

For some reason he looked familiar.

Wilde couldn't put his finger on it.

SECRET STARTED SINGING.

Her voice was incredible.

Wilde hardly heard her; he was more focused on the man. Suddenly he realized why the guy looked familiar.

It was Robert Mitchum.

35

THE STORM WOULD KILL HER. Waverly knew that, deep down. Her core temperature was dropping and the wind was pounding the rain through her clothes and straight into her bones.

"I need to get out of the weather."

"Can you hold on another half hour until we're sure he's asleep?"

"No."

A beat.

"Okay, stay here a second."

Su-Moon crawled to the front of the boat, hung over the edge and studied what was below. Then she came back, slowly.

"There's no way down except to jump," she said. "It's not far but there's no way he won't feel it."

Waverly's heart raced.

She couldn't outrun anyone.

She could barely move.

"We have three options," Su-Moon said. "We can climb down the ladder, get in the water, make our way to the finger, and climb up."

"I can't swim."

"I'd have to hold you up."

"No, you'll drop me."

"You'll be fine."

"No, I won't. I already had a vision about drowning."

"Okay," Su-Moon said. "The other option is for you to get to the front of the boat. I'll climb down the ladder and get on the swim platform. I'll beat on the door to distract him. You jump down and head down the dock."

"How about you?"

"I'll dive in the water."

"What if he comes after you?"

"He'll still be half asleep. I don't think he will."

"What's the other option?"

"Okay," Su-Moon said. "The third option is that we both crawl to the front of the boat and drop down. As soon as we land, you head down the dock and disappear as fast as you can. I'll stay there. If he comes out, which he probably will, I'll pretend that I'm drunk and I'm on the wrong dock, I'm looking for D-22."

Waverly chewed on it.

Her core temperature dropped even more.

"Let's do it," she said. "Number three. I'll stay behind, though, not you."

"Can't do it that way," Su-Moon said. "He'll see your face."

"So?"

"So, you'll be working at his shop tomorrow, remember?"

Waverly hesitated.

"I just won't show up," she said. "Forget work. I don't want you taking the risk. This is my issue, not yours."

SUDDENLY THE BOAT SHIFTED, EVER so slightly, the kind of shift that would come from the movement of weight.

The black silhouette of a man appeared over the edge of the roof where the ladder came up.

A hand darted out and grabbed Waverly's ankle with the force of a vise.

"Got you!"

36

DAY ONE
JULY 21, 1952
MONDAY NIGHT

THE POOL CUE SMACKED UPSIDE River's head with a force that dropped him to his knees. Colors exploded deep in his brain and little hammers pounded at the inside of his skull. He was hurt and hurt bad. The hearing shut off in his left ear. He raised his hand to find it filled with blood.

Voices hollered.

They were deafening and jumbled and overlapped to the point where he couldn't understand anything except an occasional word.

A boot landed in his ribs.

"How's it feel, little girlie?"

His brain spun.

"You want some more? Huh? You want some more?"

Another kick came, lower, more in his stomach.

He braced for another one.

It came from behind him, from a second man.

Then an iron fist grabbed his hair and pulled his face up. Spit landed in his eyes.

"Cut his eyes out!" someone shouted.

A man's face got close to his.

"You want me to cut my dick off? I'll cut a dick off all right. It's not going to be mine, though."

"Do it!" someone shouted. "Cut it off."

River tried to get to his feet but couldn't.

His muscles wouldn't work.

His head was dark with pain.

Three guys held him down.

A fourth one grabbed his belt and undid it.

River struggled with every working molecule left in his body.

It did no good.

He wasn't even close.

SUDDENLY THE ROARING DIALED DOWN a touch, then abruptly fell to almost nothing.

Stop!

Stop!

Stop!

Stop!

Stop!

The voice came from a female somewhere behind him.

"Leave him alone!"

Now he recognized it; it came from January. He twisted his head and saw her, clutching what was left of her white dress to her body.

"Those men raped me," she said. "Him and him."

"Bullshit."

"Jesus, Jackson, look at her."

"She's lying."

To prove it, he punched her in the face.

She raised her hand, staggered back, and dropped to the ground. The dress fell to the side. She wore no panties. Between her legs there was blood.

She didn't move, not a muscle.

THE HANDS CAME OFF RIVER.

He staggered to his feet.

"Fair fight," someone shouted. "One at a time." A hand shook River's shoulder. "Is that good with you, mister? A fair fight, one at a time."

River said nothing.

Instead he picked January up and got her to a booth.

Her eyes opened.

She was hurt but she wouldn't die.

"Stay here," he said.

THEN HE WALKED BACK.

On the pool table he spotted a bottle of beer, half-empty. He drank what was left in one long swallow. Then he held the bottle by the neck and busted the bottom off. Jagged glass was left.

He set it down on the edge of the table and shook the blood out of his left ear.

He squared off to the two men.

"Now, cut your dicks off, both of you. Use that to do it. Cut 'em off or I'll do it for you. If I have to do it, I'm going to cut your eyes out too. First your dicks, then your eyes. Do you understand?"

One of the men tried to bust out.

The crowd closed in and pushed him back.

37

DAY ONE
JULY 21, 1952
MONDAY NIGHT

FROM HIS POSITION AT THE drums, Wilde watched helplessly as Alabama slipped off her barstool and made her way to the left. When she got to Robert Mitchum, she leaned into the bar, ostensibly to order a drink. Her ass was so close to his hand, it might have been touching.

Wilde knew what she was doing.

She was being stupid—the exact thing he told her not to be.

Sure enough, now they were talking.

She was instantly fascinated with this stranger in a white shirt and letting her chest brush up against him to prove it.

She smiled her smile.

She tossed her hair.

It wasn't clear if Mitchum was responding; but if he wasn't yet, he would be soon.

Alabama was hard to resist.

Even with all his strength, Wilde could hardly do it half the time.

Damn it, Alabama.

WHEN THE SONG WAS OVER, Secret got mobbed, she got mobbed so badly that Wilde didn't even try to squeeze in. One of the mob turned out to be Rex Sailwood, the owner of a local record label called Sky Records. He bought her a drink and chewed on her ear for fifteen minutes before she was able to break free.

"Don't tell me," Wilde said. "Sailwood's going to make you a star."

Secret was surprised.

"You know him?"

Wilde nodded.

He did.

"Is he legit?"

"Actually he is," Wilde said. "He's not as big as what you'll find in Chicago or New York, but he can get a record made and played."

She ran a finger down his nose.

"I'm going to take your advice and sleep with the drummer."

Wilde frowned.

"Do you see that guy over there at the bar in the white suit? The one molesting Alabama—"

She did.

"Is that the guy you saw on the roof?"

"I told you, I couldn't make him out."

"Could it be him?"

"It could be, but so could you. Why, is that him?"

"That's our friend Robert Mitchum," he said. "Alabama's making a move against my direct orders. Short term, if we stumble into them, pretend you don't know her. We can't blow her cover."

"What's long term?"

He lit a cigarette.

"Long term, we need to be sure she stays safe tonight, which is going to put a crimp in those plans you have for the drummer." He blew smoke. "To be more accurate, *I* need to be sure she stays safe tonight."

Secret kissed him.

"You had it right the first time—*We.*" A pause, then, "We need to find out if he recognizes me."

"That's a dead issue," Wilde said. "At this point he obviously will and we'll never know if it's from the other night or from the stage or from both."

"We'll know if he hunts me down," Secret said.

Wilde nodded.

"Yeah that would answer the question."

Secret punched him.

"Don't be so laid-back about it."

"Trust me, I'm not."

38

DAY ONE
JULY 21, 1952
MONDAY NIGHT

WAVERLY TWISTED AND JERKED AND did everything she could to get away from the grip that had her ankle. That did nothing but send her over the edge headfirst into the cold black waves.

Water filled her eyes and ears and nose.

She couldn't breathe.

Panic gripped her body and made it jerk.

Her head stayed under.

Her lungs burned.

She wanted one thing and one thing only: to breathe.

Seconds, that's all she had left.

Suddenly an arm came around her from behind. She tried to twist around and climb up the person but couldn't break loose.

Her head came above water.

Air.

Air.

Air.

She sucked it in so fast that water came with it and sent her into a coughing fit. She got a second breath, a clean one this time. Then she was over by the finger, the solid finger, and held on for dear life.

"Boost yourself up."

It was a man's voice.

Bristol's.

She tried.

"I can't!"

"Yes, you can. Do it."

She pulled again with all her strength. This time Bristol pushed from behind. Her chest got up onto the wood; then she pulled herself until her whole body was safe. Face down, she breathed. Nothing had ever felt so good. Splashing sounds came from behind her. Bristol was muscling his way out of the water. Then he was out, standing over her, dripping even colder water onto her already freezing-body.

He tapped a toe into her ribs.

"Get up."

The finger rocked—someone was running down it toward them. Waverly looked in that direction and saw the black silhouette of Su-Moon charging. The woman flung her body in the air over Waverly, hitting Bristol and sending him into the water.

She pulled Waverly to her feet.

"Come on."

That was last night.

NOW IT WAS TUESDAY MORNING and she opened the copper designer door of The Bristol Group and stepped into the frantic offices as if nothing happened. Last night had been dark and her face had been down. It was doubtful Bristol got a good enough look at her to recognize her in a different environment.

She'd find out soon enough.

Most of last night had been for naught. The only thing of interest in Bristol's boat was an architecture file relating to some kind of terminal and docking layout for a ferry company on the Hong Kong side of Victoria Harbour. Even that wasn't of much interest, being noteworthy only in the fact that it was at Bristol's house rather than at the office, and was three years old.

Why would he have a three-year-old architecture file at home in the bottom drawer of his dresser?

SEAN WATERFIELD SPOTTED HER AND headed over.

"You look nice," he said.

She lowered her voice.

"What do you know anything about a Hong Kong project?"

"You mean an architecture project, here at the firm?"

Right.

That.

He scratched his head.

"No."

"It was three or four years ago."

Three or four years ago.

He reached back.

"Wow, I hadn't thought about that in years," he said. "It wasn't a project. It was something we bid on. It never materialized. Another firm got the bid."

"Who."

"I can't remember. Why?"

A MAN'S FACE APPEARED.

"Are you the temp?"

Yes.

She was.

"I need you to make a donut run. Please and thank you." He handed her money. "Two dozen assorted."

Ten minutes later, picking out two dozen from behind a glass display at Rudy & Summer's World Famous Donuts, she had a nagging thought that she might not be able to take Bristol down if he turned out to be the dropper.

How could she do that to someone who snatched her out of the water?

39

DAY TWO
JULY 22, 1952
TUESDAY MORNING

RIVER WOKE TUESDAY MORNING IN a panic. He was supposed to take the target, Alexa Blank, no later than yesterday. That didn't get done. He needed to take her this morning, right now, before anyone found out he'd screwed up.

He rolled out of bed.

January reached over and grabbed his hand.

The covers fell off her body. The tattoo of a dragon started on her stomach, wrapped around her hip and over her ass, then around her left leg, ending slightly above the knee. Unlike the tattoos on her arm, which were a jumbled mess, this was a work of art with perfect colors and a fascinating imagination.

"Where you going?" she asked.

His instinct was to take her.

His body was strong enough now.

It hadn't been last night.

He shook it off.

"Business."

"This early?"

He nodded and kissed her.

"I'll be back by noon," he said. "Go back to sleep."

She curled up and closed her eyes.

He was halfway out the door when he heard, "River, come back here a minute. I lied to you about something."

He headed back.

"Lied about what?"

"About me," she said. "My initial plan was to kill you. I was just going to be nice and bide my time until the right moment came. What you did last night to those two guys, that made everything even. You don't have to worry about me anymore."

A beat passed while he processed it.

"Fair enough."

HE HEADED FOR THE SHOWER boxcar, got the temperature as hot as he could stand it, and lathered up.

Don't do anything stupid.

That was the important thing.

He needed to get Alexa Blank this morning but had to be careful to not be in such a rush that he did something stupid.

He had to be sure she didn't see his face.

He had to be sure no one saw him.

More than that, he had to be sure no one even connected him.

How was he supposed to do that in the daylight?

Even thinking about it was stupid.

HE TOOK THE CAR DOWNTOWN and swung by the Down Towner on foot.

There she was, pouring coffee into someone's cup.

She was fit.

Pretty, too.

She had a nice smile.

How did she factor into anyone's equation? What made her important enough to be a target? She was basically a walking nobody. She hardly registered on the world. Did she see something she shouldn't have? Did she know something she shouldn't?

Maybe River would question her after he took her.

The answer might turn out to be a lot more lucrative than the payment. The information might be something he could use to blackmail someone. He'd just need to be careful that it never got traced back to him. Maybe he'd let January take the lead if it got that far—set her up as the blackmailer.

Interesting.

Should he bring her in as a partner?

40

DAY TWO
JULY 22, 1952
TUESDAY MORNING

TUESDAY MORNING AT THE OFFICE, Wilde paced, chain-smoked and drowned his stomach in coffee. When Alabama walked through the door at 8:15 wearing the same dress as last night, Wilde hugged her tighter than tight and said, "You're alive."

Alabama knew the reason for the statement.

She had left the Bokaray with Robert Mitchum last night before Wilde could intercede. She spent the night with him.

"I was going to call and let you know I was okay," she said, "but I didn't want to blow my cover."

"Blow your cover? You're not supposed to have any cover. You're supposed to be doing one thing and one thing only, namely not doing anything stupid. Do you remember when my lips moved in that direction, when they said plain as day, don't do anything stupid?"

Yes.

She did.

But things got out of control.

She got dressed up last night to come down to the Bokaray. She spotted Mitchum at the bar and wandered over to see if he called himself Robert.

He did.

"He liked me," she said.

"He wasn't supposed to know you exist," Wilde said.

She poured a cup of coffee and took a long slurp.

"You would have done the same thing if you were me," she said.

Wilde set a book of matches on fire and lit a cigarette.

"Look," he said. "We're going to have this conversation one time and one time only. When I tell you what the risk boundaries are, you have to respect them. I set the boundaries and you stay in them, that's the way it is. I can't have you going rogue and doing your own thing. I can't be worrying about you when I need to be thinking about other things. When I tell you not to do something, you have to not do that something."

She smiled ever so slightly and wrapped her arms around his neck.

"You were worried about me?"

"Alabama, I'm serious."

She pecked a kiss on his lips.

"You're so cute when you're all protective," she said. "Do you want to know what I found out?"

Wilde took a long drag and blew smoke to the side.

"Just don't tell me you slept with him."

She ran a finger down his chest.

"Maybe you didn't get a good look at him," she said. "He actually is Robert Mitchum, only better."

SHE DRANK THE LAST OF what was in her cup and went to get another. Over her shoulder she said, "He's not the killer."

"How do you know?"

"I can't tell you. You'll get mad."

41

DAY TWO
JULY 22, 1952
TUESDAY MORNING

TOM BRISTOL PASSED BY WAVERLY three or four times and didn't once emit a glimmer of a reaction to indicate that he recognized her from the little fiasco at the houseboat last night. Every time Waverly saw him, she pictured his hand slapping down on an ass.

She needed to find the owner of that ass and warn her.

Bristol was dirty.

Waverly could feel it.

At 9:30, Su-Moon called with some unexpected news. "I'm down the street from the marina. I'm going back to the houseboat."

"Are you nuts?"

"He's at the office right now, right?"

Yes.

He was.

"Write this number down," Su-Moon said. Waverly picked up a pencil and wrote numbers on the top sheet of a scratch pad. "That's Bristol's home phone number. If he leaves the office, call that number and let it ring twice. That will be my cue he's loose."

"What are you trying to find?"

"Whatever·it was we missed last night."

Waverly exhaled.

"Don't do it."

"Talk to you later."

"I'm serious. I have a bad feeling."

"You always have a bad feeling."

AN HOUR PASSED, THEN ANOTHER. Bristol didn't wander from the office haunts and Su-Moon would have been long done by now. Still, when Sean Waterfield swung by and asked Waverly if she wanted to go to lunch, she dialed Bristol's number and let the phone ring twice before leaving, just to be safe.

They ended up at Fisherman's Wharf with takeout plates of shrimp and rice, which they ate on the edge of a dock.

Their legs dangled over the water.

The boats were out to sea.

Mooring posts were wrapped in tires.

Seagulls filled the air.

The street buzzed with vendors.

The sky was clear but the temperature wasn't more than seventy.

"That Hong Kong deal was weird from the get-go," Waterfield said. "We were big in Europe but hadn't done anything in Asia yet. This would be our first. Tom Bristol went there to personally meet with the owners and go over the specs. He came back as excited as I've ever seen him. He worked up all the drawings and bid documents himself, working until who-knows-when every night after the rest of us left. The bid got submitted and then he crossed his fingers and waited. In the end, another firm got the project."

"Which firm?"

"I can't remember," Waterfield said. "It doesn't really matter. It wasn't ours."

SUDDENLY A FIGURE APPEARED IN Waverly's peripheral vision and sat down next to her.

It was the last person in the world she expected.

Tom Bristol.

He looked at Waterfield and said, "Sean, are you putting the moves on our new temp?"

Waterfield nodded.

"Got to," he said. "Look at her."

42

DAY TWO
JULY 22, 1952
TUESDAY MORNING

WITH NO GOOD WAY TO abduct the little-nobody-waitress target at the moment, River headed back home to the rail spur to find January scrubbed up and looking pretty damn nice. She handed him a sealed envelope and said, "This was taped on the outside of the door."

"Did you see who put it there?"

"No, why?"

"Just curious."

Inside was a short, sweet message: "You missed the deadline. Contract is rescinded."

River tore it in half, then another half and another, and threw it on the ground.

"What's wrong?"

River heard the words coming out of January's mouth but his brain was on too much fire to process them.

"What's wrong?" she repeated.

"Later," he said.

His body was already in motion, trotting for the car.

January was suddenly running at his side.

"Let me come with you."

"No."

"River—"

He swung her to a stop and held her at arms length. "Stay here."

"But—"

"I'll explain when I get back," he said. "Right now it's best if no one sees your face."

"Why?"

He kissed her.

"Just trust me," he said. "Stay here till I get back."

Then he was in the car and gone.

HE POINTED THE FRONT END downtown, paying just enough attention to traffic to not bend someone's fender.

Worst-case scenarios pounded through his brain.

He'd never had a contract rescinded before.

This was bad.

Bad.

Bad.

Bad.

Bad.

Bad.

It might even be the end.

Not just the end of his tenure but the end of his life. If they weren't going to use him anymore, why would they let him keep breathing? What was the upside?

There wasn't one.

He'd be a lot less risky six feet under in a wooden box. Let the spiders crawl over his face.

How would they take him out?

A cowardly bullet from the distance?

A knife in the back?

A rope around the neck?

More importantly, when would it come?

Tonight?

Yeah.

It would be tonight.

He could feel it moving in, like an ugly black sky.

One thing was clear, crystal clear, crystal clear beyond belief, namely he'd been a fool for working all these years without knowing who he was working for. He should have never let the money lure him in. That would never happen again, guaranteed.

He parked a block down the street and headed to Alexa Blank's restaurant at a brisk pace.

Through the window he saw her.

She was in a white dress and a black apron carrying two plates of food to a table.

HE OPENED THE DOOR, STEPPED inside and took a seat in the corner booth.

She smiled at him and said, "Be right there."

"No rush."

43

DAY TWO
JULY 22, 1952
TUESDAY MORNING

WHEN WILDE PRESSED ALABAMA TO tell him how she knew Mitchum wasn't the dropper, she eventually relented even though he'd get mad. "I told him I had a secret place where you could see all the lights of Denver. When he asked where it was, I said, *It's up on a roof over on Market Street. You want to go there with me?*"

Wilde frowned.

"That was stupid."

"Yeah, well, if he'd said yes, I wasn't really going to go," she said. "I was going to pretend to sprain my ankle or something. The important thing is that he wasn't interested. He was more interested in a nice soft bed."

"And that's what happened, the bed?"

She nodded.

Wilde pictured it.

He must have had a look, because Alabama punched him on the arm and said, "You're jealous."

"No, I'm not."

"Yes, you are."

"No, I'm not."

"Just say the word," she said.

"What word?"

"Tell me I'm yours."

Wilde lit a book a matches on fire, let them burn down to his fingertips and threw them out the window.

"I don't want you to see him again," he said. "This isn't a game."

"See, you are jealous."

"No, I'm not. The thing is, just because he didn't want to go to a roof doesn't mean he's not the dropper. Who knows how these guys think? Maybe he'll just store it away for a week and jack off to it. Then one night seemingly out of nowhere he'll say, *Hey, didn't you mention once about wanting to see lights?*"

"*Jack off to it*," Alabama said. "You're such a poet."

Wilde nodded.

"I'm a poet and don't know it," he said. "I can make a rhyme any time." He put a somber expression on his face. "I'm serious when I said not to see him again."

"He's a good lover," Alabama said. "You're probably better, but then again I don't really know."

"Alabama—"

"Look at it this way," she said. "If he's not the dropper, no harm done and I get a little very-much-needed R&R. If he is, he'll suggest that roof thing at some point. I won't go up, don't worry, I'm not that stupid. Either way, we win."

Wilde lit a cigarette.

"I'll fire you if I have to."

"Go ahead and try."

"Fine, remember it was your idea," he said. "You're fired."

She ran her fingers through his hair.

"Looks like it didn't work," she said. "I'm going to pick up some donuts. You want any particular kind?"

He paused.

"White cake with chocolate frosting."

She tweaked his nose.

"I'll see what I can do."

TWO MINUTES AFTER SHE LEFT, the door opened and Secret walked in wearing white shorts and perfect golden legs. She pulled a pink tank top up and rubbed her stomach on Wilde's.

"Tonight," she said.

Wilde knew what she meant.

They hadn't done it last night thanks to Alabama's little disappearing trick.

"Tonight?" Wilde said. He put his arms around her waist. "What's wrong with right now?"

"You're kidding, right?"

No.

He wasn't.

He wasn't at all.

To prove it, he flung her over his shoulder, locked the door, took her into the adjacent room, and kicked the door shut with his foot.

There were no windows.

The darkness was pure magic.

He laid her on the floor, stuck a knee between her legs, and kissed her deep.

She responded.

Slowly.

Then she responded more.

Suddenly a terrible thought entered Wilde's head—Alabama; she'd be back with donuts right in the middle of everything.

He got to his feet and said, "Don't go anywhere."

"Wilde—"

"I'll be right back."

At the main door, he hung his tie on the outside knob and relocked everything tighter than tight.

Figure out the code, Alabama.
Figure it out or I really will fire you.

BACK BETWEEN SECRET'S LEGS, HE picked up where he'd left off, except the woman had something to say. "I remember what I wanted to tell you. Something popped into my head this morning. I think I read something back in New York a couple of years ago about a woman falling from a building."

"You mean like here?"

"I don't know about that," she said. "All I remember is thinking that it would be a horrible way to go."

Yeah.

Right.

He didn't care.

At this second he cared about one thing and one thing only.

His mouth went to hers.

His hand went between her thighs.

44

DAY TWO
JULY 22, 1952
TUESDAY AFTERNOON

THE TALK AT FISHERMAN'S WHARF was small and inconsequential, neither focused on business nor anything of significance. In the end, Waverly wasn't sure if Bristol's appearance was planned or accidental. When she got back to the office, however, the top sheet of the scratch pad—the one she had written Bristol's home number on—was gone.

Had Bristol spotted it as he walked past?

Did he wonder what his home phone number was doing on Waverly's desk?

Did he tail her and swing by, as if by chance, to get a feel for her?

Did he connect the dots between the number and the events of last night?

Bolt.

That's what her gut said: bolt.

Something ugly was headed her way.

The phone rang with calls all afternoon. A good number of them were for Bristol, who never tipped a hand when Waverly patched them through. Then an unexpected call came, for none other than Waverly herself, from Su-Moon.

"I'M OUTSIDE THE BUILDING ON the street," she said. "Find an excuse to come down here. I need to talk to you."

Five minutes later, Waverly slipped out, bypassed the elevator, and bounded down the stairs two at a time to street level.

Su-Moon was clearly excited.

"Big news," she said. "I wasn't finding anything, not for a long time, but my mind kept going back to this Land Camera that was stashed in the top dresser drawer. At first I didn't know why it kept nagging me, then I realized that it was because I hadn't come across any photos— only the camera, no photos. That's when I started to dig deeper."

She pulled an envelope out of her purse.

"I found this taped underneath the bottom drawer of the dresser. Take a look."

Waverly opened it.

Inside were dozens upon dozens of black-and-white Polaroid film photos.

All of them were of women.

Most of them were naked or close to it, posing in lewd positions.

"There are at least five different women in these photos," Su-Moon said. "I'll bet dollars to donuts that one of them is Kava Every. That's what you need to find out."

"How?"

"I don't know, just do it."

Waverly handed the envelope back.

Su-Moon wouldn't take it.

"You keep it," she said.

Waverly shook her head.

"You need to go put it back," she said. "He's going to find it missing."

"Who cares?"

"We care."

"No, we don't," Su-Moon said. "Wait, give it to me a minute." She took it, flipped through the photos until she got to one near the back and said, "These. These are the ones that interest me."

Waverly studied them.

THERE WERE SEVEN OR EIGHT photos. In each one, the woman wore a dress. A fan was underneath her, blowing the dress up.

They were very erotic.

"What about them?" Waverly said.

"Look at their dresses."

"I am."

"And what do you see?"

"They're blowing up."

"Does that strike you as strange?"

"They all strike me as strange."

"Let me put it this way," Su-Moon said. "That's what their dresses would look like if they were falling off a building."

She handed the envelope back to Waverly.

"Go find out if one of these women is Kava Every."

45

DAY TWO
JULY 22, 1952
TUESDAY MORNING

ALEXA BLANK WAS A BLUE-eyed princess with strawberry pigtails and a spring in her step. Looking into her eyes, River was glad the contract had been rescinded. She'd be a hard one to kill. She pulled a pencil and pad out of her apron and said, "What'll it be, cowboy?"

"Coffee." A beat, then he added, "But not here."

She wrinkled her forehead.

"Not here?"

"No, not here," he said. "Down the street."

"Down the street?"

He nodded.

"At a different restaurant. With you."

She shifted into a sexier position, edging in ever so slightly.

"With me, huh?"

"Right. With you."

"You're hitting on me."

"I am."

She studied his eyes and found no lies. A smile worked its way onto her mouth.

"Be careful," she said. "I might call your bluff."

"Start calling, because I'm dead serious."

She stood there deciding, then slipped out of her apron, tossed it across the counter next to the donuts and said, "Mary, I got to run a quick errand. Be a peach and take my tables for ten minutes, will you?"

OUTSIDE, SHE LOCKED HER ARM through River's as they headed down the street.

"I don't do this with just anybody," she said.

"Me either."

"Really?"

"Really."

She moved her hand up and felt his muscles. "You remind me of Tarzan."

"You mean I'm someone who belongs in a jungle?"

She punched his arm.

"No, I mean it in a good way. What's your name?"

He hesitated.

"River," he said. "Dayton River."

She shook his hand.

"I'm Alexa Blank."

"I know."

She furrowed her eyes.

"You know? How do you know?"

"I know because someone hired me to abduct you," he said.

46

DAY TWO

JULY 22, 1952

TUESDAY MORNING

ALABAMA WAS SITTING BEHIND THE desk munching on a donut with her feet propped up when Wilde opened the door into the main room. By the look on her face, she was getting a kick out of the one on his. "How long have you been here?"

She ignored him, looked at Secret, and said, "I hope he's better than he sounds."

Secret smiled.

"He was okay."

Wilde looked at her.

"*Okay?*"

She nodded.

"*Just okay?*"

"There's nothing wrong with okay," she said. "Especially for your first time. You'll get better."

"*My first time?*"

"Right," she said. "We all have one. We're clumsy and awkward; then we improve."

Wilde lit a cigarette and blew smoke at her.

"Not funny."

Alabama picked a tie off the desk and threw it to Wilde. "You forgot that on the doorknob." To Secret, "Don't count on him improving. He's not all that trainable."

"I already figured that out."

WILDE HATED LIBRARIES.

He hated the musty smells and the squeaky wheels of the shelving carts and most of all he hated the quiet air. He couldn't think when it was that quiet. Well, that wasn't completely true: he could think, but what he usually thought about was the fact that he needed to keep quiet.

After Secret left, Wilde told Alabama that Secret remembered reading something about a woman falling from a building in New York two or three years ago.

"Go down to the library, dig through the old New York papers and see what you can find out about it."

"Why?"

"I'm curious if the woman was wearing a red dress."

"You think there's a connection to what happened here?"

He shrugged.

"That's what you're going to find out."

She pecked a kiss on his cheek and headed for the door

"Yes, master."

Then she was gone.

HE STOOD THERE IN SILENCE.

Something was wrong.

His brain was trying to grasp a thought but was having trouble.

Then it came to him.

He leaned out the window and waited for Alabama to appear at street level.

"Hey, 'Bama."

She looked up.

"What?"

"I really don't want you to see Robert Mitchum again."

She blew him a kiss.

"I won't if you don't see Secret again."

"That's different, and you know it."

"Actually, I don't."

47

DAY TWO

JULY 22, 1952

TUESDAY MORNING

WHEN WAVERLY ASKED WATERFIELD IF he knew where she could get a good recent picture of Kava Every, at first he had no idea. An hour later, he led her to a storage room and shut the door. Leaning against a box was an eight-by-ten group photo framed in glass, now broken. "This was taken at the firm's retreat," he said. "That's Kava right there."

Waverly's heart raced.

She was ninety-nine percent sure that the woman was one of the same ones from the envelope under Bristol's dresser.

She looked at Waterfield.

"Can I take this?"

He narrowed his eyes.

"Okay."

He pulled it out, rolled it up, and hid the frame behind a box.

"Are you okay?"

A beat.

Then she nodded.

"Bristol was having sex with her," she said.

"How do you know?"

"I'll explain later."

"When?"

"Tonight."

When they opened the door and stepped out, something happened they didn't expect.

Tom Bristol was leaning against the wall.

His arms were folded.

He was waiting for them.

HIS EYES FELL TO WAVERLY'S purse.

She followed them down.

To her horror, the end of the photograph stuck out. Bristol grabbed it, snatched it out and unrolled it. "This is firm property," he said. "What else do you have in there you're not supposed to?"

He grabbed her purse.

Then he pulled out the envelope and waved it in front of her face.

"That's not yours either," he said. "I called the temp agency. They never heard of you." To Waterfield, "You knew that, didn't you? You knew she wasn't a real temp."

Waterfield's eyes flickered.

Then they got hard and he said, "If she's not a temp, that's news to me."

"Oh, really?"

"Yeah, why? What's going on?"

"Then what's she doing with the photo?"

"What do you think? I'm sending her out to get it reframed."

"Bullshit."

Waterfield softened, as if caught.

"Okay, the truth is that I brought her back here in the hopes of coping a feel," he said. "Then I got worried about someone seeing us coming out together. I gave her the photo to have an excuse for being in here, that I was giving it to her to get it reframed."

"Bullshit," Bristol said. "Get out of my sight, you're fired." Then to Waverly, "As for you, you better learn to swim, because the next time you're in the water I'm not going to pull you out."

Waverly couldn't breathe.

She couldn't move.

"Get out of here and don't come back," Bristol said.

Her lips quivered.

Leave.

Leave.

Leave.

She couldn't make her feet move.

"Get out," Bristol said.

Suddenly something snapped in Waverly's head. Thunder rolled through her veins at what she was about to do.

Then she snatched the envelope out of Bristol's hand and ran.

"Get back here, you bitch!"

Go!

Go!

Go!

Go!

Go!

48

DAY TWO

JULY 22, 1952

TUESDAY MORNING

WHEN RIVER TOLD ALEXA BLANK that someone hired him to abduct her and await further instructions as to whether to kill her or not, it took her a moment to realize it wasn't a joke. "After I got hired, I got fired," he added. "That's because I was supposed to get the job done by last night and didn't. What that means is that someone else now has the job. Since the target time was last night, my suspicion is that he's already on your tail." He looked around. "He might even be watching us right now."

She stared in disbelief.

Then she walked away and said over her shoulder, "You're cute, but you're way too weird for me. Have a nice life."

River caught up to her, grabbed her arm, and jerked her to a stop.

"I'm here to help you," he said. "You need to trust me."

She shook her arm free.

"Get the hell away from me or I'll call the cops."

Then she was gone, heading down the street and disappearing into the restaurant.

River waited for five minutes before following her in and taking a seat in the corner booth.

She was back in uniform.

Shaken.

Confused.

River waved at her and said, "Coffee, please."

She ignored him.

She didn't disappear into the kitchen and out the back, though. Nor did she head over to the phone to call the cops. River flagged down the other waitress, ordered coffee, and sipped it.

He eased back in the booth and stretched his legs out on the bench.

He didn't stare at the woman.

He kept his eyes pointed out the front window, watching the skirts and suits parade past, ready to get up if someone looked too much like a killer.

Ten minutes passed.

He got a second cup.

More time passed.

A half hour.

An hour.

Alexa Blank was beginning to look his way with greater and greater frequency. Then, when River was hardly paying attention, she slipped in and locked eyes.

"Who hired you?"

River shook his head.

"I don't know," he said. "That's what I want you to help me figure out."

"How?"

He shrugged.

"Who wants you dead?"

"I don't know."

"You have to know."

"Well, I might *have to*, but I *don't*."

RIVER STUDIED HER EYES and found no lies.

"What I propose is that you and me slip out the back right now and sort this out someplace quiet." She was about to say something when River interrupted her. "Think long and hard before you say no. I'm only going to give you this chance one time." A beat, then "You have ten seconds to give me your answer. After that I'm gone and you're on your own."

She darted her eyes.

"How do I know this isn't a trick to get me to leave with you?"

"You don't," he said, standing up. "Five seconds."

49

DAY TWO

JULY 22, 1952

TUESDAY AFTERNOON

THE DARK BEAUTY LONDON MARSHALL bounded through the door early afternoon looking like a hundred crazed banshees were on her tail. "Someone broke into my house," she said. "It's trashed."

"When?"

"I don't know," she said. "When I left for work this morning everything was fine. When I swung by just now, it was trashed."

Wilde swung his suit jacket over his shoulder and dipped his hat over his left eye.

"Let's have a look."

At street level, Wilde pointed to Blondie and said, "That's mine, the little green one."

London headed to the passenger side and slipped in to find the steering wheel in front of her.

"It's English," Wilde said. "Everything's backwards."

They got rearranged and Wilde merged the front end into thick noon-hour traffic.

He exhaled and said, "I have to be honest. I haven't had ten seconds to work on your case."

"That's okay."

"I'm sorry."

"It's okay, I understand."

"I'm on it now, though," he said.

"You still have the map, right?"

He put a confused expression on his face and shot her a sideways glance.

"I thought I gave that back to you."

Her mouth opened.

"Just kidding," he said. "Yeah, I have it."

THE WOMAN SMELLED NICE.

Her voice was a song.

She was a vision in white—a white skirt, a matching white jacket, a white blouse, and white high-heels.

The skirt rode up as they drove.

Wilde kept his eyes off her nylons, but it was a struggle.

Her house turned out to be a two-story Tudor in a nice section of town out by Colorado Boulevard. The tree-lawns were wide and lined with shady elms. Vines crept up wrought-iron fences. It wasn't Capitol Hill, but it wasn't anything to sneeze at.

London led him around to the back.

The door had been jimmied.

"This is how he got in," she said. "From the get-go, he didn't care if I knew he'd been here. The first time was different—he was discrete. This time, he was out for blood."

Inside, a bomb had gone off.

Everything in the kitchen cabinets had been swept out and smashed on the floor. The drawers were pulled out, tipped upside down, and dropped.

Cushions were cut open.

Clocks and TVs were smashed.

Furniture was overturned.

"I HAVE SOME BAD NEWS," Wilde said. "This was his last chance trying to find the map on his own. You're next. He's going to grab you and make you tell him where it is. I'm sorry to be so blunt, but I don't want to sugarcoat it. You need to know what you're up against."

She flipped a couch back upright, put the cushions in place, and sat down.

"I can't run," she said. "I have a job, friends, everything. My whole life is here in Denver. I have a trial starting next week."

Wilde lit a cigarette.

"In that case, we'll have to go to Plan B."

"Which is what?"

"There are two options."

"Which are what?"

"The easiest one is to just give him the map."

She shook her head.

"That's not going to happen. What's the other option?"

"The other option is that we trap him."

"How?"

"By dangling the bait."

"Meaning me."

Wilde nodded.

"You and the map."

"How do we do that?"

"I don't know, but we need to do it tonight. Like you said, he's out for blood."

She stared out the window, then back at Wilde.

"What happens if we actually get him trapped? Do we kill him?"

Wilde shrugged.

"Maybe he'll put us in a position where we have no choice. Self-defense and all that." A beat, then "In the meantime, you'll need to go down to the police department and file a report."

London shook her head.

"I don't want anyone to know about the map."

"You don't have to tell them about the map," Wilde said. "Just get the report on file and let 'em come out here and investigate. Then if the guy shows back up and ends up dead, they'll know it was self-defense." He frowned and added, "Keep in mind that the guy is probably just a hired gun. If he ends up dead, he'll get replaced. We need to get to the source."

"How?"

"I don't know."

"You must have some idea."

"Well, there is one thing," he said. "The guy probably knows who hired him. If we ask him nice and polite and put a cherry on top, maybe he'll tell us."

London smiled.

"I'll pick up some cherries this afternoon."

"They're in the produce section."

50

DAY TWO

JULY 22, 1952

TUESDAY AFTERNOON

WITH THE ENVELOPE CLENCHED IN her fist, Waverly got to the stairwell and bounded down three at a time, with Bristol no more than a heartbeat behind. With every step, she expected a fist to lock into her hair and snap her neck back so hard that her body yanked out.

Two seconds went by.

No fist came.

Then more seconds passed.

She made it to street level and ran with every molecule of strength she could summons.

Her lungs burned.

Her muscles cried.

The streets were crowded. She weaved through pedestrians as best she could.

A cup of coffee flew out of a hand.

An elderly lady tumbled to the ground.

Bristol didn't let up.

He stayed behind her.

He didn't care that people were staring.

He didn't care a damn.

A half block went by.

Waverly swung onto the tail end of a moving trolley, dangled dangerously, then got a foot planted. A look back showed Bristol sprinting at full strength but dropping back.

He slammed one fist into the other.

Then he bent over, braced his hands on his knees, and sucked air.

WAVERLY CHECKED THE ENVELOPE TO be sure the photos hadn't dropped out.

They hadn't.

They were all there.

She already knew what she had to do.

She had to find out who they were.

She also had to find out if they were still alive or had met a strange death like Kava Every.

She shoved the envelope in her purse.

Got you, Bristol.

Got you by the balls.

51

DAY TWO
JULY 22, 1952
TUESDAY MORNING

RIVER DRANK COFFEE WHILE ALEXA Blank tended to tables, deciding whether he was angel or demon. It was several minutes before she swung by with an answer. "Let me see your driver's license."

"Why?"

"Just do it."

He obliged.

She studied it and said, "Dayton River, like you said." She handed it back. "Get your car and pick me up behind here in the alley in ten minutes. You see that other waitress over there?"

River nodded.

"I told her that if I end up dead, you're the one who did it. I told her your name, Dayton River."

"You won't end up dead."

"I can't believe I'm doing this."

Heading out of Denver, they didn't talk much. River concentrated on the rearview mirror, studying every car, looking for a killer behind a wheel. At the edge of the city he made several evasive turns. No one followed. The woman kept a sideways eye on him and had her body pressed against the door as far away as she could.

"Relax," he said.

"How?"

"I'm not going to hurt you," he said. "My assignment was to abduct you and not let you see my face. I would be contacted later and told whether I should kill you or let you go. My question is why?"

"I don't know."

River frowned.

"This is important," he said. "Think."

"I am thinking."

"Do you have any enemies?"

"No."

"Boyfriends?"

"No."

"Did you see something you shouldn't have?"

"No."

"Do you know something you shouldn't?"

"No."

"Are you blackmailing someone?"

"No."

"Did you steal something?"

"No."

"Are you a mistress?"

"No, I'm a waitress," she said. "That's all I am, just a waitress."

"That might be true, but you're a waitress who's on someone's radar screen."

She stared out the windshield.

"According to you," she said.

"Not according to me," River said. "You are, trust me."

"I am trusting you, but it's hard."

River patted her hand.

"I know," he said. "I wish I could say something encouraging. Unfortunately, it's going to get harder before it gets easier."

THE CITY GOT SMALLER.

The country got bigger.

Black and white magpies appeared in the sky.

Rabbit brush grew in number and size.

"Where are we going?"

"We're going to your new home, until we can figure this out."

"What is it, a house?"

"No, it's something you're not going to like." A beat, then "If you want to live, you're going to need to be strong. I'll help you all I can, but most of it's going to depend on you."

52

DAY TWO
JULY 22, 1952
TUESDAY AFTERNOON

ALABAMA HAD BIG NEWS WHEN she returned from the library. "You're like a monkey pecking at a typewriter," she said. "Sooner or later you were bound to spell a word."

Wilde smiled.

"So what word did I spell?"

"Connection."

"Connection?"

Right.

Connection.

Wilde scratched his head. "I'm glad I did it pecking, then, because I'm not sure I could do it on purpose."

She handed him a printout of a newspaper article.

"Read it and weep," she said.

It was a short article dated August 14, 1949, about a thirty-year-old woman named Brittany Pratt who had been found at the bottom of a six-story office building in lower Manhattan the previous morning. Police were investigating to try to determine the cause of the fall.

"This happened three years ago," he said.

"Right."

"That's a cold trail," he said. "There's nothing in here about whether she was wearing a dress or not."

"She was," Alabama said. "It was red, too."

"How do you know?"

"I can tell."

"How?"

"The same way I can tell that you want to see me naked," she said. "Instinct."

Wilde smiled.

"I've already seen you naked," he said. "Besides, that's a totally different analogy. The reporter's name is Michael Hyatt. Call the paper and see if he's still there. If he is, find out if he knows anything that isn't in the article. Maybe he did a follow-up investigation or kept in touch with the police."

"That can be arranged."

"Good."

"I'm talking about seeing me naked," she said.

"I thought you were saving that for Robert Mitchum."

"I'm saving that for you," she said. "Mitchum's just a fill-in until you come to your senses."

"Call the reporter."

"Now?"

He handed her the phone.

"Yes, now."

"What are you going to do while I'm doing that?"

He lit a cigarette.

"Smoke."

SOMETIMES THE UNIVERSE WORKS THE way it should. Not only was the reporter still with the paper, but he actually had something to say.

"It's so funny that you ask whether she was wearing a dress," he said. "She was. A red one."

"Short or long?"

"Short," he said. "It was up around her waist."

"Was she wearing panties?"

Yes.

She was.

"White."

"How do you know?"

"I was the person who found her."

"You're messing with me."

"I'm not. I was out walking and there she was," he said. "I'll never forget it, not as long as I live. At first I thought she'd just passed out or something. There wasn't as much blood as you'd think. Then when I got closer I could see the blood under her head and matted in her hair. The back of her skull was crushed like an eggshell."

He talked to the woman's neighbors and friends afterwards.

"Not a one of them thought it was suicide," he said. "It was either an accident or murder. My money was and still is on murder. The funny thing is, though, she was squeaky clean in every way. No one had a motive to kill her, not even a tiny little one. Believe me, I checked. Being the one who found her, the whole thing became pretty personal for me."

"Was she pretty?"

"Very," he said. "Here's the bad part about it. She had a five-year-old daughter. She was a single mom. The kid—her name's Mandy—ended up in the orphanage right down the street from where her mom was killed. She's still there. I go by every day and take her a candy bar."

"That's nice of you."

"The truth is that I do it as much for me as for her," he said. "What's your interest in her?"

Alabama explained.

They might have a related case.

"I'll help any way I can," he said. "I'd give my right nut to catch the guy, especially now that I know he did it again."

"Thanks for the visual."

He chuckled.

"I have more if you need 'em."

"No, that one will be enough."

She almost hung up.

"Hey, you still there?"

He was.

"Where was she, the night she got dropped?"

"She went out to a bar."

"Alone?"

"As far as I know."

"What bar?"

A beat.

"I'd have to pull my notes and get back to you," he said. "I'm drawing a blank. Give me your number."

She did.

They hung up.

TO WILDE, "NEXT TIME I tell you I know something because of my intuition, I want to see a little respect from your end."

"Yes, Ma'am."

"That's better."

"I'll give you even more respect if you can reach into your bag of intuition and pull the guy's name out."

She ran a finger down his chest.

"For that, I'd need my crystal ball. Unfortunately, it's in the shop right now."

"In that case, why don't you do this? Find out if your little lover-boy friend Robert Mitchum was in New York when the woman got dropped."

She frowned.

"He's not the one."

"In that case, indulge me."

53

DAY TWO

JULY 22, 1952

TUESDAY AFTERNOON

WAVERLY HAD NEVER SEEN MURDER in someone's eyes, but recognized it as crystal as crystal can be in that last, long, hateful look from Bristol. He would kill her. Nothing else mattered other than killing her and feeding the rage in his brain.

He was a snake.

She was a mouse.

The sun was bright, but the railing on the back of the trolley was cold.

The wind blew straight into her bones.

The city looked the same as always but was different.

It was cold.

It was foreign.

It was as if it could care less if she was alive or dead.

Suddenly a hand grabbed her arm.

"Lady, you're too close to the edge."

She looked over.

It was a young Asian kid in a baseball cap, about ten or eleven.

"You're going to fall off."

He directed her into the guts of the trolley. The wind disappeared except for what came through the windows—just enough to sweep her hair.

She looked at him.

His eyes were kind.

They were the opposite of Bristol's.

The city softened.

Her bones warmed.

"Thanks," she said.

SHE MADE HER WAY TO the Green Dragon Oriental Massage Parlor to find that Su-Moon hadn't returned yet, so she waited in the woman's apartment and kept one eye on the street from behind closed blinds. Something happened that she didn't expect, namely Sean Waterfield came into sight.

He disappeared into the massage parlor for a time, then reemerged and leaned against a building on the sunny side of the street.

Waverly paced for a few minutes, then headed down.

The man's face was serious.

"Bristol calmed down. I'm not fired, but we need to get those photos back to him," he said.

"Why?"

"Because they're his," Waterfield said.

"They prove he knew Kava. Not just knew her, but knew her intimately."

Waterfield hardened his face.

"I'm going to be honest with you," he said. "I have my job back, but only if I return with that envelope."

He let the words hang.

Waverly retreated in thought, deciding.

"Let me ask you something," she said. "Was Bristol in Denver last weekend?"

He scratched his head.

"Not that I know of. He never mentioned anything. We don't have any clients there—"

"Did you see him in town—last weekend, I mean?"

Waterfield shrugged.

"He was out of the office Friday. As for Saturday and Sunday, I didn't go in, so I don't know. He might have been there, he might not have."

Waverly focused.

"He was in Denver," she said. "I'll bet anything. He flew in Friday and killed a woman there Friday night. Then he flew back Saturday or Sunday."

"A woman was killed there?"

She nodded.

"The same way as Kava," she said. "She was dropped from a roof. She was wearing a red dress, the same as Kava. A lot of his pictures had women in dresses blowing up. That's how they'd look if they were falling."

She waited.

Waterfield retreated in thought.

"This is a serious game you're playing," he said. "Give me the photos, I'll return them to Bristol and you two can go your separate ways." He held her hand. "I'm not doing this so much to keep my job, but more to prevent anything from happening to you."

"What does that mean?"

"What do you think it means?" A beat, then "Don't back him into a corner."

"He killed Kava."

"You don't know that."

"Yes, I do."

"All you know is that they had a relationship," Waterfield said. "In hindsight, he had the exact same relationship with lots of women."

Right.

True.

"Here's what I'm going to do," she said. "I'm going to keep the photos. I'm going to find out who the other women are besides Kava. I'm going to find out if they're alive or whether they met some strange demise."

Waterfield shook his head.

"Go tell him," Waverly added. "Tell him exactly what I'm going to do. Tell him one more thing, too. Tell him to get that look out of his eyes."

"What look?"

"Just tell him, he'll know what I'm talking about."

Waterfield shifted his feet, looked down at them and then back up.

"I guess this is it between us."

Waverly sighed.

"I can't give the photos back."

Waterfield nodded.

He understood.

"We did have something, though, didn't we?"

She squeezed his hand.

"We did."

Waterfield looked into her eyes.

Then he turned and was gone.

54

DAY TWO

JULY 22, 1952

TUESDAY AFTERNOON

RIVER KEPT ONE EYE ON the ground for rattlesnakes and cactus and the other eye on Alexa Blank walking beside him. As the graveyard of rusty machinery loomed closer and closer, the woman's eyes took on a more pronounced edge. She was picturing what it would be like out here alone at night.

"Do you get out into the country much?"

She shook her head.

"No."

"You'll hear coyotes," he said. "Sometimes they bark like dogs and sometimes they yelp like wolves. Most likely they'll be far off. If they get your scent, though, they might come close to try to figure out what you are. They might even sound like they're circling and getting ready to attack. They won't, that's the thing to remember. No matter how many of them there are or how close they get or how loud they get, in the end they'll just go away. Do you understand?"

"I don't think I can do this."

River put a hand on her shoulder.

"This is the safest place in the world for you right now. Trust me."

"I don't like being alone."

"You'll be fine," he said.

"What about mountain lions?"

"They're rare."

"But they might come around, right?"

"Theoretically I guess it's possible."

A HUNDRED STEPS LATER, THEY passed the first rusty hulk and then wound deeper into the guts of the mess. River pointed to a trailer.

"That's your new home."

The woman stared at it in disbelief and shook her head.

"No, no, no. I can't do this."

River grabbed her hand and kept her in pace. "Come on, I want to show you something."

Inside the dead hulk he showed her rope, chains, food, toilet paper, and all the rest.

"I set this up to keep you here," he said. "This proves that I wasn't joking when I said I was hired to take you. Take a good look around, because this is what my replacement is going to do if he gets his hands on you." A beat, then "Wait here."

He stepped outside.

Thirty seconds later, he came back and handed her a gun.

"I had this stashed for emergencies," he said. "You take it, you keep it with you at all times. Use it if you have to. Do you know how to fire it?"

No.

She didn't.

"I'll show you before I leave," he said. "Here's the important thing. Stay inside this structure. You need to look like you're being held captive."

"Why?"

"Because, what I'm going to do is say I took you before I got the message that the contract was rescinded," he said. "Someone might demand proof. They might make me bring them here. If that happens,

I can't have you sitting around outside getting a suntan. Do you understand?"

Yes.

She did.

"I'll be back tomorrow to check on you," he said. "Well, correction, it will either be me or a woman named January."

The woman's face contorted.

"I can't do this," she said. "I can't be alone out here at night. There's no way."

"This is the best place."

"I want to go to a hotel or something."

"No, you need to be here. It needs to look like you're being held captive."

She shook her head.

"I can't stay here."

River shifted his feet and frowned.

"I hate to do this, but you're not giving me a choice."

With that, he flung her over his shoulder, carried her to the back wall, and chained her leg.

"You tricked me!"

"No, I didn't. This is for your own good." He tossed her the gun. "To fire, you flick the safety off and pull the trigger. Spend tonight figuring out who wants you taken. The sooner we figure that out, the sooner we can deal with it."

SHE FLICKED THE SAFETY OFF and pointed the barrel at River's chest.

"That wouldn't be a good move," he said. "I'm the only one who knows where you are."

He turned and headed out.

The gun exploded.

A bullet passed so close to his head that his hair moved.

"You better come back tomorrow," the woman said.

River turned and looked at her.

"I already told you I would."

Then he left.

55

DAY TWO

JULY 22, 1952

TUESDAY AFTERNOON

DOLLFACE.

That was the name of the bar Brittany Pratt was at in New York the night she died, according to the reporter's notes. It was an upscale jazz club in Manhattan. "Sounds something like the Bokaray," Wilde said as he dialed.

A gruff man's voice answered on the third ring.

It turned out to be the manager, a guy named Marty Brown. Wilde explained that he wanted to know if a man who looked like Robert Mitchum had been in the club on August 14, 1949, the night a woman named Brittany Pratt took a dive off a roof.

"You're asking me about something that happened three years ago? That's nuts."

"Yeah, I know. But—"

"Ask me what I had for breakfast. That I might remember. I'd have a fifty-fifty chance."

Wilde exhaled.

"This is important," he said. "Let me rephrase it. Have you *ever* seen a man in there that looks like Robert Mitchum?"

A beat, then "Yeah."

"You did?"

Yeah.

He did.

"When?"

"I don't know. He shows up once a year, maybe twice. He'll be here for two or three days in a row then he disappears."

"You remember him, though?"

"I remember him. He gets my share of the ladies."

"Do you know his name?"

"No."

"Do you know anyone who might know his name?"

"Not offhand."

"When was the first time you remember seeing him? Was it at least three years ago?"

Silence.

"It could have been." A beat then, "Eggs. That's what I had for breakfast this morning. I just remembered."

"Eggs."

Right.

Eggs.

"I had coffee and three Camels," Wilde said.

"Did you remember right away or did you have to think about it?"

Wilde smiled.

"I had to think about it."

"There you go."

WILDE HUNG UP, LOOKED AT Alabama and said, "Mitchum's the killer."

"No, he's not."

"Yes, he is, and he's been at it for at least three years. The only question is how many more has he done besides the one in New York and the one here in Denver."

"None, that's how many."

Wilde tapped a Camel out of the pack, set a book of matches on fire, and lit up.

He blew smoke.

When the flames got to his fingertips, he shook them out and tossed them in the ashtray.

"Stay away from him," he said.

Alabama hardened her face.

"You're wrong about him."

"This isn't negotiable."

"Good, because I'm not negotiating."

"I'm serious, Alabama."

She opened the door, stepped through, and said over her shoulder, "So am I."

The door slammed.

Wilde was alone.

From the window he watched Alabama huff down the street and disappear around the corner.

He didn't go after her.

He knew that she knew he was right.

The best thing he could give her at this moment was time alone, time to work through it.

HE FINISHED THE CAMEL, MASHED it in the ashtray, then leaned back in his chair. His feet went up on the desk and his hat went over his face.

He closed his eyes.

The darkness was cool water for his brain.

Tonight he'd guard London.

Something was going to happen, something bad, Wilde could feel it in his bones. He reached into the drawer, pulled his gun out, and set it on the desk.

"Rest up."

56

DAY TWO

JULY 22, 1952

TUESDAY AFTERNOON

MOUTHING OFF TO SEAN WATERFIELD about what Waverly was going to do was one thing; gathering the intestinal fortitude to figure out if she was bluffing or not was something else. She stayed hidden in the apartment until Su-Moon showed up. The woman got filled in and then said something unexpected. "Tom Bristol and Sean Waterfield are in cahoots."

Waverly grunted.

"That's not the impression I got."

"Think about it," Su-Moon said. "Whose side is he on now that everything's hit the fan?" Silence. "Answer, not yours, and that's been true from the start. Don't trust him, don't talk to him, and don't see him. That's my advice."

"Well, you're too late. We already decided that ourselves."

"He'll be back with a big apology and a dozen roses," Su-Moon said. "When he does, keep him at bay. In the meantime, I have a plan. You're going to wander around Chinatown. I'm going to follow and see if Bristol or one of his dogs follows you."

"One of his dogs?"

"He knows you'll be watching for him," Su-Moon said. "He'll hire someone."

Waverly tilted her head.

"How do you come up with this stuff?"

"It's called growing up on the streets." She patted Waverly's knee and said, "It's time for you to get outside and start playing rabbit."

Waverly used the facilities.

Then she hid the envelope in a box of cereal and headed out.

LESS THAN AN HOUR LATER, they had their answer. "You were being followed by two Chinese guys," Su-Moon said.

Waverly wrinkled her forehead in shock.

"I didn't see anyone."

"You weren't supposed to."

"Two?"

Su-Moon nodded.

"I didn't recognize either of them. They had tattoos. One of them had a long braided ponytail and was wearing a blue bandanna. The other one—the muscular one—had short hair and was wearing a white muscle shirt." A pause, then "The fact that they knew you were here goes back to my prior comments about your little lover-boy. He knew you were here, Bristol didn't."

Right.

Damn.

"What we need to do is get back into Bristol's houseboat," Su-Moon said.

Waverly looked for a trick but didn't see it.

"You're serious."

Su-Moon nodded.

"Dead," she said.

"Why?"

"Because we're going to find out who the women are in those photos, right? To see if any of them mysteriously disappeared?"

"Right."

"To do that, we need to get names. That means we need to get ahold of Bristol's little black book. That's either in his pocket or at his office or at his houseboat. He'll be out hunting for you tonight. While he's doing that, we'll pay a visit to the boat."

"We already checked it."

Su-Moon considered it.

"Okay, fine," she said. "We'll do his office."

57

DAY TWO

JULY 22, 1952

TUESDAY AFTERNOON

WITH HIS GUN IN THE hands of Alexa Blank, River was naked. From the graveyard he headed to Mile High Guns & Ammo on Colfax to fix that little problem. Luckily they had a duplicate of the one he already had—a Colt .45—meaning he wouldn't have to get familiar with a different action and kick. A copy of the *Beat* was sitting on the counter. River flipped through it as the clerk wrapped everything up.

"Woman Falls to Death" caught his eye.

According to the article, a woman named Charley-Anna Blackridge had fallen to her death from the roof of a building on Curtis Street late Friday night. Police were investigating.

He closed the paper.

His head spun.

This wasn't good.

It wasn't good at all.

From the store he headed to the first phone book he could find and looked up Charley-Anna Blackridge. She was listed at 1331 Clayton.

He headed over and knocked on the door.

No one answered.

The structure was a small brick bungalow with no driveway or garage, slightly elevated from the street. A twist of the knob showed that the door was locked. He looked around for nosy neighbors and found none. What he was about to do was stupid. He tried to talk himself out of it, but it didn't work.

His feet took him around the side of the structure to the back. An alley ran behind the houses. That's where the owners parked.

Two houses down, a German shepherd tugged at a chain and barked.

The noise was for River.

He'd been warned.

"Screw you."

He tried the back door, expecting it to be locked.

It wasn't.

The knob turned.

He opened the door a foot, shouted "Anyone home?" and got no answer.

He looked at the neighboring houses, saw no prying eyes, and stepped inside

HE WAS IN A KITCHEN.

A yellow refrigerator vibrated with a soft hum that rose slightly above the absolute quietness surrounding it.

On the Formica counter was a bowl of fruit—apples, oranges, and bananas. Everything was fresh, purchased within the last day or so.

Dishes were piled in the sink.

A frying pan sat on a cold burner. Next to it was pizza box. River opened the top to find two slices inside. He picked one up to see if it was stiff. It wasn't, it was flexible. He closed the top and took a deep breath.

"Anyone home?"

No one answered.

He headed upstairs.

The steps bent slightly under his weight.

The third one creaked.

58

DAY TWO

JULY 22, 1952

TUESDAY AFTERNOON

LATE AFTERNOON, WILDE GOT AN unexpected call from Michelle Day, the bartender from the El Ray Club, and pulled up an image of her wiggling on the bed with her hand between her legs. Halfway through the conversation, he wrote *Gina Sophia* on a notepad and underlined it twice, then once more even bigger. Two heartbeats later, he was bounding down the stairs two at a time with his hat in hand and the paper in his shirt pocket.

At street level, he dipped the hat over his left eye and tried to figure out where he'd parked Blondie.

He couldn't remember.

It wasn't in sight, either direction.

He tapped a Camel out of a pack, lit up, and walked west toward 14th. Thirty steps later, Blondie's back end came into sight, parked on the opposite side of the street, peeking out from behind a delivery truck. As soon as he saw it, he remembered where he'd parked—right there.

The top was up, mostly to keep the riffraff from using it as a waste can for butts and candy wrappers and RC bottles. The sky above was a tasty crystal blue. He briefly played with the thought of taking it down before deciding that he was too cramped for time.

Instead, he removed the window curtains and took off, almost clipping some drunk zigzagging on a bicycle with a beer in his left hand and a battered White Sox cap up top.

He drove into the financial district, found a parking spot on 17th Street near the Brown Palace, and killed the engine. Three minutes later, he walked into the offices of Jackson & Reacher, Denver's second-largest law firm.

A bun-haired receptionist with a wrinkled face looked up.

"I'm here to see Gina Sophia," Wilde said.

"Is she expecting you?"

"I doubt it."

TWO MINUTES LATER, HE WAS in the office of the law firm's only female attorney, about twenty-eight. Her face had minimal makeup and her attire was gray and conservative. That didn't stop Wilde from seeing the beauty underneath. She looked at him without saying anything, then closed the door and sat on the desk, dangling nylon legs.

"I've seen you around," she said. "You play drums down at the Bokaray."

Wilde nodded.

"Guilty."

"You tried to pick me up once," she said.

Wilde didn't remember.

"Did it work?"

"No."

"My loss."

"Maybe you'll have better luck next time," she said.

"One can only hope." A beat, then "How come it didn't work the last time? Did I use a corny line or something?"

"Actually, you did," she said. "If I remember right, it was something like, *How do you like me so far?*"

Wilde smiled.

That was one of his staples.

"That *is* pretty bad by the light of day."

She nodded.

"Blame it on the alcohol," he said. "So, what line would have worked better?"

She pondered it.

"I don't know. I don't pick up girls."

WILDE SHIFTED HIS FEET AND explained that he was a private investigator working on the murder of Charley-Anna Blackridge, who got dropped to her death from the roof of a building after leaving the El Ray Club last weekend.

"I talked to the bartender, Michelle Day," he said. "She said you were in there last night and told her about leaving Friday night with a guy who looked like Robert Mitchum. Is that true?"

"Why do you want to know?"

"Because he's my main suspect," Wilde said. "If he was with you, then everything I'm thinking is wrong."

"Then everything you're thinking is wrong."

"Are you saying it's true?"

"I'm saying it isn't for public disclosure," she said. "You see where I work and what I do."

"It's not going beyond me, I assure you," Wilde said.

She looked for lies.

"He picked me up, we left and spent the night at his hotel," she said.

"The whole night?"

"Every single minute."

"You're sure?"

She smiled.

"Trust me, it's not the kind of thing I'd forget."

Wilde paced.

"He has a tattoo," he said.

She nodded.

"That's true."

"Can you tell me what it is?"

"It's on his arm," she said. "It's a pinup girl standing in front of a warplane."

Wilde nodded.

That was him all right.

"What's he in town for, did he tell you?"

She shrugged.

"We didn't pick each other up to talk."

"No, I guess not."

"Any other questions?"

Wilde thought about it.

Yes.

There was another question.

One more question.

"WHAT DID HE USE FOR an opening line?"

She smiled.

"He said, *How do you like me so far?*"

"So, it worked for him?"

"Right."

"But it didn't work for me?"

"Not the first time."

"How about the second time?"

"We'd have to wait and see."

WILDE WAS ALMOST AT THE lobby when he came back and knocked lightly on the door of the woman's office. She looked up from a pile of papers.

He said, "How do you like me so far?"

She smiled.

"Get out of here before I call your bluff."

59

DAY TWO

JULY 22, 1952

TUESDAY NIGHT

TUESDAY NIGHT AFTER DARK, A mean thunderstorm rolled off the Pacific and pounded San Francisco with heavy fists. Waverly and Su-Moon kept their faces down and held tight to the railing as they climbed the fire escape at the back of Bristol's building. The city was dark, almost black. They were nothing more than deep shadows in an equally deep world.

At each floor, they tried the exit door.

At each floor, the knob wouldn't turn.

They climbed to the top, which stopped at the highest occupied floor.

That door was locked too.

Waverly's heart raced.

She didn't know whether she'd be able to do the next step.

The wind was fierce.

Her clothes were soaked to the skin and her skin was soaked to the bone. Next to her, Su-Moon was fighting to get the rope and grappling hook out of a black bag. The plan, when they talked about it earlier, seemed simple and straightforward—hook the roof parapet, then climb up.

Now it didn't seem so simple.

Now it seemed insane.

Su-Moon coiled the rope loosely and said, "Watch your head in case this comes back down."

"We should just forget it."

"It's too late."

"We'll come back tomorrow when the weather's better."

"We're here now."

The grappling hook wasn't heavy, five pounds or thereabouts. The rope was half-inch braid, knotted every two feet for grip.

"Here goes."

She twirled the grappling hook twice then sent it flying at the parapet. It hit the side, two feet short, and tumbled back invisibly, ricocheting off Waverly's arm.

"Go down a ways until I get this done," Su-Moon said. "There's no use both of us being exposed."

"No."

"Just do it," Su-Moon said.

"Let me throw it. You go down."

"Fine."

On the third try, Waverly got it hooked on something. She tugged and found it secure.

"Got it."

True, she had it, but there was a problem. It was off to the side instead of directly above them. She let the rope slacken and found that it fell to the right of the landing. If they lost their grip climbing, the fall wouldn't be ten or fifteen feet to the landing, it would be all the way to the ground.

"No harm," Su-Moon said. "I'll go up first, then move it over."

"Let's just forget it. I got a bad feeling."

"We're fine. Just relax."

SU-MOON TUGGED ON THE ROPE and then put her full weight on it.

"It seems secure."

She climbed up on the railing, grabbed the rope just above the highest knot she could reach, and said, "It's slippery."

"Don't do it."

"Just be careful when it's your turn."

With that, she shifted her weight off the railing and onto the rope, dangling in the darkness two or three feet to the right of the landing.

Then she climbed.

The wind whipped rain into her face with all the subtlety of a hundred needles.

60

DAY TWO

JULY 22, 1952

TUESDAY AFTERNOON

FIVE MINUTES. RIVER DIDN'T WANT to be in the house of Charley-Anna Blackridge any longer than that. If he couldn't hit dirt in five minutes, he'd abort.

Five minutes came and passed.

River didn't abort.

There was something here.

He could smell it.

He was careful to put everything back as he found it, except for a photo of the woman from one of a hundred he found in a shoebox in the closet, which went into his wallet. Several minutes further into the search, he found something of interest, namely two spent airline tickets, four months old, roundtrip from Denver to San Francisco, one in the name of Crockett Bluetone and the other in the name of Charley-Anna Blackridge.

Crockett Bluetone.

River had heard that name before.

Where?

For some reason it pulled up an aura of power and money.

Who are you, Crockett Bluetone?

River stuffed the tickets in his wallet and kept searching. Five minutes later, he hadn't found anything else of interest and left.

No one saw him, at least that he was aware of.

HE PULLED NEXT TO THE first phone booth he came to, left the engine running, and checked the book. Crockett Bluetone, it turned out, had two numbers. One was for a residence in Capitol Hill, the coordinates of choice for Denver's rich and relevant, an area replete with lush lawns, tree-lined boulevards, wrought-iron fences, and stone lions guarding cobblestone drives.

The other number was a work number.

It was for the law firm of Colder & Jones, one of Denver's largest law firms if not the largest, with offices in the swank Daniels & Fisher Tower on 16th Street.

So, you're a lawyer.

What were you doing taking a trip to San Francisco with Charley-Anna Blackridge four months ago?

Was she a client?

A witness?

A lover?

RIVER DROVE OVER TO 16TH Street, found a place to park two blocks over on 14th, and doubled back on foot. The Daniels & Fisher Tower was the highest structure in downtown Denver, in fact in all of Colorado.

He approached it with a quick step.

Five minutes later, he was in Crockett Bluetone's office behind closed doors.

The man—in his late thirties—had a square jaw and predator eyes. His sleeves were rolled up enough to show strong forearms and hands. At six-two, he was bigger than River expected, better-looking too.

River bypassed the leather chair in front of the lawyer's desk, instead walking to the window, looking down for a beat, then back at the lawyer.

"I'm not really here about a legal matter," he said.

"No?"

"No. Does the name Charley-Anna Blackridge mean anything to you?"

A beat.

"No."

"No?"

"No."

River raked his hair back.

"Let me help your memory," he said. "I'm talking about the Charley-Anna Blackridge you went to San Francisco with four months ago."

The lawyer didn't move.

Then he leaned back in his chair, put his hands behind his head, and said, "What's your connection to her?"

"Nothing, just a friend," River said. "She got murdered last weekend."

The lawyer nodded.

"I know."

River walked over and sat on the edge of the desk.

"Are you the one who did it?"

"Wow, that's quite a question."

"Yes, it is."

61

DAY TWO

JULY 22, 1952

TUESDAY AFTERNOON

ALABAMA SHOWED UP LATE AFTERNOON, tapped a Camel out of Wilde's pack, lit it, and handed it to him. Then she sat on the edge of the desk and dangled her legs. "I talked to Mitchum point-blank and asked him where he went after he left the El Ray Club," she said. "He said he left with a woman and they spent the night at his hotel."

Wilde blew smoke.

"Who?"

"He wouldn't tell me her name," Alabama said. "He said she was a lawyer and she made him promise to be discreet."

"So, no name?"

"No, but he was telling the truth," Alabama said.

"How do you know?"

"Because I could tell, that's how."

"Well, that's an interesting story."

"Why?"

He told her about getting a call from the bartender, Michelle Day, who gave him the name of Gina Sophia, a lawyer at Jackson & Reacher. "I went over to her office to get the story straight from the horse's mouth. She left the club with him and was with him all night. She even knew about his pinup-plane tattoo, so there was no question we were talking about the same man."

Alabama jumped off the desk, turned around and shook her hips.

"You hate it when I'm right," she said.

Wilde nodded.

"Luckily it doesn't happen that often."

"Actually it happens more than you know."

"I'm not sure it happened this time, to be honest with you," he said.

"What do you mean?"

"What I mean is, Mitchum was at the El Ray Club the night Charley-Anna got murdered," he said. "He also frequented Dollface in New York, where Brittany Pratt was the night she got murdered."

Alabama wasn't impressed.

"No one says he was there *that* night," she said. "Two people went to the same club on occasion, big whoop-de-do. As far as Denver goes, Mitchum was with the lawyer all night. That means case closed, end of discussion, done deal."

"Maybe not," Wilde said.

Alabama shook her head in confusion.

"What are you talking about?"

"What I'm talking about is that maybe the lawyer was lying. Maybe she's in cahoots with Mitchum and she's giving him a false alibi."

Alabama wrinkled her face.

"You don't quit, do you?"

Wilde got up, walked to the window, and looked down. A hillbilly song came from the radio of a car sitting outside.

WILDE FLICKED THE BUTT OUT the window, tapped another stick out of the pack, set a book of matches on fire, and lit up from the six-inch flame.

He turned to Alabama.

"Find out if Mitchum and the lawyer, Gina Sophia, knew each other before the night in question. If they did, she's giving him a false alibi. If she's giving him a false alibi, it's because he needs one." A beat, then "Don't let him know you're looking into it. Don't let him know that you know the lawyer's name. Any questions?"

"One. Are you crazy?"

Wilde nodded.

"I am, but that doesn't mean I'm wrong," he said. "The more I think about it, if she went to the club so she'd be in a position to give him an alibi, that means they had to set it up beforehand. That means she's not just giving him an alibi after the fact, she was in on the alibi from the start, meaning she's more in the nature of co-conspirator."

"Why would she?"

"I don't know," Wilde said. "In fact, the more I think about it—"

"You already thought about it more."

He smiled.

"Right; now I'm thinking about it more a second time, and what I'm thinking is that maybe she's not giving him an alibi at all. Maybe he's the one who's giving the alibi. Maybe he's giving it to her."

"Are you saying she's the killer?"

He shrugged.

"Maybe I am."

Alabama shook her head in wonder.

"Do me a favor, will you?"

He nodded.

Sure.

"Shoot me if I ever get as twisted as you."

62

SU-MOON MADE IT TO THE roof without dropping to her death. She disappeared over the parapet, checked the access hatch to be sure it wasn't locked, and shouted down to Waverly, "Come on!"

"Move the rope over."

"Can't. There's nowhere to hook it."

Waverly swallowed.

Su-Moon had barely made it, and she was stronger.

A gust of rain lashed at her face and pushed her body sideways. She waited for it to subside, then got up on the railing, shifted her weight onto the rope, and climbed up hand over hand with every ounce of strength she had. At the top, Su-Moon grabbed her arm with both hands and pulled her over the parapet.

She landed on her back.

The weather pelted her face.

She didn't care.

She was up.

She was alive.

"Come on," Su-Moon said. "No time for naps."

The access door led to a steel interior stairway. On squishy feet they took it down to Bristol's floor, hearing no one, seeing no one, encountering no cleaning crews or guards. A trail of dripping water followed them.

So far, so good.

The door to the Bristol office suite was locked. Su-Moon busted the glass with her foot, reached through and unlocked the bolt.

They were in.

She shut the door and relocked it.

"Which way to Bristol's office?"

"Follow me."

They ended up in a corner office that faced the street. The windows had blinds, but they wouldn't completely seal the lights.

"We should have brought flashlights."

"Too late now."

They moved a banker's lamp from the top of the desk to under it, then turned it on. That gave them enough to see by without overdoing it.

Then they searched.

They weren't careful.

They weren't neat.

TEN MINUTES INTO IT, THEY still hadn't found anything of relevance. Then Waverly had an idea to pull the drawers out of Bristol's desk and see if anything was taped on the backside or underneath.

There wasn't.

Five minutes later, they found a hidden compartment under a piece of removable wood in the top drawer. Inside was a black address book together with an envelope.

Su-Moon slapped Waverly on the back.

"Bingo."

SUDDENLY A NOISE CAME FROM the hallway outside Bristol's office.

"Shit!"

Su-Moon flicked off the banker's lamp.

The room fell into darkness.

The women froze.

They didn't make a sound.

63

DAY TWO
JULY 22, 1952
TUESDAY AFTERNOON

THE LAWYER, CROCKETT BLUETONE, DENIED killing Charley-Anna Blackridge. He had a brief affair with her four months ago and took her to San Francisco for a long weekend out of sight of the wifey-poo. Shortly after that, the fire went out for both of them. He hadn't seen her in over three months. "We parted on amicable terms. That was it."

River had a question.

"Is anyone after you for any reason?"

"No."

"Are you sure?"

Yes.

He was.

Absolutely.

"Why?"

"Because sometimes people kill one person not to get to that person but to get at another person."

The lawyer frowned.

"No one's after me. If what happened to Charley-Anna was murder, it had nothing to do with me."

River studied the man's eyes, found no lies, and headed for the door.

"See you around."

The lawyer stood up.

"There's a saying," he said. "Discretion is the better part of valor."

"Don't worry about it. I could care less who you stick your dick in."

RIVER GOT HOME TO FIND January in white shorts and a white tank top. She hadn't come across any mysterious envelopes taped anywhere. No one had called. If a hitman was lurking around, she hadn't seen him.

She ran a finger down River's chest.

"I've been waiting for you."

He frowned.

"It's dangerous for you here."

"Too bad."

He studied the horizon. The mountains were a dark jagged band against the sky. The sky above was filled with light.

"Let's take a walk," he said.

"Where?"

"Down by the river. I want to see how good you can shoot a gun."

"You're so romantic."

He nodded.

"The first rule of being romantic is to not be dead."

WALKING WITH HIS ARM AROUND January's waist, River told her about an old friend named Charley-Anna who got dropped from a roof last weekend. That's where River was this afternoon, checking the woman's house and subsequently feeling out a hotshot lawyer named Crockett Bluetone.

"Do you think he did it?" January asked.

"I'm not sure. He admitted having an affair with her four months ago but says they split up amicably shortly after that."

"You don't believe him."

No.

He didn't.

"Why would he kill her?"

"It could be any number of reasons," he said. "The obvious one is that she might have been blackmailing him. She might have threatened to tell the wife about the affair unless he paid her off. She might have even set that up from the beginning. Maybe that's why she was keeping the airplane tickets—they were the proof. Or she might have found out some dirt on him during pillow-talk time and was blackmailing him about that. There's also the possibility that he was in trouble with some third party and they sent him a message by killing her. For all I know, he was still seeing her. He says he wasn't, but who knows? She might have been precious to him and someone else knew it."

"So what are you going to do?"

"I don't know," he said. "I need to chew on it."

"You want me to seduce him? I can get him to talk."

River laughed.

"No, no seducing."

"Why not?"

River picked her up, flung her over his shoulder and slapped her ass.

"Because."

64

TUESDAY EVENING, WILDE HEADED OUTSIDE under a darkening sky for a jog. The air was moist, just short of rain. To the west, charcoal clouds churned over the mountains and worked their wicked way toward Denver. A storm was coming, a mean storm. Blondie's top was up, but it wouldn't hurt to make sure the window curtains were tight.

Alabama had left the office shortly after four and hadn't come home yet.

As usual, Wilde ran too fast starting out and used up all his wind, which forced him into a more sustainable beat. His best distance was the quarter-mile. He'd never been fast enough out of the blocks to be competitive in the hundred or two-twenty. Nor could he keep up a full sprint for a half-mile.

The quarter-mile, however, was his.

He was fast enough out of the blocks and had the stamina to sprint the whole thing. His best time so far was 55.3, which wasn't world-class by any means but respectable enough.

The streetlights kicked on.

Right now, the dark beauty London Marshall was holed up in Wilde's office with the lights out and the door locked. After the jog, Wilde would go over to her house to check and make sure no little surprise visitors were waiting for her in the closet. Then he'd call and tell her the coast was clear.

She'd come home.

Wilde would spend the night on the couch.

With any luck, whoever was after the woman would make his move.

London.

London.

London.

She was a striking woman, every bit as striking as Secret.

Secret was the one for Wilde, though.

She'd gotten there first.

Wilde needed to focus on her and not get distracted.

That was his problem, he always allowed himself to get distracted. "That's why you're still single," Alabama told him at one point. "Women come too easy to you."

"That's not true."

Those were the words that came out of his mouth, *That's not true.*

Down deep, though, it was true.

Even now, focused on Secret, there was an uncontrollable corner of his brain that wondered what it would be like to unwrap London.

WHEN HE GOT HOME, ALABAMA still wasn't there. Wilde took a long hot shower, dried his hair just enough to get the drip gone, and stepped out with the towel wrapped around his waist.

Alabama was upside down on the couch, with her back on the cushions and her legs up. Her hair hung over the edge and hung down toward the floor. She looked at Wilde with upside-down eyes and said, "I found out some stuff."

Wilde headed over.

"Like what?"

With a lightning reach, Alabama grabbed the towel, yanked it off, and tossed it over the edge of the couch.

She laughed.

"Seven."

"You need to stop doing that."

"And counting."

Wilde fetched the towel, rewrapped it, and sat down next to her.

"So, what did you find out?"

ALABAMA SPREAD HER KNEES EVER so slightly. Wilde detected the movement in his peripheral vision but didn't react.

"First," Alabama said, "I went to Gina Sophia's law firm and had a little talk with a bun-haired receptionist. I told her I was trying to track down a friend of mine who looked like Robert Mitchum. I told her he uses a lot of lawyers and asked her if he was using anyone there at Jackson & Reacher. She told me that no one like that had ever been there—she would have remembered, Robert Mitchum was her favorite actor. She would have seen him, too, because she was the only receptionist."

Wilde grunted.

"All that shows is that Mitchum and the lawyer didn't meet at work," he said. "It doesn't prove they didn't know each other."

Alabama smiled.

"I'm going for eight later, so be warned."

Wilde guarded the towel with his hand.

"Not now," Alabama said. "Later. Anyway, the other thing I did was talk to the desk clerk at Mitchum's hotel. At first he didn't want to say much, so I had to show him my boobs. Then he opened up."

"Tell me you're kidding."

She shrugged.

"No can do," she said. "Anyway, according to him—his name's Dick by the way, ironic, huh?—Mitchum did in fact return to the hotel with a woman. The person he described sounds like Gina Sophia. They were in the room together all night."

"How does he know that?"

"Because they were drunk and loud and playing music and dancing," Alabama said. "People in the adjoining rooms were complaining. Dick went up personally and knocked on the door four or five times to get them to knock it off."

"Did he actually see Mitchum?"

Alabama nodded.

"Every time he went up, Mitchum opened the door. Every time, Mitchum apologized and said he'd knock it off, but he always started back up again. Finally, about four in the morning, Dick called the cops. A half hour later, a cop showed up. Dick took him up to the room and the cop knocked on the door. Mitchum opened it, the cop told him to knock it off or else. That got his attention and things settled down."

Wilde chewed on it.

"So he was there continuously until at least four," he said.

"Four-thirty. That's when the cop showed up, four-thirty. Oh, Dick had one more thing relevant to the issue, but he wanted to squeeze my boobs. I let him and here's what he told me—"

"You let him?"

"God, Wilde, they're just boobs. Calm down and listen. The cleaning crew started at five and a housekeeper named Maria went into Mitchum's room by mistake. He was passed out in bed with a woman. They were both naked. Maria eased back out. Mitchum never knew she'd opened the door."

"How did Dick know?"

"One of the other housekeepers ratted on Maria," Alabama said. "Apparently they don't get along."

"Apparently not."

Alabama exhaled.

"I have a theory," she said. "Maybe there's another guy who looks like Robert Mitchum. Maybe he's the one who frequented that New York club."

"So you're saying there are two Robert Mitchums?"

"Three, actually, if you count the original."

65

DAY TWO
JULY 22, 1952
TUESDAY NIGHT

THE NOISE TURNED OUT TO be someone rolling a cleaning cart down the hall, singing mumbled words in a terrible, raspy voice.

Josephine, oh Josephine,
Get your big old lips off of me.
Josephine, oh Josephine,
Get your big old lips off of me.

It's turning you on, baby,
But it's making me want to go to sea.

The singing stopped at Bristol's door, followed by a twist of the knob, a twist that found the bolt thrown from the inside. Waverly and Su-Moon didn't blink or breathe. The singing started again, glass got swept up, then the voice disappeared down the hall. The women waited until it was good and gone, then got the hell out of there.

Outside, the storm was even meaner.

Traffic lights swung in the force of the weather.

Except for a few muddled headlights, all the sane people of the world had retreated.

Leaving on Su-Moon's scooter wasn't an option.

What to do?

Half a block up the street was a blue neon sign that said California Hotel. They ran for it through sloppy puddles and slippery concrete. It turned out to be a nice place with a crowded bar at the far end of the lobby. They paid more than they wanted but ended up with a nice room on the fifth floor. The concierge managed to wrangle up dry clothes—nothing fancy, just Ts and sweatpants—which he delivered personally with a smile.

"Just leave them in the room when you check out," he said. "No charge."

"Thanks. You're a prince."

They tipped him good.

TECHNICALLY, THE BLACK BOOK FROM Bristol's desk was an address book. To its credit, it did have that type of information, namely names—female names, to be precise—together with addresses and phone numbers.

But there was more.

Much more.

There were dirty little notes about what Bristol had done to them and when.

Red dress spanking 4/22/51
Tied spread on bed 11/4/49
Staked out, Baker Beach, 7/11/52.

Hogtied 2 hours, 9/28/48

"The guy's a dirty little freak," Waverly said. "He has a dark side two miles long."

Su-Moon nodded, then tapped a finger and said, "Look at this one."

Waverly did.

Michelle

Rooftop blowjob, 3/19/48.

"Rooftop," Su-Moon said. "There's our connection, right there."

"You think?"

She did.

She did indeed.

"I'll bet you dollars to donuts that *blowjob* is code for *dropped*," she said. "Notice that all the other women have last names and addresses and phone numbers. This one only says Michelle. That's because he didn't want too much incriminating evidence in case this ever got in the wrong hands." She tapped her finger again. "Even the name Michelle might be code. The date, though, is probably accurate. We need to find out if anyone got dropped on 3/19/48."

THEY CHECKED THE ENVELOPE.

Inside was a passport and $10,000 cash.

"This was his ticket to ride in case he had to get out of Dodge fast," Su-Moon said. "He's not going to be happy about this being gone."

66

DAY TWO
JULY 22, 1952
TUESDAY NIGHT

ALMOST ALL COMMUNICATIONS RECEIVED BY River from the man behind the assignments came in written form anonymously delivered in envelopes. River had spoken to the man only twice, but it was enough, so when phone rang early in the evening, he recognized the caller as *him*. "The contract was terminated."

The voice was deep and controlled.

It made River pull up an image equal to his own.

"I was all set to take her last night," River said. "A friend of mine got in trouble—something serious. I had to attend to it. That's why I was late."

"I buy results, not efforts."

"You got the result, it was just this morning instead of last night. It was a few hours late. I don't see the problem."

"Do you have the woman?"

"I do."

"You shouldn't have done that. When a contract is rescinded, you're to step down. Not doing that interferes with your replacement."

"I had completed the contract before I got the message," River said. "When I took the woman this morning, I didn't know you'd rescinded the contract. I didn't find that out until I got back home."

Silence.

"Where is she?"

"I have her."

"Where?"

"Someplace safe," River said. "Everything's on track. I can release her or kill her, whichever you want."

A pause.

"Tell me where you have her."

"I can't," River said. "That's not the way we do it and you know it. Like you said, you buy a result, not an effort. The result is that I have her." A beat, then "I don't understand what anybody wants with her. She's a nobody."

"What you understand or don't understand is not relevant."

River exhaled.

"We need to meet, face to face."

"Why?"

"Because it's time. I'll buy you a beer."

A pause.

"You're playing a dangerous game."

The line went dead.

Suddenly a hand appeared on River's shoulder—January's hand. "Trouble?"

"He's going to take me out." He swung the woman around onto his lap. "You too if you're in the line of fire."

CLOUDS SWARMED IN FROM THE Rockies and switched the Denver sky from twilight to night. The wind swept up and the streetlights kicked on. Distant lights that had been only a pale glimmer ten minutes ago were now bold and dominant.

River grabbed his gun, then January's hand, and headed for the car.

The woman fell into step.

"Where are we going?"

"Charley-Anna's house."

"Why? What's there?"

"Not what, who."

On the way over, large isolated splats of rain smashed on the windshield—just a few. Within thirty seconds, the wipers were swinging at full force, bringing a watery mess of a world in and out of focus. January snuggled closer and rested her head on River's shoulder.

"Let's just go somewhere and disappear," she said.

"That's not an option."

"Sure it is."

"No, it isn't."

"Why? Because you have all your money wrapped up in that so-called place of yours?"

"No."

"What then?"

"Just because."

"Come on, River," she said. "Let's go to California. I've never been there. I want to see the beach."

River patted her leg.

"I'll show it to you, but first things first."

"Promise?"

Good question.

The answer surprised him.

"Yeah, I promise. Put it in the bank."

She kissed him on the cheek.

"It's in." She got serious and said, "Don't end up dead on me."

"I'll see what I can do."

AT CHARLEY-ANNA'S HOUSE, JANUARY waited in the car while River headed over alone. On the third knock, a young woman opened the door. River explained who he was—a friend of the victim's—and got let in. The woman turned out to be someone named Alley Bender.

"I just found out about Charley-Anna earlier today," River said. "I'm going to tell you something you probably don't want to hear, but here goes. I broke into the house this afternoon to see if I could find a connection to whoever it was who killed her." He saw the expression on the woman's face and added, "I only went into Charley-Anna's room, not yours."

The woman studied him.

"Do you want some wine?"

No, he didn't.

The woman poured herself a glass, tilted toward River in salute, and took a long sip.

"What do you know about a lawyer named Crockett Bluetone?"

"How do you know about him?"

River explained.

He found two airplane tickets to San Francisco.

He paid a little visit to the attorney this afternoon.

"He said he had a brief affair with Charley-Anna but it died out more than three months ago. Is that true?"

She woman wrinkled her forehead.

"Let me see the tickets."

River pulled them out of his wallet.

The woman took a quick look and stuffed them in her bra.

"I'll hang on to these," she said.

River almost pulled them out but decided he didn't need them. He needed information more.

"So, were they having an affair and did it die out three months ago?"

"No."

"No affair?"

"Yes, affair, but no, it didn't die out three months ago. *Exploded* is more the word. And the explosion wasn't three months ago. It was last week."

River looked at the wine bottle.

"You know what? Is that offer still open?"

It was.

She got him a glass.

It was red and sweet and dropped tingly down his throat, then straight into his blood.

Everything softened.

"WHAT CAUSED THE EXPLOSION?"

"I don't know. She was pretty private about it."

River studied the woman's eyes.

They darted.

"Was she blackmailing him?"

The woman looked away as if contemplating an exit, then held River's eyes for a heartbeat before diverting.

"Maybe."

"Maybe?"

"Okay, *yes*."

"Was she threatening to go to the wife about the affair?"

"No."

"What, then?"

"I don't know. It was something else."

"What?"

"I don't know."

"Was it something she found out about him?"

The woman nodded.

"Yes, but I don't know what."

"Sure you do."

"Honest, I don't," she said. "All I know is that it was something big. Charley-Anna kept a diary. I tore this place apart looking for it but couldn't find it."

River took a long swallow of wine.

"Did you tell all this to the police?"

No.

She didn't.

"Why not?"

"I didn't think it was relevant."

River tilted his head.

"Bullshit," he said. "You didn't tell them because you were in on the whole thing with Charley-Anna."

"You have a wild imagination."

"That's why you just now took the tickets," he said. "If nothing else, you can threaten to tell the wife about the affair."

"That's crazy."

River stood up.

"My guess is that Charley-Anna never told Bluetone about your involvement," he said. "That's why you're still alive. My advice is to drop the whole thing while the dropping's good."

The woman wrinkled her nose.

"If everything was as you say, why would I have told you all the stuff I just did?"

"Because you're scared."

She shook her head.

"You have a wild imagination."

River headed for the door.

Over his shoulder he said, "You got yourself in deep. Get yourself out if you can."

Then he was gone.

Ten seconds later, he was back.

"Give me a pencil."

She did.

River scribbled something down.

"That's my phone number," he said. "Use it if you need it."

"Sure."

"Promise me."

"I said sure."

"Sure isn't a promise."

The woman exhaled.

"Okay, I promise."

River nodded.

"That's better."

Then he was gone.

BACK AT THE CAR, HE slid behind the wheel, gave January a kiss, and cranked over the engine.

"Where's the gun?"

She handed it to him.

"Prepare to get wet," he said.

"Why?"

"We're going home, but we're going to park a half-mile out and head in on foot."

Silence.

"You're going to let me come with you?"

"Yes."

"Why?"

"Because if I say no, you're not going to listen anyway."

She smiled.

"You're starting to get to know me."

67

DAY TWO

JULY 22, 1952

TUESDAY NIGHT

WILDE SNEAKED SILENTLY THROUGH THE raven-haired lawyer's back door using the key she had given him. He listened for intruders and heard nothing, other than the storm slamming against the windows. With the lights out, he made a pass through each room and then dialed his office.

A tender, timid voice answered.

"Hello?"

"London, it's me," Wilde said. "Are you still up for this?"

A pause, then "Yes."

"Are you sure?"

"Pretty sure. Don't let me get killed."

"I won't."

"Promise?"

"I'll tell you what," he said. "If you get killed, I'll give you your retainer back."

She laughed faintly and said, "Fair enough."

"Okay, I'm at your house now and the coast is clear. Come home and follow your normal routine when you get here. I'll be upstairs lying on the floor behind the bed. Don't worry about turning on the lights, no one from outside will have a line of sight on me."

"Okay."

"Do you normally close your window coverings at night?"

"Yes."

"Leave one or two of them open a crack so he can see you moving around. I want to be sure he knows you're home."

"Okay."

"You sound nervous."

"I'm okay."

"Are you sure?"

"No."

Wilde smiled.

"See you soon." A beat, then "One more thing. Don't talk to me if your face is pointed toward a window. I don't want him to see your lips moving."

"Good idea. You brought a weapon, right?"

Right.

He had.

"A gun?"

Right.

That.

HE LAY IN THE DARK behind the bed, memorizing every sound, every play of light from the streetlights, every engine in the night.

Fifteen minutes later, a car pulled into the driveway.

The front door opened and the lights downstairs kicked on.

Curtains swung closed across rods.

More lights kicked on.

A refrigerator door opened. An ice tray got cracked and ice fell into a glass, followed by something poured over it. The sound made Wilde thirstier than he already was. A bottle of RC would be nice—no, not a cola, a beer; an ice-cold beer, straight from the freezer right before it froze.

The suit jacket was next to him on the floor.

Inside the left pocket was the pack of Camels.

Wilde resisted the urge to tap one out.

The resistance lasted all of a minute before he broke one loose and lit up. The smoke in his lungs was so damn perfect. The roughness in his brain softened.

The bedroom lights suddenly turned on.

Curtains swung closed across rods.

With his head at floor level, Wilde had a view of the woman's feet. They walked toward him and turned at the bed, followed by the woman's body sitting on the mattress.

"So far, nothing unusual," she said.

"He'll wait for you to go to bed. Just keep doing what you do."

Wilde watched as shoes came off followed by nylons.

A dress dropped to the floor.

Then a blouse.

Then a bra.

Then panties.

"I usually take a shower before I go to bed," London said.

"Then do it. Don't break your routine."

THE BATHROOM WAS ACROSS THE hall, in line of sight from Wilde's position. As the woman walked to it, her body came into view.

She was naked.

Her ass was taut and smooth.

Her back was strong.

Her raven hair cascaded.

Her left hand carried a glass of wine.

She left the bathroom door open, got the shower up to temperature, and stepped in. The curtain didn't close all the way. Wilde had a good reflection of her in the mirror. He watched her until his conscience made him stop. Then he rolled onto his back, lit another Camel, and stared at the ceiling, being careful to blow the smoke under the bed where it wouldn't be seen from the outside.

The shower shut off.

Don't look.

Don't look.

Don't look.

That's what his brain said.

His eyes didn't listen.

He watched the woman's every move as she toweled off, swallowed the rest of the wine, and slipped into a T-shirt—nothing else, just the T. When she headed back across the hall, Wilde didn't drop his eyes. The woman's body was still moist. Her breasts pressed against the cotton.

She flicked the lights off.

The room dropped into darkness.

Then she stepped over him and got into bed.

"Good night," she said.

Before Wilde could answer, lightning exploded outside, so close that the walls shook.

"Good night."

"Thanks for being here."

"No problem."

68

WAVERLY PULLED THE HOTEL CURTAINS back just far enough to get a sideways peek of the nightscape, saw nothing but the storm and a few errant headlights punching through it, and let them fall back. On the bed was Bristol's money, being pushed around by Su-Moon's index finger. Ten thousand dollars was a lot, more than Waverly made in six years. It made her palms sweat. "If Bristol isn't out to kill us yet, he will be when he finds his little friends gone."

Su-Moon looked up.

"We'll split it evenly," she said. "Five G's apiece."

Waverly shook her head.

"I don't want it. It's all yours."

"What's wrong? Are you afraid he's going to call the cops?" She laughed. "Don't worry, his reputation's worth more than that." She tapped a finger on the black book. "That's his reputation, right there. That's every bit of everything he is and ever will be."

"That's my point."

"What's your point?"

"He'll kill to get it back," Waverly said.

Su-Moon pushed the money and then looked up.

Her face was serious.

She scooped the bills up, stuffed them back in the envelope, and stood up.

"Come on."

"Where we going?"

"Out."

"You mean down to the bar?"

"No, I mean out."

"Outside? I'm just finally getting dry—"

THEY TOOK A CAB TO Chinatown and pulled over two blocks short of Su-Moon's apartment. Su-Moon paid the fare, then tore a ten-dollar bill in two, gave half to the driver and said, "Me and my friend are going to take a little walk. We'll be back within a half hour. If you're here when we get back, you get the other half." The driver turned off the headlights and killed the engine.

"I'm already waiting," he said.

The women stepped out.

The storm assaulted them.

They walked briskly, hugging the lee side of the street and taking as much refuge as they could. Inside Waverly's left sweat-pants pocket was Bristol's black book. Su-Moon had the money in hers.

The streets were empty.

By the time they got to the corner, Su-Moon's pants were close to dropping off from the weight. She stopped long enough to tighten the drawstring as she studied the street.

No one was there, not a soul.

Su-Moon grabbed Waverly's hand and pulled her into the street, on the opposite side of the massage parlor, which was closed.

Suddenly she stopped.

"My apartment lights are on," she said.

Waverly looked.

The curtains were drawn.

Light came from behind them.

"Did you leave them on?"

"No."

"Are you sure?"

Yes.

She was.

Positive.

"So what do we do?" Waverly said.

Su-Moon exhaled.

"We'll walk past and see if we can see who's inside," she said.

They did.

They saw no movement.

They kept going and stopped at the end of the street.
When they looked back, the lights were off.

69

DAY TWO

JULY 22, 1952

TUESDAY NIGHT

RIVER DUMPED THE CAR AT the BNSF service lot a half-mile from his place and walked west through the pitch-black silhouettes of boxcars and gondolas. The gun was in his left hand, cold and wet. January followed two steps behind, saying nothing, hunkered against the rain.

The storm was dangerously wicked.

Wild arcs of lightning flashed low and mean.

His heart raced.

Someone was positioned to kill him.

Someone was waiting silently in a black recess with one thing and one thing only on his mind.

River could feel him.

He slowed from a brisk walk to a timid one, then stopped altogether and put his arms around January.

"Stay here," he said.

"No."

"Yes."

He kissed her hard and headed into the darkness without looking back. The gun was slippery in his hand. His aim—if he got a chance to have one—might well be off, in fact would probably be.

Shoot again.

Fast.

A hundred yards away, that's how far he was now. *Where are you hiding, you little bastard?* His blood raced. *You're watching for my headlights, aren't you? You're going to shoot me in the back while I'm walking to the door.*

Yeah.

That was it.

That was definitely it.

That's how River would do it.

You're positioned but not all the way in. You won't crawl all the way into your little crack until you see the headlights. That little mistake is going to cost you. It's going to cost you big-time.

RIVER GOT TO THE END boxcar, took a position under it on his stomach with the gun pointed outward and waited for an explosion of lightning. It didn't take long. A wild electric jolt punched the nightscape.

Shapes lit up.

Tracks.

Cars.

No killer.

River turned his eyes slightly to the right and waited for the next jolt.

Come on.

Show yourself.

Storm lights exploded in the distant skies, this way and that, but not close enough to cut through the mess and light the immediate area.

Thunder rolled over Denver.

Come on.

Get closer.

A chill worked its way into River's bones. He was getting stiff. That wasn't good. He needed to be limber. He rolled over to get the circulation flowing. Just as he got back to his stomach, the world shook with a violent explosion and lit up brighter than daylight.

No human shapes appeared.

River saw nothing he shouldn't.

Maybe tonight wasn't the night.

Or maybe it was the night but the attack was something different than River thought. Could the guy have anticipated River coming in on foot?

January.
January.
January.

River crawled out from under the boxcar. The storm pounded him with a wild force but he paid no attention. Every fiber of his being was focused on getting to January. He needed to know she was all right. He needed to know he hadn't been outsmarted.

Ten steps into the open, lightning exploded.

The yard lit up.

Every inch of River's face and body lit up.

He dove.

Gravel cut into his face.

The gun flew out of his hand.

70

DAY TWO

JULY 22, 1952

TUESDAY NIGHT

LONDON WAS RIPE FOR THE taking, that's what the whole shower-in-sight thing was all about. Wilde could swing up into her bed right now and take her like she'd never been taken in her life. He could turn her into a sweaty, lust-soaked animal. It wouldn't blow his cover. No one from outside would be able to tell.

The problem was Secret.

She was in his blood.

His blood needed to be sure he didn't screw things up. An hour of pleasure, no matter how pleasurable that pleasure might be, wasn't worth turning Secret into someone who trusted the wrong man.

No.

No.

No.

If things didn't work out with Secret, it wouldn't be because of anything Wilde had done.

That's what his brain said.

Still, the rest of his body couldn't stop thinking about what it would be like to swing up top.

"ARE YOU STILL THERE?"

The voice came from above.

It was laced with erotic vibration.

"Yeah."

"If the floor's too hard, you can come up here. There's room."

Wilde exhaled.

"The floor's fine."

"Are you sure?"

"I'm sure. Go to sleep."

"I can't," London said. "I'm too wound up."

"Try."

The storm raged against the windows, rattling them to the edge of shattering. In other circumstances, Wilde would have nestled into the MG with a couple of beers and let the weather beat down on the rag inches above his head. Tonight, however, all he could do was try to hear over it, listening for sounds of intrusion.

Something seemed off.

He grabbed the gun and stood up.

"I'm going to check the house," he said.

"Okay."

"I'll be right back."

"Hey, can you do me a favor?"

"Sure, what?"

She handed him the empty wine glass. "Can you fill this back up for me? The bottle's in the fridge—"

He hesitated.

It was a bad idea.

He didn't feel like arguing, though.

"Sure."

DOWNSTAIRS, THE DOORS WERE SHUT and locked, as were the windows. There were no signs of entry. Outside, nothing showed that shouldn't. No menacing silhouettes lurked in the shadows.

Wilde filled the wine glass, headed upstairs, and took his place back on the floor. The carpet was harder than he remembered.

London propped against the headboard and nursed the wine in silence.

"He's coming tonight," she said.

Wilde frowned.

"I don't think so."

"Why not?"

"Because the storm's too perfect."

London set the glass on the nightstand and snuggled into the covers.

"Good night."

TIME PASSED.

The storm intensified.

Wilde listened to it as London's breathing got deeper and heavier, then he shut his eyes just to rest them for a second. A slap of thunder forced them open. He listened for sounds, found none, and closed them again.

The jagged edges in his brain softened.

Don't fall asleep.

I won't.

Keep your eyes open.

I'm just resting.

You're falling asleep.

No, I'm not. Leave me alone.

AT SOME POINT LATER, WHICH could have been ten seconds or ten hours, a hand shook his shoulder and brought him out of a deep sleep.

He frantically fumbled for consciousness.

"Someone's in the house," London said.

Wilde felt around for the gun in the dark but couldn't find it.

Then he had it.

The steel was cold and heavy.

"Where?"

"Downstairs."

Wilde focused with a pounding heart.

He heard nothing.

Suddenly a heavy silhouette bounded into the room. An arm raised and a knife stabbed down at London's head. Wilde jerked the woman to the side with one hand and pulled the trigger with the other.

71

DAY TWO
JULY 22, 1952
TUESDAY NIGHT

THE DARK SILHOUETTE OF A man emerged from the shadows of Su-Moon's building. He pulled a black hood over his head, hunched his shoulders against the storm, and headed up the street at a brisk walk.

He was coming their way.

Waverly and Su-Moon wedged into the shadows.

Twenty seconds.

That's how long they had, twenty seconds, then he'd be on them. He almost certainly had a gun, that or a knife, not to mention his fists. He hadn't seen them yet, but he would. He'd catch strange shapes in his peripheral vision.

He'd turn.

He'd focus.

He'd see two women.

He'd focus harder.

He'd recognize them.

"He found the photos," Su-Moon whispered.

Waverly's veins pounded.

It was too late to run.

It was too late to do anything.

She closed her eyes and held her breath. The storm was too loud to hear footsteps.

Any second, that's when he'd be on them.

She pressed her back against the building and kept her body motionless.

A swift menacing figure emerged in her peripheral vision. She fought to not turn her head toward it, but her muscles didn't listen.

Her eyes focused.

Her face twisted.

A dark hood turned in her direction. Inside that hood, Waverly could see no face, only an empty blackness. Suddenly the man stopped. The hood turned directly toward her.

A beat passed.

Then a hand grabbed her neck.

PYTHON-STRONG FINGERS WRAPPED AROUND her throat, squeezing and lifting at the same time.

Her oxygen stopped.

Her lungs froze.

No air went out.

No air came in.

She let her legs fall out from under her and twisted her body wildly in an effort to break free.

It did no good.

The grip tightened even harder.

SUDDENLY GLASS SHATTERED AND SU-MOON had the broken edge of a bottle pressed against the man's face.

"Don't move!"

The fingers around Waverly's neck stayed in place but loosened.

"Let her go!"

The fingers loosed even more.

Waverly punched them off and choked out stale air, then sucked in oxygen, sweet sweet oxygen. The man's face came into focus, at first no more than a shadowy blur, then more pronounced.

It wasn't Bristol.

It was someone she'd never seen before.

His eyes drilled into hers.

They were predator eyes.

"Search him," Su-Moon said. "Get the envelope."

Waverly heard the words.

She understood them.

She didn't move, though.

She couldn't.

"Damn it woman, do it!"

72

DAY TWO
JULY 22, 1952
TUESDAY NIGHT

GET TO COVER, GET TO cover, get to cover—that was the one thought and the only thought that River allowed his brain as he hit the dirt. There was no time to worry about losing the gun. There was no time to feel the gravel cuts in his face. He rolled, took a long leap and rolled again, waiting for an explosion of gunfire followed by a bullet tearing into his body.

No shots came.

No bullets landed.

The storm pummeled down, but no one killed him.

He got to a boxcar, made his way underneath to the other side, and ran to January.

She wasn't there.

"January!"

No voice called back.

"January, where are you?"

She didn't answer.

HE SEARCHED, FIRST FRANTICALLY, THEN methodically.

She wasn't where he'd left her.

She wasn't at the parking lot.

She wasn't at the boxcars.

She wasn't anywhere.

He crumpled to his knees and put his face in his hands. The storm raged down, nipping at his skin with sharp little teeth.

He didn't care.

January was gone.

She'd been taken.

He'd let it happen.

73

DAY THREE

JULY 23, 1952

WEDNESDAY MORNING

THE B-17G FLYING FORTRESS WAS a bomber equipped with four Wright supercharged radial engines and a distinctive roar that could be heard two counties away. For much of the war, Wilde had sat in the rear turret of that firebird with his hands on the trigger of the 50-caliber machine guns. Most of the men he'd killed in his life had

176 · R.J. JAGGER

gotten killed from there. Although they got taken from a distance, they weren't necessarily impersonal.

Wilde would watch the flames and smoke and death spirals.

He would picture their terror.

He didn't regret doing it, even today.

He didn't enjoy it, though.

Not then.

Not now.

Not tomorrow.

Since the war, he'd taken two additional lives, both fully justified, both with his back against the wall in a him-or-them situation. The events of last night brought that number to three.

"Had it coming."

Those were the exact words of Casey Ballard, the barrel-chested, yellow-cigar-teethed homicide detective who had responded to the scene last night for all of fifteen minutes, just long enough to ask a few questions and get the body out of there.

The words were true.

The guy had it coming.

No question.

No doubt.

Still, Wilde's heart wasn't quite right, exactly like it wasn't quite right when one of his 50-cal presents found their mark. It wasn't quite right, even though London was alive this morning because of him and only because of him.

HE GOT TO THE OFFICE early, just as the sun crept into the sky. He took a shower, changed into fresh clothes and sucked down coffee and smoke. None of it cleared his head. He couldn't get the dead man's face out of his brain.

He needed to know the guy's name.

So far, that was still a mystery.

The man carried no identification.

London didn't recognize him.

Neither did the cop.

He was in his mid-thirties with a rough, no-nonsense face. That's all Wilde knew about him; that and the fact that he died with a bullet in his neck.

ALABAMA SHOWED UP AN HOUR later wearing a pre-caffeine face. She headed for the pot, filled up, and took a noisy slurp. Then she looked at Wilde over the edge of the cup and said, "So, how'd it go last night?"

Wilde wrinkled his face.

"Not good."

He filled her in.

She listened without interrupting then said, "The guy actually stabbed at her head with a knife?"

Wilde struck a match.

"Right."

The smoke snaked toward the ceiling.

"Why?"

Wilde waved the flame out and tossed it in the ashtray.

"What do you mean, why?"

"He was after the map, right?"

"Right."

"So how was he going to find it if he killed the only person who knew where it was? It doesn't make sense. I could see him going there to interrogate her. I could even see him killing her after she told him where it was—but before that? No, no way." A beat, then "Something funny's going on."

Wilde tapped a cigarette out and lit up.

He blew smoke.

"You love complicating my life, don't you?"

"That's not the question."

"Okay, then, what's the question?"

"The question is, why aren't you on your way over to the little lawyer's house to ask her point-blank what the hell is going on?"

"Why, what do you think she knows?"

"I don't know. What I do know, though, is that she's keeping it from you, whatever it is."

74

DAY THREE
JULY 23, 1952
WEDNESDAY MORNING

A THROBBING PAIN BEHIND WAVERLY'S left eye pulled her out of a fitful sleep. The room was dark and silent except for the heavy breathing of someone sleeping next to her. The crazy storm of last night had diminished to a drizzle or had disappeared altogether. She raised her hand to the ache in her head and felt dried blood. Then the memory of last night flashed.

She recalled reaching for the man to see if he had the envelope.

She recalled his sudden move.

She recalled Su-Moon being knocked violently to the ground.

She recalled a scream coming from her throat followed by a heavy punch to the side of her head.

She recalled her legs buckling.

She recalled her face hitting the ground so hard that water splashed into her nose and choked the oxygen out of her mouth.

In hindsight, the man didn't kill them.

He took what they had—the black book and the money—but he didn't kill them.

They made their way to Su-Moon's and confirmed that the envelope was in fact gone. Then they washed their wounds and went to bed.

That was last night.

Now it was dawn.

ALL THEIR PROOF WAS GONE—the pictures, the black book, the money, everything. Bristol was too smart to try to hide it again. He'd destroy it. He'd burn it or rip it to shreds or something equivalent. It was forever gone.

Waverly flipped onto her back and closed her eyes.

Now what?

Nothing, that's what.

It was over.

Over.

Over.

Over.

Wait—

Maybe it wasn't.

No, it definitely wasn't.

They had one more thing to do, namely warn the woman from Bristol's houseboat—the one who was draped across Bristol's lap in the red dress getting spanked.

They owed that to her.

Plus, maybe Bristol actually had feelings for her. If she left him, it might actually hurt.

He had it coming.

SUDDENLY WAVERLY HAD A WILD thought, so wild that she shook Su-Moon awake.

"I have a plan," she said.

Su-Moon exhaled.

"What time is it?"

"I don't know."

"Go back to sleep."

"I have a plan," Waverly said.

"Good for you," Su-Moon said. "Tell me in the morning."

"It is morning."

"The afternoon, then."

75

DAY THREE
JULY 23, 1952
WEDNESDAY MORNING

AT THE BREAK OF DAWN, barely awake before a shower or coffee, River threw on sweats and scouted the grounds for January. Last night's storm was now a humid mess up top and sloppy puddles down below. A light breeze was breaking up remnants of gray-bellied clouds and herding them to Kansas.

January was nowhere to be found.

Her live body wasn't there.

Her dead body wasn't either.

The latter brought enough relief to let him set out on a run, almost a sprint, letting his stride lengthen and his lungs dig. A mile clicked off, then another. The sky softened and an eerie mist lifted off the ground.

It was possible that January had left of her own volition.

Maybe she spotted the guy but couldn't call out.

Maybe the guy spotted River and called it off.

Maybe January followed him.

Maybe she'd show up any minute and tell him where to find the guy.

The run turned into six or seven miles, all Tarzan style. Back home, everything was the same.

January wasn't there.

No notes were on the door.

He took a shower.

AS HE WAS DRYING OFF, the phone rang and a deep, menacing voice came through. "Listen carefully, asshole, because what you do in the next thirty seconds is going to determine whether your tattooed little friend lives or dies. Do you understand?"

River exhaled.

"Let me talk to her."

"She's alive, don't worry about it," the man said. "Now, where is Alexa Blank?"

River pulled up an image of the woman chained in the graveyard. She should still be there, alive and well, unless something went wrong.

He needed time.

"I'll take you to her," he said.

A beat.

"Just tell me where she is and then stay put. After I have her, I'll release your little friend. You have my word. All I want is a fair exchange, nothing more."

River shook his head.

"Drive south out of town on Santa Fe, about twenty or twenty-five miles," he said. "You'll see my car at the side of the road. Be sure January's with you. Be smart and we'll both get what we want. Be stupid and I'll rip your heart out and throw it to the maggots. Go now. I'll be waiting."

He slammed the receiver down.

His blood raced.

Someone was going to die.

TEN SECONDS LATER, THE PHONE rang. River watched it without answering as he threw on clothes, then grabbed his gun and headed for the car with his hair dripping. Halfway there, he turned back long enough to get an eight-inch serrated knife from the top dresser drawer.

The knife and gun got thrown on the seat next to him.

Then he squealed out.

The traffic was thick.

Everyone in the universe was in his way.

The minute he passed someone, some other idiot popped up in front.

Calm down.

Calm down.

Calm down.

That's what his brain said, *Calm down.*

Calm down and be smarter than him.

Calm down and come up with a plan.

Calm down and kill the little prick.

TRAFFIC LOOSENED.

River actually got some breathing room and opened it up. Then a car at a crossroad turned right in front of him. The jerk could have waited—*should* have waited—but was just one more of those selfish bastards who thought they owned the road.

River got on his tail and honked his horn.

The guy looked in his rearview mirror.

His hand came up.

His middle finger came up.

The finger waved back and forth.

River put every muscle of his leg into the accelerator and swung violently into the other lane to get alongside.

The massive grill of an oncoming eighteen-wheeler suddenly appeared from out of nowhere directly in front of him.

Shit!

He slammed on the brakes.

The rear wheels locked and went into a fishtail.

76

DAY THREE
JULY 23, 1952
WEDNESDAY MORNING

WILDE WENT TO THE LAW firm to find that London hadn't shown up for work, to the puzzlement of the receptionist. Wilde found her at home, packing a suitcase. Her face was stressed. Her eyes wouldn't look into his for more than a heartbeat.

"Going somewhere?" he asked.

"It's over, Wilde."

"What's over?"

"Everything."

He lit a cigarette, blew smoke and said, "Last night was close, I'll admit. You're alive, though."

"This time," she said.

He tilted his head.

"So you're going on the run?"

She nodded.

"As far and as fast as my legs will take me." She looked into his eyes, then away. "You can come with me if you want."

The words rolled through Wilde's brain with the force of a freight train. He pulled up the image of them getting into her car, heading down the road and never looking back.

"That's quite a statement," he said.

She walked over, put her arms around him, and laid her head on his chest.

Her body trembled.

"I have some money saved up," she said. "We'll go down to Mexico and find the treasure. I'll cut you in. We'll be fifty-fifty partners."

Wilde pictured it.

The picture was intoxicating.

Secret would be history, but London was every bit her equal. The only reason he hadn't fallen for London yet is because he'd let Secret in first.

He'd made no commitments to Secret.

If he left, it wouldn't be a violation.

There was chemistry with London.

He couldn't deny it.

It was the same as with Secret, maybe even more so.

FINDING THE TREASURE AND GETTING it out of Mexico would be dangerous, in fact damn near impossible. In all probability they'd be caught and end up in rat-infested prison cells, either that or dead. But if they actually pulled it off, if they actually got away with it, the math would be fun.

"Come with me," London said. "Say you will. After we get the treasure we'll buy an island and spend the rest of our lives on the beach." A beat then, "Or first we can travel. I want to go to Hong Kong." She pulled her stomach tighter to his and looked into his eyes. "How about you, Wilde? Have you ever wanted to go to Hong Kong?"

He grinned.

"I never really thought about it."

"If we get the treasure, that's what our lives will be," she said, "thinking about things we never thought about before. Not just thinking about them, either—actually doing them. We'll make the world ours. Everyone else will just be a trespasser."

He kissed her forehead.

"When you think, you don't mess around, do you?"

"No, I don't."

She kissed him on the mouth.

Her lips were soft and moist.

"So, what do you say?" she said. "Are you in?"

77

DAY THREE
JULY 23, 1952
WEDNESDAY MORNING

WAVERLY'S PLAN WAS TO MAKE contact with the woman Bristol had spanked in his houseboat, not just to warn her but also to solicit her help.

She was on the inside.

She could get information they couldn't.

Su-Moon wasn't enthused.

"What makes you think she'd do that?"

"Maybe she won't," Waverly said. "But we're going to warn her anyway. What's the harm of asking?"

Su-Moon pulled the blinds back and looked out.

The alley was full of life.

A thick fog was lifting.

She turned to Waverly and said, "The harm is that Bristol might use her against us. When she confronts him—*which she will*—he'll deny any wrongdoing, then persuade her to go in with him to get rid of us, under the guise of saving his reputation, hence his money, hence whatever it is that he's giving her on the side. She lets him spank her. Remember?"

True.

Waverly remembered.

"That doesn't just happen," Su-Moon said, "not without some kind of connection, an emotional connection. Emotions trump reasoning every time. I don't mind warning her. If we do and she doesn't take it, that's her problem. Getting mixed up with her beyond that is a train wreck."

Waverly exhaled.

"Let's do this," she said. "I'm going to go downtown and shadow Bristol. In the meantime, you go down to the library. Remember that entry in Bristol's journal about the rooftop blowjob?"

"Yes."

"That was dated 1948, March or April or May, somewhere in that time frame."

"March I think."

"Okay, March. Go through every big-city newspaper that the library carries and see who was murdered in that timeframe, no matter where in the country."

A CROWDED BUT UNEVENTFUL TROLLEY took Waverly into the guts of the financial district, where she bought a coffee and took a position as far down the street from Bristol's building as she could while still maintaining surveillance. Thirty steps farther down, next to an alley, a bad sax player squeaked out jagged notes with a bent rhythm. Passersby occasionally tossed coins into an open case.

Waverly didn't know what she expected to see.

It was possible, though unlikely, that the man who had attacked them last night would show up and disappear into Bristol's building, confirming that Bristol was behind it—as if there was any question.

If that happened, she'd follow him. If she could find out who he was, it might be worth breaking into his house.

She wore a blue, long-sleeve shirt tucked into gray cotton pants.

A black baseball hat tilted down over her face.

Ten minutes passed, then half an hour.

Bristol's face didn't show—not going in, not coming out.

A sliver of sun cut between two buildings.

Waverly stepped over and got in it.

Suddenly a man emerged from Bristol's building.

It was Sean Waterfield, the Marlboro man who took her to dinner, the one who may or may not be in cahoots with Bristol. He turned in her direction and walked at a brisk pace on the opposite side of the street with his hands in his pockets. She leaned against the building, brought the coffee up to her mouth and kept the brim of the hat low. Her instinct was to trust him, to intercept him, to tell him everything that had happened, to solicit his help, to let him take her in his arms, to let his lips meet hers.

She resisted the impulse.

He passed without looking her way.

She watched him as he walked away.

Did she just make a mistake?

Maybe.

It wasn't irreversible, though.

She could call him later if she wanted.

Maybe she would.

TIME PASSED, THEN MORE.

Lots of people came in and out of Bristol's building. None of them were Bristol or the man from last night, or anyone else of interest.

Fifteen minutes later, a cab pulled up.

Street parking was full.

It double-parked in the traffic lane.

A car behind it paused, then honked and swung around.

There was a woman in the back of the cab. Her face was pointed toward the building. Suddenly Bristol emerged, wearing a dark suit and carrying two briefcases, one in each hand. He walked quickly to the cab, opened the door, and slid in. Almost immediately the vehicle took off.

Damn it.

He was getting away.

Suddenly Waverly spotted a cab heading her way. She jumped in front of it, smacked the hood as it skidded to a stop and jumped in.

"Do a one-eighty."

The driver stared as her, astonished he hadn't run her over.

"Now!"

The vehicle spun around.

"Follow that cab up there," she said.

"You want me to catch up to them?"

"No, just stay back and follow."

"Okay."

A beat, then "I'm a Russian spy," she said. "That's my target up there."

The man laughed.

"You speak pretty good English for a Russian spy."

"They teach it to you at spy school."

78

DAY THREE

JULY 23, 1952

WEDNESDAY MORNING

IN THE WRONG LANE AND heading directly into the front end of an eighteen-wheeler, River had one thought and one thought only: to avoid a head-on hit at all costs. It wasn't even a thought, really. It was more of a chemical reaction in his brain, a reaction that made him jerk the steering wheel to the left with all his might.

The vehicle reacted like a startled snake.

The center of gravity shifted violently.

River felt it in his gut but kept his eyes on the mountain of steel speeding at him.

He might clear.

He might not.

He closed his eyes at the last second and tightened his grip on the steering wheel until there was no squeeze left. Then, whoosh. The front ends didn't lock. The vehicles passed by each other, so closely that River felt the vacuum suck him to the right.

Then he flipped.

His body left the seat and slammed into another part of the interior, then another and another.

Everything spun.

It was too fast to make out images.

All he could see were violent blurs.

Then the vehicle almost tipped again but didn't. Instead it twisted, reset on the wheels and sped into the topography with a wild bumping motion.

River's brain lightened at that second.

The vehicle wouldn't flip again.

He wasn't dead and whatever happened in the next few seconds wouldn't kill him.

He'd survived.

He might be hurt—hurt badly, in fact—but he wasn't dead.

THE VEHICLE SLOWED AND FINALLY came to a stop. River was in the back seat, half on the floor, twisted. He bowed his forehead onto his hands and closed his eyes.

Everything was silent.

It was the deepest silence he'd ever heard.

Thunder rushed through his veins.

He was alive.

That's all that mattered.

Alive.

Alive.

Alive.

Then a warning sounded inside his head, a warning that said he had no time to relax.

Something was wrong.

A pain from his side made him focus. He looked down and saw a knife sticking out of his body.

There was blood, lots and lots of blood, enough to scare him.

He grabbed the knife as fast as he could, pulled it out and dropped it.

There.

The bastard was out.

He twisted upright and pulled his shirt up to see how deep the wound was.

He couldn't tell.

There was too much blood.

It felt deep, but he couldn't tell.

SUDDENLY HIS RIGHT EYE BLURRED.

He wiped the back of his hand across it.

When he pulled it away, there was blood, dripping down from somewhere above.

He felt around until he found the wound. It was on his head, under his hair, two or three inches back. He ran a finger along it to gauge how bad it was.

It was bad.

79

DAY THREE
JULY 23, 1952
WEDNESDAY MORNING

"SO, WHAT DO YOU SAY? Are you in?"

London was waiting for an answer.

Her stomach was pressed to Wilde's.

Her lips were open.

Her breathing was shallow.

Wilde was at a crossroads, the kind that lasts only a few seconds and then ripples forever. Part of him said yes, go; screw his whole existence, disappear with London and let whatever happens happen. The other part said no, don't even think about it; he hardly knew the woman, certainly not enough to throw away everything he'd built up in Denver.

He blew smoke.

Then he looked down into her eyes and opened his mouth to talk.

He still didn't know what the answer would be, but knew it was time to give it.

The silence was over.

It was time to decide.

It would come to him as he mouthed the words.

SUDDENLY A NOISE CAME FROM behind him. He turned to find a man in the room, a man he knew—Crockett Bluetone, the hotshot lawyer, the head of London's firm.

London was as surprised as Wilde and took a step back.

"The door was open," Bluetone said. Then to Wilde, nodding at his cigarette, "You got another?"

Wilde hesitated; then he tapped one loose and extended the pack.

Bluetone pulled it out, said "Thanks," and lit up from a fancy gold lighter.

His eyes were on London.

He flicked the lighter shut, stuck it in his pocket, blew smoke at London, and looked at Wilde.

"She's a beautiful woman. I wouldn't take her offer, though, not if I was you." He focused on London and said, "Tell him why."

Wilde turned to London.

Her face was a mixture of hate, fear, and confusion.

"Get out of here," she said.

"Sure, partner, whatever you say. We'll be talking, though. Trust me on that."

Then he was out of the room and down the stairs.

The front door opened and slammed.

He was gone.

PARTNER.

Partner.

Partner.

The word ricocheted through Wilde's brain.

"What did he mean, partner? He didn't mean law partner, did he?"

London took a step back.

The wall stopped her from going farther.

"He's scum," she said. "The guy who tried to kill me last night—Bluetone hired him. That's why I'm getting out of Denver. That's why I can't practice law anymore."

Half of Wilde wanted to take the woman in his arms.

The other half wanted answers.

"Answer my question," he said. "What did he mean, partner?"

London exhaled, then slumped to the floor.

Wilde sat next to her.

"Talk," he said.

London took his hand in hers, brought it to her mouth and kissed it.

"Partner refers to the Mexico deal," she said. "Technically we were partners in that."

Wilde nodded.

That's what he thought.

"Go on," he said. "Keep talking."

A beat.

"It's not pretty," she said.

"Fine, I've been warned. Now keep talking."

"If I keep talking, you'll hate me."

Wilde took a drag on the smoke.

"Let's find out."

80

BRISTOL'S CAB HEADED SOUTH, AWAY from the skyscrapers of the financial district, and then even deeper to where the insane congestion of the city began to ease. Waverly stared through the windshield as they followed, being sure she didn't break the line of sight. The driver was staying back just the right amount. "You're doing good," she said.

The man moved the rearview mirror.

His eyes suddenly appeared in it, looking into Waverly's.

"We try our best for Russian spies," he said.

"Good."

"You never said thank you, by the way."

"For what?"

"For not running you over."

She smiled.

"Thanks."

"No problem."

"The last person I didn't run over gave me a pretty good tip," he said.

"I'll see what I can do."

"I'm not suggesting, I'm just stating a fact."

"I understand."

A photo of a woman with two blond girls was taped to the dash.

"Is that your wife and kids?"

He looked into her eyes for a heartbeat, then back at traffic.

"Yeah."

"They're nice."

"I married out of my league," he said. "What can I say?" A beat, then "You got a family?"

"No."

"Get one," he said. "That's my advice."

"I'll keep that in mind."

"A family keeps you sane."

"I've heard the opposite, too."

WAVERLY SUDDENLY REALIZED WHERE THEY were headed—the San Francisco Municipal Airport, on the east side of the bay thirteen miles south of downtown. That had to be it. There was nothing else down in this section of the world worth going to.

"They're going to the airport," she said.

"That'd be my guess."

Her heart raced.

There would be at least some minimal wait before they boarded a plane. The woman would powder her nose at some point.

Waverly would be there when she did.

SHE TURNED OUT TO BE half right—they ended up at the airport, but Bristol and the woman bought tickets and boarded a plane almost immediately.

The flight was headed for Denver.

Waverly's first instinct was to get a ticket and jump on. Her second instinct was that her first instinct was insanity. There'd be almost no possibility of Bristol not spotting her. In fact, with her luck, the only seat left would be right next to him.

She headed to the ticket counter.

"When's the next flight to Denver?"

A man in a brown suit checked.

"Two hours," he said. "At 12:15."

"I'll take a ticket."

DENVER.

Denver.

Denver.

Of all the places in the world, why was Bristol headed to Denver?

81

THE ENGINE WAS DEAD AND the world was quiet. River got out and found he was fifty yards off the road. A magpie flew overhead, and clouds were building up over the mountains. The windshield was spiderwebbed with cracks, the rear glass was gone, the metal looked like someone had taken a hundred-pound sledge to it. The eighteen-wheeler was down the road so far, it was barely a speck. The key was still in the ignition. River turned it and the vehicle started. He smiled, listened for strange noises, and got none. The tires weren't flat. He surveyed the terrain from there to the road and picked the path least likely to get him stuck. Three stressful minutes later, he was back on the road heading south.

A wobble came from the tail end.

Something was bent.

It felt like the wheel, that or the axle.

At fifty, the shaking got violent enough that he had to ease back to keep from tearing the stupid thing apart. He kept his right hand pressed against the knife wound.

In the rearview mirror, he checked his face.

It wasn't pretty.

He didn't care.

Suddenly a thought came to him.

The gun—where was it?

The knife was there, on the floorboard to the right, but the gun wasn't visible.

He twisted to see if it was on the back seat.

It wasn't.

Damn it.

He pulled to the side, left the engine running with the clutch in neutral, and searched under the seat. It wasn't there. It wasn't anywhere.

It was gone.

It must have flown out the window during a roll. If he went back, he might be able to find it, but then again—maybe not.

What to do?

He was weak.

The sane thing to do was to abort before he ended up dead. He kept the front end pointed south with his foot on the pedal. There were no other cars. He was alone in the universe.

Five minutes passed.

The knife wound was losing its pain, receding more into a dull throb.

HE CHECKED THE REARVIEW MIRROR and saw something he didn't expect.

A car was back there, a quarter-mile or so, too far to see how many people were inside or if they were male or female.

It wasn't closing.

It wasn't dropping back.

It was a perfect shadow.

River watched it for a number of heartbeats, then took his foot off the pedal, coasted to the side of the road, and stopped. He picked the knife off the floorboard, secured it behind his back under his belt, and stepped out.

The sky spun.

He leaned against the vehicle to keep from falling.

A drop of blood dripped into his eye.

82

DAY THREE
JULY 23, 1952
WEDNESDAY MORNING

WILDE STOOD UP AND PULLED London to her feet, then put his arms around her. "Tell me," he said. "Tell me what it is that's not pretty."

London squeezed him and looked up into his eyes for a heartbeat before pulling away.

"I wish I hadn't done it," she said. "Believe me when I say that."

"Done what?"

She slumped onto the bed next to the suitcase.

"Me and Crockett were partners in the Mexican deal," she said. "It was actually my idea, not his. I was the one who approached him, not the opposite. The deal was simple. He bankrolled all my trips down there over the years. He greased the skids so that I could be away from the law firm for months at a time without getting fired. He was also in the wings to help me if I got caught or ended up in jail or something like that. In return, if it turned out that I actually did come across something of value, we'd split it fifty-fifty. On my last trip down there, I came across the map. You already know about that part."

The cigarette was down to Wilde's fingertips.

"Hold on."

He stepped into the bathroom and threw the butt in the toilet after lighting a new one from it.

He blew fresh smoke.

"You said he hired the guy who tried to kill you last night."

"That's right."

"Why?"

LONDON EXHALED.

"Okay, when I got back from Mexico, I didn't tell him about the map—not at first," she said. "I pretended like nothing out of the ordinary had happened."

Wilde wrinkled his face.

"So you double-crossed him."

"No," London said. "Well, yes, but only at first. He could tell I was lying and kept pressuring me to find out what I was hiding. Then someone broke into my house."

"Him?"

London shrugged.

"Maybe, but I don't think so," she said. "I think it was some third party."

"Who?"

"I don't have a clue," she said. "Anyway, I was scared at that point. I came to you for protection."

Wilde nodded.

"Right, I know."

Her eyes held his briefly, then flicked away. "I wasn't completely honest with you, though," she said. "I gave you a map to hold. It wasn't the original one. It was a decoy."

"What are you saying, that it was a copy?"

"It wasn't even a copy," she said. "It was just something I made up."

"So it doesn't show the location of a treasure?"

London shook her head.

"No, it's just a worthless piece of paper," she said.

Wilde tilted his head.

"So where's the original?"

"I have it," London said. "It's somewhere safe."

"Where?"

"That's something I can't tell you," she said. "Here's the thing—at the same time I was going to you for protection, Crockett was putting more and more pressure on me. I decided to do the same thing with him that I did with you, namely give him a false map."

"Did he think it was real?"

She nodded.

"Yes, the same as you."

"So you double-crossed him at that point."

HER BREATH SHORTENED.

"I'm not proud of it," she said. "But I was the one taking all the chances. I was the one with my ass in the dirt. I was the one who figured out where to look." A beat, then "I was going to pay him back in the end, everything he'd invested—tenfold. The only thing I didn't want to do was to cut him in for a full fifty percent. He hadn't earned it."

Wilde frowned.

"But that was the deal."

London hardened her face.

"Well, the deal changed."

Wilde inhaled deep and long, then blew a ring.

"Let me fill in the next part," he said. "Crockett figured out what you did and hired someone to kill you."

London shook her head.

"No."

"No?"

"No."

"What, then?"

"He actually thought he had the original map," she said. "At the same time, he denied that he was the one who'd broken into my house. I think he was telling the truth when he said that. If he was, then there was definitely a third party in the mix."

"Okay."

"We came up with a plan," she said. "This is the part where it starts to not get pretty, at least where you're concerned. The plan was that I would have you come over to my house last night to protect me."

WILDE'S CHEST TIGHTENED.

"Go on."

"I was supposed to slip something into your drink." She pulled a pill out of her purse and held it up. "This. It wouldn't make you pass out completely, but it would slow you down to the point where you wouldn't be able to hold your own in a fight."

She put the pill back in her purse.

"I don't remember feeling groggy," Wilde said.

"That's because I never slipped it to you," London said. "Like I was saying, the *plan* was that I would slip it to you. Then, at exactly one o'clock in the morning, Crockett would break in. He'd attack you. He wouldn't kill you or hurt you too bad, but you'd know you were attacked. Then he'd abduct me. I'd disappear and you'd make a police report the following morning. I'd never show back up again. Then, whoever the third party was, they'd think I was actually gone forever. They'd get off my tail."

Wilde frowned.

His vision blurred.

Then he focused and said, "So I was your witness?"

"Right."

"That was wrong."

She nodded.

"To a point," she said. "Remember, though, I was fighting for my life. I hired you to protect me. The plan—if it had actually gone as planned—would have gotten the result. You would have played your part, although I admit it wasn't the way you envisioned. You also got paid pretty well."

Wilde shook his head.

"That's bullshit," he said. "Don't try to justify what you did."

LONDON SHRUGGED.

"If you're looking for an apology, I'll give you one," she said. "But someday when it's your neck on the line, you'll understand."

"I already understand."

"Do you? Deep down?"

"Yes," he said.

But he wasn't sure.

Not really.

Not down in his bones.

"Anyway," London said, "I didn't go through with the plan."

True.

Very true.

"Why not?"

"Simple. I had a feeling that Crockett was going to double-cross me," she said. "He had the map, or at least he thought he had the map. He didn't need me anymore. I had a sneaky feeling that what he was actually going to do was kill me instead of pretending to abduct me." Her lower lip trembled. "So instead of slipping you something, I kept you as you were. Then when he came in, I woke you. Good thing too, because I was right. He actually tried to kill me. Not directly—the guy who showed up was hired by him."

"You still don't know that."

"Wake up, Wilde," she said. "It's for sure. If it was a third party looking for the map, they wouldn't kill me. I wouldn't be any use to them dead. The only person who had a motive to see me dead is someone who thought they already had the map. That's Crockett Bluetone."

It made sense.

"That's why he showed up this morning," she said. "Everything went wrong last night. He knew I was skipping town and headed over to grab me. The only thing that stopped him was you being here."

Wilde chewed on it.

It fit.

It all fit.

His fingers were hot.

He looked down to see the cigarette almost burned to the end.

He threw it in the toilet.

Then he lit a book of matches on fire, watched the flames for a few heartbeats and lit another cigarette. He waved the flames out and threw the matches in the toilet.

HE LOOKED AT LONDON.

"You set me up to kill Bluetone last night. You knew he'd show up. You knew I'd kill him. You turned me into a murderer. You did it so you could have the whole treasure for yourself."

London buried her head in her hands.

Then she looked up and held his eyes with hers.

"I told you it wasn't pretty," she said.

"Well, you were right."

"I felt bad afterwards," she said. "When I said I was going to cut you in on half, that was the truth. That part of it was real. It still is real, Wilde. Let's do it. Let's go get the treasure and then live the rest of our lives on an island. Come on, just you and me. Screw the rest of the world."

83

DAY THREE
JULY 23, 1952
WEDNESDAY MORNING

WAVERLY PUT A NICKEL IN the payphone every ten minutes but never got anything except ringing until just before her flight was called for boarding—then Su-Moon answered. She had big news. "A woman named Bobbi Litton got killed in Cleveland in May of last year," she said. "She fell off a building in the middle of the night. Bristol killed her, I can feel it in my gut. Where are you, by the way?"

Waverly explained.

She was getting ready to board a plane to follow Bristol and the spanked woman to Denver.

"Why are they going to Denver?"

"I don't know," Waverly said.

Silence.

"I know," Su-Moon said. "He killed the woman there Friday night, but now something's gone wrong. For some reason it's coming unraveled. He's going there to clean it up."

"What do you mean, unraveled?"

"I don't know," Su-Moon said. "Maybe there was a witness and he found out about it. Maybe he figured out that a hotel clerk or someone had too much information. I don't know. Did you call that guy you know at Bristol's firm, the Marlboro Man—"

"—Sean Waterfield—"

"—right, him. Did you call him to see if Bristol has business in Denver?"

"No."

"Do it. If he doesn't have business there, that means he's going back to clean up a mess." A beat, then "We're to blame, no doubt. It's because of the pressure we're putting on him that he needs to be extra careful."

"You think?"

Yes.

She thought.

"I'm going to go to Cleveland and run down Bobbi Litton's murder," Su-Moon said.

Waverly wrinkled her forehead.

"Why? This isn't your fight."

"It is now. We're too close. Are you going to be staying at your house in Denver?"

"Apartment, not house."

"Give me the number there."

She did.

"I'll call you," Su-Moon said. "Be careful."

"You too."

WAVERLY DROPPED ANOTHER NICKEL IN the phone and dialed the Marlboro Man. "Where's Bristol?"

A beat.

"Let's have lunch," he said.

"Can't."

"Sure you can."

"Not today, honest. Where's Bristol?"

"I don't know. He left the office."

"To where?"

"I don't know," he said. "He just up and left. Supposedly he won't be back for a day or two."

"Did he go somewhere on business?"

"Not that I know of."

"Would you know, if that was the reason?"

"Yes, I'd know."

Waverly exhaled.

"Thanks," she said. "I don't know if it means anything, but I actually do like being with you."

"Then prove it."

"Maybe I will, but I can't at the moment."

THIRTY MINUTES LATER, SHE WAS buckled into a window seat of

a shaky four-prop plane with the armrests in a death grip, swooping up into a turbulent cloudy sky.

Bristol.

Bristol.

Bristol.

I'm going to nail your ass so hard that they'll hear your screams in China.

84

DAY THREE

JULY 23, 1952

WEDNESDAY MORNING

THE VEHICLE FROM RIVER'S REARVIEW mirror skidded to a stop next to him. A man in a black T-shirt with a rough, no-nonsense face got out. He flicked a butt to the ground and headed over. It wasn't until he came around the front end that River saw his right hand.

In it was a gun.

It came up and pointed into his eyes.

"Do you know who I am?"

River studied him.

He was cold.

He was capable.

A scar ran down his forehead, across the right eye, down the cheek and over the upper lip. He wasn't nearly as big as River but was still a good size, six-one or more. His body belonged to a street cat, sinewy and hard. The cuffs of his T were rolled up, flaunting taut arms built for pull-ups. A red rose was tattooed on his left forearm. Sticking in the rose was a black dagger. He looked like he'd been kicked around and had learned how to kick back ten times harder.

River didn't know him.

He didn't want to know him.

"Where's January?"

"You mean the little tattoo bitch?" The man tilted his head toward the trunk. "In there."

"Let me see her."

"She's a crappy lay. You can do better."

River fought down thunder in his blood.

"I want to see her."

The man pulled a pair of handcuffs out of his back pocket and tossed them to River. "Sure, put these on first, behind your back."

River hesitated.

The man hardened his face.

"Do it, or things are going to get real ugly real fast."

River's chest tightened.

He'd been stupid to stop. He should have aborted. He should have set a trap. He should have done anything except what he did.

"Do it, I said!"

River pictured the cuffs on his wrists. He'd be totally beaten at that point. He'd be defenseless. He'd be a mouse in the tiger cage.

The man twisted his face, pointed the barrel of the gun at the trunk, and cocked the trigger.

"You have three seconds. Then she gets some air holes."

River swallowed.

IT COULD BE A FAKE. January might not even be in there. River didn't know that for sure though.

He snapped a cuff on one wrist.

It was cold as death.

"Behind your back."

River exhaled and then complied.

He was cuffed.

Everything in the world was instantly different.

The man smiled.

"There, that wasn't so hard now, was it? Now we can get down to the business we came here for. Where's Alexa Blank?"

"I'll take you to her."

"Damn right you will."

"First let January go."

"That's good, a sense of humor. I like that."

"I'm serious," River said.

The man whipped the weapon, so fast that it caught the side of River's head in spite of his pull back. Rage exploded inside his skull.

He'd kill the little bastard.

He'd kick him to death.

"There's a lot more of that if you want it," the man said. "Take me to Alexa Blank."

"Screw you."

The man opened the trunk. Inside was a woman, tightly hogtied with multiple wraps of rope. Her mouth was gagged. Her eyes were open and flicked with life but had so much fear in them that they were hardly recognizable as January's. The man put the gun to her forehead and looked at River.

"I'm done being nice, asshole."

85

DAY THREE

JULY 23, 1952

WEDNESDAY MORNING

"WHEN I SAID I WAS going to cut you in on half, that was the truth. That part of it was real. It still is real, Wilde. Let's do it. Let's go get the treasure and then live the rest of our lives on an island. Come on, just you and me. Screw the rest of the world."

Screw the rest of the world.

Get the treasure.

Live on an island.

The images filled Wilde's brain. He let himself get drunk on them, just for an instant, then broke loose. He took a deep look into the woman's eyes, those beautiful eyes, those tricky little eyes. Then he headed for the door.

"Good luck."

He was gone.

Walking to Blondie under a crisp blue sky, on his mind was one thought and one thought only, namely Secret St. Rain. He needed her in his arms. He needed her breath on his lips. He needed her body against his. He'd been a fool to think about London, even for a moment. That particular piece of weakness was over, dead and buried and forever gone.

He headed to Secret's hotel.

She wasn't there.

"She left a half hour ago," the guy at the front desk said.

"Did she say where?"

"No, but she was dressed to kill."

Wilde tilted his head.

"She couldn't have been *too* dressed to kill. After all, you're still alive."

The man smiled.

"Barely."

WILDE HOPED SECRET WAS AT the office. She wasn't, but Alabama was. Wilde dangled a Camel from his lips, set a book of matches on fire, lit the cigarette from the flames, and let them burn as he poured a cup of caffeine. Alabama dangled her feet off the edge of the desk and watched. Then she said, "How'd it go with London?"

"Bad."

"Bad?"

"Right, bad."

"How bad?"

"Real."

"I knew it."

Wilde filled her in on what a fool he'd been. Alabama's face got tighter and tighter. When the full story was out, she said, "She set you up to kill someone? That bitch is going to rot in hell."

Wilde couldn't disagree.

Alabama hopped off the desk.

"You want me to go over and beat the shit out of her?"

Wilde frowned.

Then he opened the desk drawer, pulled out an envelope full of money—London's retainer—and counted what was inside. It was drawn down $75 from when it was fresh. He took that amount out of his wallet, shoved it in, and handed the envelope to Alabama.

"Do me a favor and deliver this to London."

The woman grabbed it.

"With pleasure."

Wilde squeezed her arm.

"Don't hurt her. Don't even say anything. If she's not home, just slip it under the door and leave."

SUDDENLY THE DOOR OPENED AND the last person Wilde expected to see stepped in—London. She hesitated briefly as she caught the look on Alabama's face and then walked toward Wilde.

She didn't get two steps before Alabama grabbed a fistful of hair and yanked her to the floor.

86

DAY THREE
JULY 23, 1952
WEDNESDAY AFTERNOON

WAVERLY DIDN'T GO TO HER apartment when she landed, just in case Bristol was laying in wait. She couldn't rule out the possibility that his trip to Denver was orchestrated, knowing the whole time that she was watching and would follow. It would be brilliant, actually. Luring her out of town would split her from Su-Moon plus get her away from whatever evidence was still in San Francisco that she hadn't yet found. More importantly, by luring her to Denver as opposed to some other city, he'd know where she'd be staying. It would be easier to kill someone in an apartment than a hotel.

The money Shelby Tilt had given her was almost gone.

Denver was hot.

The sky was packed with sunshine.

From an airport payphone, she called Emmanuelle LeFavre at the Clemont and got patched through to her room. The phone rang but no one answered.

"Would you like to leave a message?"

"No. She's still registered there though, right?"

"Yes."

"Thanks."

She took a cab into the city and checked into the Ambassador Motel on Larimer Street under the name Marilyn White. For 25 cents she got the key to room 212, which turned out to be a smoke-stained cube with a squeaky bed and a cracked window. She checked the hot water to see if it worked.

It did.

So did the door lock.

She headed outside to a phone booth, opened the yellow pages, and started calling the most expensive hotels. Bristol and his little spankee woman, it turned out, were staying at the Brown Palace.

"Would you like me to ring their room?"

"No, that's okay. What room are they in?"

A beat.

"Four-sixteen."

"Four-sixteen."

"Right."

"Do me a favor, will you? Don't tell them anyone called. I'm going to surprise them later."

"Sure."

"Thanks, you're a peach."

The man chuckled.

"Then peaches smoke cigars."

Waverly pulled up an image, one that made the corner of her mouth turn up.

"What's your name?"

"Jake."

"You have a good day, Jake."

"You too, whoever you are."

WAVERLY HAD BEEN INSIDE THE Brown Palace on only a few occasions—all for work, never for pleasure. It was historic and opulent, full of dark wood, important conversations, and pockets stuffed with money. She wouldn't fit in, not dressed the way she was.

She headed over to 16th Street and bought a black dress, matching high heels, and fresh lingerie, then took a shower back at the hotel, towel-dried her hair, fluffed it out with her hands, and painted her face.

There.

The room had only one mirror, a small book-sized deal over the bathroom sink. She checked herself out as much as it allowed and found the reflection passable, assuming she kept moving and put on airs.

Then she headed down the dark cinderblock stairwell.

The man at the front desk—a study of grease framed in a white sleeveless undershirt—was impressed.

"You changed," he said.

She sensed trouble.

"Nice of you to notice."

"I can stop up later if you want." He smiled, pulled a half-empty bottle of wine out from under the counter, and waved it seductively. "Me and my friend, that is. Room 212, see, I remembered. I don't remember everyone's, so take it as a compliment."

"Maybe tomorrow."

His face tightened.

"Okay, but your loss."

"Have a nice evening."

"I'll see you around."

OUTSIDE, THE CITY SMELLED LIKE a combination of exhaust fumes, French fries, and bar carpet. Seventeenth Street was two blocks north;

the financial district was five or six blocks to the right. That's where the Brown Palace was—a cab ride for someone with money, within walking distance otherwise.

For her it was a walk.

She spotted a street vendor and stopped long enough to buy a hot dog and an RC.

The streets buzzed.

The workday had just ended.

Everyone was scampering to get home or to the bars or wherever it was they were headed.

The Brown Palace appeared up ahead.

Waverly wiped grease off her mouth with the back of her hand and headed for it.

She didn't have a plan, at least nothing conscious. All she knew was that she had to make contact with the spanked woman.

That was first and foremost.

That was the priority.

She told herself it was mostly to warn her.

In reality, though, it was just as much to convert her, to solicit her help, to get inside Bristol's world without him knowing it.

She walked past a doorman dressed in a monkey suit who gave her a curious look, then pushed through heavy revolving doors before he could say anything.

The smell of money assaulted her.

Bristol wasn't in the lobby.

She walked to the elevators like she owned the place, pressed the UP button and stepped inside when the doors opened. Her hand went toward the floor buttons and almost pressed 4. Then she drew an image of the doors opening ten seconds later with Bristol standing right there.

It would be better to press 3.

Get off at 3, then take the stairs up to 4.

Then what?

She still wasn't sure.

Press her ear to Bristol's door and see if he was in?

Try to get a maid to open the door if he wasn't?

THEN, JUST LIKE THAT, A saner plan came to her. She stepped out of the elevator, headed across the lobby, and walked up to the man at the registration desk.

"Are you the cigar-smoking peach?"

He smiled.

"That's me. It's nice to put a face to a voice."

"Likewise," she said. "I need paper, pencil, and an envelope. Please and thank you."

87

DAY THREE
JULY 23, 1952
WEDNESDAY MORNING

THE MAN PUSHED THE BARREL harder into January's forehead, turned his cold steely eyes to River, and said, "You got two seconds, asshole." The tone was unmistakable. The man was serious. He'd pull the trigger and that would be that.

"Okay."

"Okay what?"

"Okay, I'll take you to her."

The man twisted his face, almost as if upset that River had given in before he got to splatter January's brains all over the inside of the trunk. He froze for a heartbeat before pulling the gun away from January's face and letting it fall to the side.

"Where is she?"

"Not far. Five or six miles up the road." A beat, then "January's not part of any of this. Let her go."

The man tilted his head.

Then he looked around, saw no cars coming from either direction, and said, "Get on the ground, facedown."

River's instinct was to resist, but he saw no rage in the man's eyes. The man's plan wasn't to shoot him in the back.

He complied.

"Don't move a muscle."

"I won't."

The man tucked the gun in his belt, snatched January out of the trunk and flung her over his shoulder. "Get up and start walking. Stay in front of me." They headed into the brush and didn't stop for two hundred yards. Then the man set January's hogtied body on the ground behind a rabbit bush and checked the ropes.

They were tight.

They were inescapable.

He patted her head.

Then he said to River, "You can come back and get her later. If you screw up, you die and she rots to death. Do we have an understanding?"

River nodded.

"Good. Let's go."

RIVER TOOK A LAST LOOK at January and said, "I'll be back. I promise." Then he turned and headed for the car with the man three steps behind. Halfway there he stopped and stared into the man's eyes.

"What's your name?"

The man smiled.

"Now there's a question I didn't expect," he said. "Keep walking."

River complied.

Twenty steps later, the man said, "Spencer."

"Spencer?"

"Right, Spencer."

"Is that your first name or last name?"

"Last."

"What's your first name?"

"Vaughn."

"Vaughn Spencer."

"Right."

"Nice to meet you, Vaughn Spencer. I'm Dayton River."

"I know. Keep walking."

AT THE CAR, RIVER GOT in the back and said, "Just drive straight. I'll tell you where to pull over."

"No tricks."

"No, no tricks. Do me a favor, though. If you kill me, come back and let January go. She doesn't have anything to do with any of this."

The man tilted the rearview mirror down until he got River's face in the glass.

"What's your obsession with that girl? She's dirt."

"We're all dirt," River said.

The man chuckled.

"Can't argue with that."

"She won't rat you out if you let her go," River said. "She'll just disappear. Give her that."

"Just do what you're supposed to and you can let her go yourself."

The vehicle sped forward.

A thought sprang into River's head.

"You killed Charley-Anna Blackridge," he said. "You put her in a red dress and dropped her off a roof."

The man turned from the road long enough to look into River's face.

"Someone got dropped off a roof?"

"Don't play dumb."

"Not by me."

"Sure by you."

"Nice try, but you're wrong."

"Friday night," River said.

"Friday night I was in San Francisco. Whatever you think happened, it didn't happen by me."

RIVER STARED AT THE BACK of the man's head.

He could twist his foot up and kick him hard, right in the back of the skull. If he got a good enough contact, he might knock him out. Even if he only got a glancing blow, he might get enough contact to make the guy lose control of the wheel. The car would roll and eventually come to a stop. River might get a chance to kick the guy to death. The key to the cuffs was probably in one of his pockets. He'd get loose, then go back and get January.

His heart raced.

Try it or not?

"How much farther?"

River looked out the windshield.

"Just around that bend."

"There's nothing out here."

"Trust me."

The man raised his hand over the edge of the seat. In it was the gun, held in a tight grip. The barrel pointed into River's face. "If she's not there, you had your last chance."

"She's there."

"We'll see." He continued, "Keep your feet flat on the floor and don't even breathe."

River swallowed.

It was time to decide.

The man had told him his name.

Vaughn Spencer.

He wouldn't have done that if he was going to let River live.

88

DAY THREE
JULY 23, 1952
WEDNESDAY MORNING

ALABAMA WASN'T A MATCH FOR London, not in the long run, but had enough anger and surprise going to get the woman to the ground and then use the momentum to pin her arms above her head.

London struggled, but Alabama straddled higher up on the woman's chest and bore down with all her weight.

Wilde looked at London and said, "What are you doing here?"

"Get her off me."

Wilde exhaled.

"Okay, Alabama, enough."

Alabama didn't move, not for a few heartbeats, then stood up and said, "When I get back, you better not be here." Then she was gone, slamming the door behind her. Wilde listened to her heavy steps pounding down the stairs, then ran to the window.

"Hey, you're sexy when you're mad."

She looked up.

"Prove it."

He laughed.

Suddenly London was right behind him, straightening her hair.

"How about me? Am I sexy when I'm mad?"

"I don't know. It didn't look like you were mad." He picked up a pack of Camels from the desk, tapped one out, and lit up. "So, now we're back to my original question. What are you doing here?"

"I have something for you."

SHE PULLED A PIECE OF folded paper out of her purse and handed it to him.

"That's the original map," she said. "You were right this morning to walk out. I got weak. I let the map change me. It's time to get my old self back. Whatever riches I might get aren't worth turning into who I was becoming."

Wilde unfolded the paper.

The drawing was quicker and sketchier than the last paper she'd given him. It looked more like what you'd expect if you were alone in a dark tomb copying something by flashlight from the underside of a casket.

"It's real," London said.

Wilde took a deep drag and blew a ring.

"What am I supposed to do with it?"

London came close.

She ran a finger down the outside of Wilde's arm.

"Give it to Bluetone," she said. "Get him off my back. Negotiate a truce. He gets the map but he has to promise to leave me alone. Make him understand that the only thing I want at this point is out. I want to be left alone. He goes his way, I go mine. I'm going to stay in Denver but quit the law firm."

Wilde frowned.

"I'd do it if it would work, but it won't work so I won't do it."

London wrinkled her face.

"Why won't it work?"

He tapped ashes into the tray.

"Lots of reasons. This is a simple map. You could have a copy or even have it memorized. You might secretly have a plan to beat him to it. The only way he can know for certain that you're going your way is to kill you. That's what I'd do if I was him."

London shifted feet.

"We could go to the police," she said. "We'll tell them everything. If I end up dead they'll know he did it."

Wilde wasn't impressed.

"He could hire somebody, he could make it look like an accident," he said. "He'll have an alibi. It won't work. If he wants you dead— which he does—you're going to end up dead. The only reason he didn't kill you this morning is because I was there."

He handed the map back.

"Get out of Denver and do it now," he said. "If you want, I'll escort you down to the train station or the airport."

She laid the map on the desk.

"I don't need an escort, because I'm not going anywhere," she said. "Get Bluetone off my back, please. At least try."

She gave him a worried look.

Then she was gone.

WILDE WATCHED FROM THE WINDOW as she headed up Larimer and disappeared around the corner. As much as he hated to admit it, if Secret didn't work out, London was the one.

There was something between them.

It was animalistic but it was real.

ALABAMA SHOWED UP FIVE MINUTES later, took a quick look at the map and tossed it back on the desk. "It's another fake," she said. "All she's doing it trying to get Bluetone off her back. She's playing you again, just like before."

Wilde lit a book of matches on fire.

They burned down to his fingertips, then he tossed them out the window.

"Maybe," he said.

"There ain't no maybes about it," Alabama said. "Stay away from that woman before you end up dead." A beat, then "You said I was sexy."

He smiled.

"You were."

She came close.

"Does that mean you're ready to prove it?"

"Maybe later," he said. "Right now I have to run."

He grabbed his hat, dipped it over his left eye and headed for the door.

"Where you going?"

He almost answered.

He almost said he was chasing after London to be sure Bluetone or one of his cronies wasn't sneaking up behind her.

"I'll be back," he said.

Then he was gone.

DOWN ON THE STREET, HE heard Alabama shouting something from the window. He stopped, looked up, and focused.

"I said, she's trouble. Stay away from her."

Wilde shifted his feet.

Then he said, "I can't."

89

DAY THREE
JULY 23, 1952
WEDNESDAY AFTERNOON

WAVERLY'S NOTE WAS SIMPLE. "YOUR life is in danger. Meet me at the Flamingo Bar on Larimer Street at 10:00 P.M. tonight and I'll explain. Do not tell Tom Bristol where you are going and be sure he doesn't follow you. This is not a joke." She folded the note, put it in the envelope, licked the glue and sealed it shut. Then she handed it to the Brown Palace receptionist—the cigar-smoking peach—together with a dollar bill.

"What I need you to do is slip this to the woman staying with Tom Bristol in room 414," she said. "Don't let Bristol see you. Tell the woman to read it in private, away from Bristol. Is that something you can do?"

He took the dollar and stuffed it in his pants pocket.

"Done," he said.

Waverly kissed his cheek.

"Thanks."

"It's the least I can do, and that's what I always do."

Waverly smiled and left.

Now what?

FROM A PHONE BOOTH DOWN near Colfax she called Emmanuelle LeFavre's hotel again only to find that the woman still wasn't in.

Damn it.

SHE HEADED TO HER FLEABAG room, changed into her grungy clothes, laid the dress neatly on the bed, and took the bus to her apartment, getting off a block after the fact and circling back on foot.

From across the street, everything looked normal.

No Tom Bristols or trolls were loitering around.

She wasn't going to stay there, not tonight at any rate, but it wouldn't hurt to check things out, just to be sure everything was all right. She trotted across the street, shot into the building, and bounded up the stairway two steps at a time.

Her door was locked as it should be.

She opened it.

The place was trashed.

Someone had broken in and messed it up.

SHE PULLED THE DOOR CLOSED, relocked it, and headed down the stairs with a thundering heart.

Halfway down, she heard steps coming up.

They were heavy.

They were moving fast.

Turn around.

Turn around.

Turn around.

That's what she told herself.

Turn around.

Do it.

Do it now.

Do it now, this second.

Her body didn't respond, though.

It didn't turn around.

Instead, it did the worst thing it could do.

It betrayed her.

It froze.

90

DAY THREE
JULY 23, 1952
WEDNESDAY MORNING

"WE'RE ALMOST THERE," RIVER SAID. Fifty yards later, he added in a calm voice, "Okay, this is it. Pull over here." As expected, Spencer turned his eyes to the shoulder. At that moment River twisted his body violently and kicked at the side of the man's head with every ounce of strength he had. The man was fast and ducked at the last second but not before River connected.

The car jerked to the right and shot off the road.

The terrain shook the car so crazily that River couldn't get a second kick.

Then something bad happened.

The car slammed to a stop and Spencer stormed out.

He was stunned but wasn't hurt.

He wasn't even bleeding.

He jerked the back door open and shoved the gun into River's face.

His face contorted.

No words came out of his mouth.

He was heaving.

He was deciding.

River recoiled against the door. He didn't want to get shot in the face. He'd rather it be to his chest or somewhere else, anywhere but the face.

Seconds passed.

Spencer said nothing.

His finger twitched on the trigger.

Then he spoke.

"I ought to take you to hell right here and now."

River said nothing.

He didn't want to push the man over the edge.

"That was a stupid move," Spencer said. "What did you think? That some puny little kick was going to take me out?"

River looked into the man's eyes squarely for the first time. They were filled with rage, but not as deeply insane as before.

"Get out!"

River complied.

"Kneel down."

River didn't hesitate.

Spencer pushed the barrel into the back of the River's head and cocked the trigger.

"I'm going to ask you a question, and you better have the right answer. Where is Alexa Blank?"

"In the field, that way."

"Bullshit. There's nothing there."

"There's an old abandoned junkyard with farm machinery and trucks," River said. "She's chained in there."

Silence.

"How far?"

"A mile."

Spencer grabbed River's hair and yanked him to his feet. "Start walking. If she's not there, we're going to start by shooting your kneecaps. Then I'm going to have a little fun with my knife. Now get your ass moving."

River looked around.

There wasn't a car in sight, not in either direction.

"Move, I said."

River complied.

Within three minutes they were out of sight of the road.

The sun was an oven.

Sweat dripped down River's forehead into his eyes.

Twenty minutes into their walk, the junkyard appeared up ahead.

"I'll be damned," Spencer said. "Maybe you weren't lying after all."

THEY KEPT WALKING.

The shapes became more and more distinct.

"Which one is she in?"

"That old rusty truck trailer over there."

"Don't say a word, you hear me? Don't call out."

"Fine."

"If you do, I'll pay a visit to your little friend January and cut her eyes out. Do you understand?"

"Yes."

"You better."

RIVER HAD LEFT A GUN with Alexa Blank. What he needed to do now was let her see he was handcuffed and wasn't in control of the situation. He needed to make an expression or gesture that told her

Spencer was trouble. With any luck, she'd get the gun in hand and point it at Spencer before he knew what was happening. With more luck, Spencer's rage would come to the surface and scare the woman so badly that she'd shoot. It was a long shot, but it was the only shot River could think of.

When they got thirty steps from the truck, Spencer pushed the barrel of the weapon into River's forehead and said in a low voice, "Lie down on the ground right here on your stomach. Don't move a muscle and don't say a word."

River looked around for rattlesnakes, then swallowed and complied.

He lifted his face up and watched Spencer as the man took one careful, silent step at a time toward the rusty hulk.

With a cat-quick move, he bounded through the rear door and swung the barrel into the enclosure.

"Don't move!" he said.

"Who are you?"

"I'm here to help. Where's the key to the handcuffs?"

She pointed.

"Over there in the corner."

"I'm with the police."

"You don't look—"

"I'm undercover. You're okay now. Don't worry about anything. You're safe."

91

DAY THREE
JULY 23, 1952
WEDNESDAY MORNING

LONDON HAD A FIVE-MINUTE head start, not to mention that Wilde had no idea where she was going. His plan was nothing more than hoping to spot her randomly in the distance. The plan didn't work—she was nowhere, she was gone. She could have turned up a street, hopped on a bus, or stopped for coffee.

Wilde didn't know.

He lit a cigarette and walked up 16th Street.

Maybe he should go to her house. If she wasn't there, he could wait for her and at least be sure it was secure when she showed up.

The Daniels & Fisher Tower loomed up ahead.

As Wilde came to it, he did something he didn't expect.

He pushed through the heavy revolving door and took the elevator up to Crockett Bluetone's firm. According to the receptionist, a redhead sitting at a desk cluttered with a Royal typewriter and piles of papers, the lawyer was in a meeting.

"For how long?"

"It could be two minutes or two hours. No one ever tells me anything."

Wilde weighed the words and said, "I'll wait."

"There's coffee over there," she said. "Help yourself."

He headed over.

This was okay.

If Bluetone was here, he wasn't out somewhere killing London.

The carpet was green and thick. Mahogany molding gave the room a heavy feeling, too heavy for Wilde's taste, in fact so heavy that it seemed to suck the oxygen out of the air. The chairs were leather and oversized. The walls were filled with oil paintings, mostly Western landscapes. One in particular caught Wilde's eye and made him walk over. It was a sliver of flat desert floor at twilight dominated by a massive orange thunderhead that consumed the upper three-fourths of the painting. On closer inspection, there was a Navajo woman and flock of sheep out there in the wild. Seeing them suddenly made the sky seem a hundred times bigger.

"That's called *Evening Thunderstorm*," the redhead said. "It's by Gerard Delano."

"Never heard of him," Wilde said. "It's good, though."

She smiled.

"That's cute."

"What's cute?"

"Saying he's good." A beat, then "I've seen you around. You play the drums sometimes down at the Bokaray."

224 · R.J. JAGGER

He nodded.

"Only as a fill-in if someone's sick or something."

"You should do it full-time."

Wilde considered it.

"There isn't much money in it."

"You can say that about almost anything."

He shrugged.

"Next time you see me there, flag me down and I'll buy you a drink."

She uncrossed her legs and re-crossed them the other direction.

"Okay."

FIVE MINUTES LATER, WILDE FOUND himself in Bluetone's office with the door closed. He tossed the map on the lawyer's desk.

"What London gave you before was a fake," he said. "She didn't know if she could trust you. That's the real one. She doesn't want it anymore. It's all yours. All she wants is to be left alone."

Bluetone unfolded the paper and studied it.

"How do I know this isn't another fake?"

"You don't," Wilde said. "Here's the deal. London won't be back to the law firm again ever. She's staying in Denver, though. You're going to leave her alone. You're both going your separate ways."

The lawyer shrugged.

"Sure."

Wilde hardened his face.

"Let me be as clear as I can on this," he said. "Don't hire anyone to hurt her. Don't tell them to make it look like an accident. Don't even look at her if you pass her on the street."

A smile slowly worked its way onto Bluetone's face.

"I feel sorry for you," he said. "It's no fun to be in a woman's spell."

Wilde got up and headed for the door, turning long enough to say, "This is your only warning. Be smart and take it."

THEN HE WAS OUT, WALKING quickly down the hallway that suddenly seemed too dark and narrow. As he rounded the corner into the reception area, the redhead looked up from a magazine, startled that someone was there.

Wilde looked down at what she was reading.

What he saw, he couldn't believe.

The woman flicked it shut and shoved it in a drawer. "Our secret, okay?"

"Can I see that for a second?"

Yes.

He could.

It was a fashion magazine, one of those expensive ones with glossy paper that showed styles from New York and Paris and London. Wilde flipped through until he found the page that had been open before. On that page was Secret St. Rain, dressed to the nines with a devious smile as she sprayed perfume on her neck from an ice-blue bottle.

It was her.

There was no question about it.

Not even a little one.

His heart raced.

"Can I take this page?"

Sure.

No problem.

He ripped it out and shoved it in his pocket.

"Thanks."

Then he was gone.

92

DAY THREE
JULY 23, 1952
WEDNESDAY AFTERNOON

THE HEAVY POUNDING OF FEET continued up the stairwell toward Waverly's frozen body. Two seconds later, the 29-year-old lanky frame of Miles Rocket bounded around the landing and almost knocked her down. A cigarette fell from his lips. He picked it up and replaced it.

"You're not dead," he said.

"Why would I be?"

He shook his head.

"Damn, I thought for sure—, I mean, first you drop off the face of the earth, then that guy shows up and trashes your apartment."

Waverly narrowed her eyes.

"What guy? Did you see him?"

"Yeah, I saw him."

"Tell me."

Miles retreated in thought.

"I heard all this noise," he said. "At first I thought you were back and were having a fight with someone or something like that, but then I didn't hear any arguing so I figured you were alone. The longer it went on, the more I got to thinking that it wasn't you. When it stopped, I looked out the peephole of my door to see if someone walked by. Someone did, a man."

"What'd he look like?"

"Scary, that's the best way to describe him. Damn scary."

"Give me specifics," Waverly said. "Tall, short, fat, skinny, what?"

"Well, he was wearing a black T-shirt, although I don't suppose that helps very much," he said. "He had a scar that ran down his forehead toward his eye and then down his cheek. He was tall—over six feet—and strong too, not in a thick gorilla kind of way but more in a taut way. Oh, he had a tattoo, too. It was on his forearm. I didn't get a real good look at it on account of how fast he was moving, but it could have been a red rose or something like that."

"Did you ever seen him before?"

"No, that was it, just that one time. That was enough. There was something about the guy's eyes."

"What do you mean?"

"I don't know," he said. "They were just, I don't know—wrong, if that makes any sense."

Waverly nodded.

"Yeah, it makes sense. When did this happen?"

"Last night, about ten. No, wait, not last night, Monday night. Right, Monday night, about ten." A beat, then "What was he doing there?"

"Good question."

"You don't know him?"

"No."

"He was probably just a robber then," Rocket said. "You'd think he'd be a little more quiet though. Was anything taken?"

"I don't know."

AS MUCH AS WAVERLY DIDN'T want to be around, she wanted even less to be ignorant as to what had actually happened, so she went back to her apartment, stepped inside, and closed the door.

The sight wasn't as dramatic as before.

A lamp that could have easily been smashed was still in place, likewise for a picture frame, a radio too for that matter. Destruction wasn't the motive. On the other hand, every drawer in the place had been pulled out and dumped. If something had been taken, it wasn't obvious. A few things that should have been taken weren't— her jewelry box for one, not that any of it was worth anything, but a thief wouldn't know that at a rough glance, he'd be more prone to just take it and figure it out later. The more she looked around, the more she came to the conclusion that the man had been looking for something.

She picked a butcher knife off the floor and set it on the counter.

Then she got a pot of coffee going.

She drank a cup on the couch with the knife at her side.

Sunshine streamed through the windows.

Suddenly the phone rang.

It was Su-Moon, checking in to report that she'd arrived safe and sound in Cleveland.

WAVERLY BROUGHT HER UP TO speed on the break-in to her apartment as well as the note she was trying to get delivered to Bristol's little spankee.

"With any luck she'll show tonight."

Su-Moon wasn't impressed.

"You're playing a dangerous game."

"I'm going to scare her over to our side."

"I doubt it."

Waverly shrugged.

Time would tell.

"I won't be coming back to my apartment, so you won't be able to get ahold of me here after this. Give me the number where you're staying. I'll have to contact you."

Su-Moon read the numbers off and Waverly jotted them down and stuck the paper in her pocket.

"Call me at eight in the morning tomorrow, your time," Su-Moon said.

"Okay."

"I'll be waiting."

SOONER OR LATER, WAVERLY WOULD need to come back here. She didn't want to see the mess again and doubted the man would be back, so she resigned herself to cleaning up.

An hour into it, she found something missing.

What it was made her palms sweat.

All her files were gone, every single last one of them.

93

DAY THREE

JULY 23, 1952

WEDNESDAY MORNING

IN TEN SECONDS, RIVER WOULD be dead. He knew it in his heart, he knew it in his gut, he knew it in his mind. As soon as Spencer got the cuffs off Blank, he'd drag her outside and plant a bullet in River's head right in front of her. River would no longer be a problem and Blank would be terrified into total submission from that point forward.

Spencer had been throwing glances his way every few seconds.

River wouldn't get far if he ran.

It didn't matter.

It was his only chance.

He muscled to his feet and forced his body into an immediate full-blown sprint.

A couple of steps, that's all he got, before a bullet flew past his head.

"Stop or I'll kill the girl!"

River took more steps but there was no power in them.

Then his body was at a stop.

His lungs went deep for air.

Spencer was on him in an instant, slamming the gun into River's head and forcing him to his knees. "If it were up to me I'd kill you right now," he said. "Here's the deal. Listen hard because I'm only going to say it once. You've been retired. You won't be getting any more jobs. I'm the new you, the new improved you. Go live your life any way you want, but don't do anything stupid. Everything that's in your past, bury it there and bury it deep."

The man grabbed River's hair and tilted his face up higher.

"Here's the important thing," he said. "See that woman over there? Forget she exists, don't come after her, don't try to save her. Here's the even more important part. Don't come after me. Don't make me regret that I'm following orders right now instead of splattering your stupid brains all over the ground. Be sure I never see your face again. If I even see you walking on the opposite side of the street I'm going to assume the worst. If you make even the slightest move against me anywhere at any time, I promise you that I will hunt you to the ends of the earth and take you to a hell you can't even imagine. I already have permission to do it, so consider this fair warning."

He pulled the key to River's cuffs out of his pocket and threw it a good distance into the brush.

"Find it, unlock yourself, and have a nice life," Spencer said.

He grabbed Blank's hand, said "You're coming with me," and walked off.

Ten steps later, he turned and said, "By the way, I'm not sure if I mentioned this or not, but if you do anything stupid, your little tattoo slut January is going to meet the same fate as you."

He turned and walked.

WITH EVERY STEP SPENCER TOOK, River realized deeper and deeper that he actually wasn't going to die. Spencer wasn't just playing a final sick trick on him. When the man disappeared behind the rusted hulk of a combine, River got to his feet and scrambled over to where the key had been thrown.

The prairie grasses were thick.

River had watched the throw, but not with as much focus as he should have. From where he stood, it could be ten feet in any direction, twenty even.

He memorized where he was, namely two steps from a moss rock half the size of a coffin. He started his search from there, ever widening in a spiraling circle.

Amazingly, he found it.

It took time, but there it was.

He got it into his fingers and found just enough twist left in his hands to get the key in the lock.

Then the cuffs were off.

He was free.

His wrists were red and raw, almost to the point of bleeding. Pain that hadn't been there before suddenly materialized when the flesh became visible.

River rubbed the wounds.

Then he headed for the trailer.

INSIDE, AS HE SUSPECTED, WAS the gun he'd given Blank. He checked the chamber and found something he didn't expect, namely every bullet had been fired except one.

Blank must have shot them off to try to attract someone's attention.

Well, it didn't work.

Too bad.

One bullet.
One bullet.
One bullet.
River gripped the weapon with a steel fist and took off in a sprint.

HE CAUGHT UP WITH SPENCER all the way back at the car, just as the man was doing a one-eighty and pulling away. He was too far to catch on foot. River had to fire, there was no other option.

The window was down.

Spencer's head was in clear view.

The man was looking directly at him, surprised but defiant.

River raised the weapon, took aim, and pulled the trigger.

As soon as he did, he knew he was off.

The next second proved he was right.

Spencer's head didn't explode.

The windshield didn't shatter.

The metal didn't ping.

River had hit nothing, nothing but air.

He pulled the trigger five more times and got only the ping of the trigger against empty shells.

94

DAY THREE
JULY 23, 1952
WEDNESDAY AFTERNOON

WILDE PACED BY THE WINDOWS with an endless string of Camels dangling from his mouth and the noises of Larimer Street buzzing in his ears. Occasionally he threw a sideways glance at the magazine ad on his desk, the one of Secret trying to sell him some kind of fancy perfume in a blue bottle. Alabama showed up after lunch, looked at the ad, and said, "So she's a model?"

"Looks that way."

"She never told you?"

"No."

"How am I supposed to compete with that?"

Wilde blew smoke.

"Do me a favor: call the magazine and find out who she is."

"You already know who she is."

Wilde pulled a dollar out of his wallet and tossed it on the desk. "I'll bet you that dollar I don't."

Alabama stuffed the money in her bra and said, "You're on."

"Hold on, it's a bet. You just can't take the money."

"I'm going to win, so just chill out."

She picked up the phone and said, "Now I'll prove it."

Seven long-distance phone calls later, she had more information than she expected. Secret St. Rain wasn't really named Secret St. Rain at all, she was someone named Emmanuelle LeFavre. She was one of the most sought-after models in New York, specializing in high-fashion ads and runway struts, represented by none other than the Sam Lenay Agency. When she wasn't the stunner in front of the camera, she was busy flaunting her stuff at the latest, greatest high-society haunt. Her turf included London and Paris in addition to New York.

Alabama poured a cup of coffee and said, "So here's the question. What's a girl like that doing out here in this cow-town with you?"

Wilde shook his head.

"I don't know."

"Well, I know one thing," Alabama said. "If I was you, I'd ask."

"Trust me, it's going to come up."

He lit a cigarette.

Then he held his palm out and said, "I think you owe me a dollar—two, actually."

"No."

"No? I won."

"Yeah, technically, but I told you before that no one's named Secret, and I was right about that. So I won first." She patted her bra. "Being that as it may, if you feel strongly about it, you can take your dollar back."

He flicked ashes.

"You're too much."

SHE CALLED INFORMATION, GOT THE number for the Sam Lenay Agency, dialed, and handed the phone to Wilde.

A man with a smooth voice said, "Who am I talking to?"

Wilde froze. He expected a *hello* first.

"Is anyone there?"

"Yeah, I'm here," Wilde said.

"And who are you?"

"My name's Bryson Wilde," he said. "I'm calling from Denver."

"Do I know you?"

"No. Do you know someone named Secret St. Rain?"

"What is this, twenty questions?"

"No, just one," Wilde said. "Let me rephrase it. You represent Emmanuelle LeFavre, the model, right?"

"That's right."

"Does she ever go by the name of Secret St. Rain?"

Silence.

"Is this some kind of a joke?"

"No, she's in Denver right now, going by that name."

"Emmanuelle's in Denver?"

"Yes."

"That's impossible, she's in Paris doing a shoot. Let me give you a piece of advice. Next time you want to waste someone's time, try someone local. It'll be cheaper."

The line went dead.

95

FROM THE APARTMENT, WAVERLY TOOK the bus downtown, got change for a dollar from a magazine vendor, and headed for the nearest phone booth. There she placed a long-distance call to Chicago.

A familiar voice answered.

"Drew Blackwater, private investigator."

"Drew, this is Waverly Paige. I only have enough money for a minute of talk so this needs to be quick. Someone recently broke into my apartment and stole some of my files, the one you gave me plus a few others like it. He was a lean strong guy with a scar down his forehead and cheek. He had a tattoo on his forearm, maybe a rose or flower or something like that. Does anyone like that ring a bell with you?"

Silence.

"This is weird, but it might," he said. "For some reason it's tugging at the back of my brain."

"Can you do me a favor and dig?"

"You mean check into it?"

"Right."

"Are we talking about being on the clock?"

"Yes, I'll pay, don't worry. You can trust me."

"I know that."

"Can you do it right away? This is important."

"Are you okay?"

"I don't know."

"I'll get right on it."

"You're a peach. I don't have a phone where I can be reached. Can I call you tomorrow?"

"Yes."

"Oh, one more thing, have you ever heard of a guy named Tom Bristol? He's an architect out of San Francisco—"

"Doesn't sound familiar."

"Do me a favor," she said. "See if you can find out if he was in Chicago at the time in question."

A groan.

"That would be about impossible."

"Try anyway. Please?"

"Sure, why not? It's your money."

"Thanks. You're a double-peach."

96

DAY THREE

JULY 23, 1952

WEDNESDAY MORNING

RIVER'S CHEST THUMPED WITH LESS of a panic as Spencer's vehicle didn't slam to a stop and the man didn't jump out to carve his face off right then and there. He wasn't going to die, not right at the minute anyway. Even if Spencer changed his mind right now this second and doubled back, there was enough distance that River could sprint into the terrain. Spencer wouldn't be able to run him down in a thousand years. As the car sped farther away, however, to the point of becoming a blur, River suddenly realized why.

Spencer was going to kill January.

That would be his way to make River suffer.

He'd get to January first, put a bullet in her brain, and let River live with the guilt for a day or a week or a month. Then he'd pop out of the shadows one dark night and swing a knife into River's face.

Damn it.

Damn it.

Damn it.

River should have never made a move. Firing the gun had been stupid; he not only knew that now but even knew it while he was doing it. He'd let his rage get the best of him and now January was the one who was going to pay.

Spencer's vehicle disappeared over the horizon.

The silence was deafening.

No other cars were in sight, not a one.

River's body broke into a sprint up the road, almost of its own volition.

How far was January?

Five miles?

Six?

River could run five-minute miles. Even at that, though, he was still close to a half hour away. Spencer would have more than enough time to slam the car to a stop, trot the two or three hundred yards to where January was, say "Bye-bye, bitch. Thank your dumb-ass friend for this," and stick the barrel in her mouth.

River kept running.

There was no other option.

Getting there in time would be impossible. The best he could hope for was that Spencer had car trouble, or got confused as to where January was.

FIVE MORE MINUTES PASSED.

River kept the speed up, but his strength was draining faster than he thought. He had one more mile left at this pace, if he was lucky.

Spencer would be to January by now.

She was probably dying even as he thought about it.

97

DAY THREE
JULY 23, 1952
WEDNESDAY AFTERNOON

WILDE NEEDED AIR, NEEDED IT now and needed it bad. He grabbed his hat, cocked it over his left eye, and told Alabama he'd be back in ten. Outside, Larimer Street smelled like a bus engine on fire.

He stopped and lit a cigarette next to the water feature, the one with the cherubs that used to spit water into a bowl back when this section of town was the center of the universe.

That was a while back.

The cherubs hadn't spit for years.

The bowl was still watertight, though, and had a rancid couple of inches of liquid at the bottom. Floating in that swill were cigarette butts, candy wrappers, and at least one broken RC bottle. Wilde tossed the spent match on top of it all and headed down the street.

Secret St. Rain was really Emmanuelle LeFavre.

His first thought was to confront her.

His second thought was to ignore his first thought and not let on that he knew. Whatever it was that she was hiding, he'd be better positioned to figure it out if she didn't know he was looking.

The Denver sky was crystal blue.

He crossed to the sunny side of the street and let the sun wash over his face.

Five minutes later, he had all the air he needed and headed back to the office. He opened the door, took a step inside, got his hat in hand, and positioned his body. Then he tossed the hat for the rack.

It swung to the side and went out the window.

He looked at Alabama.

She knew the look.

She wasn't a fan.

"No way," she said. "Get it yourself."

"You never get it for me."

"I will if you do one little thing for me."

"What's that?"

"Be sure your head's still in it the next time it goes out."

He smiled.

"Ouch."

WHEN HE CAME BACK, ALABAMA met him at the door, took the hat from his hand, and tossed it on the rack, a dead ringer. "Cock it to the left," she said.

"I try."

"Try harder."

The phone rang.

Alabama answered, said "Yeah, that's him," and handed the phone to Wilde. "It's that agent from New York. He wants to know if you're the same Wilde who just called him about Emmanuelle."

Wilde lit a cigarette, blew smoke, and took the receiver.

Then he hung it up.

"That guy's an ass," he said.

Ten seconds later, it rang again.

98

DAY THREE
JULY 23, 1952
WEDNESDAY EVENING

WAVERLY SWUNG BY EMMANUELLE LEFAVRE'S hotel to see if she was in, which she wasn't, then headed back to the financial district and took up a post in an alley across the street from the Brown Palace. She hadn't been in position more than ten minutes when what she hoped would happen actually did, namely Bristol and his woman-friend swung out of the revolving doors and onto the sidewalk.

Staying back as far as she could without losing line of sight, she followed them two blocks up to where the woman stayed outside on the sidewalk while Bristol disappeared into the doors of Jackson & Reacher, Denver's second-largest law firm.

What was he up to?

Waverly crossed the street and found an innocuous spot where she could keep an eye on the woman through the glass of a parked Olds.

The spankee wore a short red dress.

Her legs were shapely.

Her nylons had a seam up the back.

Her hair was bouncy and blond.

She leaned against the building and smoked as she waited. A passing car honked at her and someone shouted, "Hey, baby!"

She ignored it.

She must have the envelope by now. Would she show up at ten?

For half an hour, not much changed. Then Bristol emerged. With him was a female, conservatively dressed, holding a pencil in her hand as if she'd been taking notes. She looked familiar. Waverly had seen her around somewhere before.

Where?

Then she remembered.

She'd seen her at the El Ray Club last weekend, Friday night, dressed like a slut and getting drunk. She was having no problem getting men to keep her glass full. One of those men had an uncanny resemblance to Robert Mitchum.

She got introduced to the red-dress blond, smiled and shook hands, mouthed a few words and disappeared back into the building.

Bristol and the red-dress walked up the street.

WAVERLY FOLLOWED, CUTTING THROUGH THE traffic onto their side of the street. Passing by the law firm, she stopped long enough to read the names stenciled on the door.

There was only one female name.

Gina Sophia, Esq.

She memorized the name and continued up the street. If she got the chance later, she'd break into the slutty little lawyer's office and see what her precious notes said; either that or somehow get her out for a drink and let the liquor loosen her up.

99

DAY THREE
JULY 23, 1952
WEDNESDAY MORNING

RIVER'S WIND WAS GIVING OUT and his legs were getting heavy. He kept running, fighting through the pain, but his body was working against him. January was either dead or dying and he was to blame. He'd hunt Spencer's ass down to the ends of the earth. That would be his life mission from this moment on.

Screw everything else.

From behind him, a noise cut through the silence, something in the nature of an engine. He twisted and saw a motorcycle approaching, still a ways off but coming fast.

He brought his body to a stop.

His chest heaved.

Sweat rolled down his forehead.

As the bike got closer, he got in front of it and waved his arms for it to stop. It slowed to twenty or so but then held steady. The driver was a man, a big man.

The man didn't stop.

He gave River a look, then swung around and accelerated.

Shit!

River grabbed a rock the size of a baseball and threw it with all his might. It connected with the driver's back near the shoulder. The front tire wobbled violently then the bike went down and raked against the road with an awful noise.

River ran over.

By the time he got there, the man was on his feet, squared off with a long blade in his grip.

"I need to borrow your bike," River said.

The man charged.

FIVE MINUTES LATER, RIVER WAS on the bike with a serious twist on the throttle. He didn't kill the biker. He just beat him enough to get him out of the way.

Miles up the road, he came to the place where January had been dumped.

Spencer's car wasn't on the shoulder.

That was good.

Maybe the man had just kept going.

River turned left off the road, into the terrain. The bike bucked violently, but River kept the handlebars in a python grip.

When he got to January, she wasn't there.

She was gone.

Spencer had taken her.

RIVER TWISTED THE THROTTLE, SPUN the rear wheel in a one-eighty and accelerated toward the road. The front end wobbled.

The tire was flat.

River kept full-speed on the gas.

That was a bad move.

The rubber shredded off and the rim dug into the dirt, jerking the bike to the left and throwing River over the handlebars.

100

DAY THREE
JULY 23, 1952
WEDNESDAY AFTERNOON

WILDE CALLED SECRET'S HOTEL, TO be told she wasn't answering her room phone. He mashed a butt in the ashtray, hopped in Blondie, and headed over. When he rapped on the door, no one answered. He paced, tapped a Camel out, and lit up. Was she inside, dead? He flagged down a maid and got her to open the room. Clothes were spread out on the bed and toiletries sat on the bathroom sink.

Secret wasn't there.

She wasn't there dead.

She wasn't there alive.

Wilde told the maid "Thanks," gave her a full dollar, got a hug and ear-to-ear smile in return, then left.

Now what?

London popped into his brain.

That wasn't exactly true, because she'd never completely left. It was more accurate to say she got bigger in his brain. Either way, he headed over to her house to see if she was okay and tell her he'd taken a run at Bluetone.

He found street parking for Blondie a block away and inhaled a cigarette on the way, flicking it on the grass as he walked up the steps.

He rapped on the door.

No one answered.

He rapped again.

A turn of the knob worked: the door was unlocked. He pushed it open and stuck his head in.

"London, you home? It's me, Wilde."

Sounds came from the upper level.

HE HEADED UP AND FOUND London sitting on the floor of her bedroom, scrunched in the corner. A bottle of whiskey was in her hand. When she looked up, Wilde saw something he had never seen in her face before, some type of strange combination of fear and despair.

"Wilde—"

He slumped down next to her and took her in his arms. Her body trembled.

"What's going on?"

"There's a woman, Alexa Blank," she said. "She's in trouble and I'm responsible."

"Alexa Blank?"

"Right."

"Who is she?"

"A friend."

"From where, the law firm?"

"No, back. Way back."

Wilde tapped a cigarette out and lit up.

"You're not making sense," he said. "I talked to Bluetone this morning."

"I don't give a shit about him any more."

"Well, you should," Wilde said. "I gave him the map and told him to lay off you. He said *Sure*, but he didn't mean it. Like I told you before, he's still going to kill you, map or no map. You need to get out of town."

She looked over.

"You gave Bluetone the map?"

"Yeah, that's what you wanted me to do."

"So he has it?"

"Right."

She brought the bottle to her mouth, took a long gulp, and handed it to Wilde. He hesitated, then took a hit, not a big one but enough to feel the sting in his mouth.

"You need to get it back," she said.

"Get what back? The map?"

She nodded.

"If I don't turn it over, Alexa's going to die."

"Turn it over to who?"

"I don't know."

"I don't get it."

"He's just a voice on the phone," she said. "He's serious, though, I can guarantee you that. He'll kill her. He let her talk for just a second so that I knew he really had her. She was terrified."

Wilde blew smoke.

"Back up and start from the beginning."

THE STORY WAS MORE SERIOUS than Wilde expected. At age fifteen, London had been walking on ice at the edge of Clear Creek on a cold February day when it caved in. She got swept into the icy waters and ended up lodged under the ice against a log. Without even a split-second hesitation for her own safety, Alexa Blank had pounded through with her feet and got London dislodged. Both of the girls got swept downstream but miraculously got out before they drowned or froze to death. They were already friends up until then, but became inseparable from that moment on.

That was back in high school, tenth grade.

After high school, they drifted socially and in almost every other way but still stayed in touch. London already had her sights on becoming a lawyer and was focused on college. Alexa took a more relaxed path and was currently employed as a waitress at the Down Towner.

Now a strange man had Alexa.

If London didn't give him the map tonight, Alexa would be dead by morning.

"How does he even know about the map?"

"I don't know," London said.

"How does he know that you and Alexa were close?"

"I don't know."

"Is Bluetone behind this?"

"No," London said.

"How do you know?"

"I don't know, I just do."

Her hand trembled.

"He's going to call me at eleven o'clock sharp tonight," she said. "I need to get the map back from Bluetone before then."

"Not I, we."

She squeezed his hand.

"You're quite the guy, Wilde," she said. "If I was you, I would already have kicked me to the curb ten different times. At this rate, I may have to give you your retainer back."

He smiled.

"That's sort of how all this started, isn't it?"

"Yeah, I guess so."

"Now it has a life of its own."

"It's the map," London said. "It's cursed. I told you that before."

Wilde blew smoke, then pulled London to her feet.

"Come on," he said.

"To where?"

"My office, for starters," he said. "You're going to make a fake map just in case we can't get the original back from Bluetone. While you're doing that, I'm going to try to figure out who took your friend."

"There isn't enough time."

Wilde opened his mouth to deny it, but the words didn't come out. "We'll see," he said.

101

DAY THREE
JULY 23, 1952
WEDNESDAY NIGHT

THE FLAMINGO BAR ON LARIMER Street was jammed with drunks of both sexes when Waverly walked in at a quarter to ten. The only light came from behind the bar, filtering through half-empty bottles of scotch and whiskey. Most of the place was dim to dark. It smelled like a forest fire that someone had tried to put out with beer. A scratchy song from a jukebox tried to rise above the noise, with little success. Waverly ordered a screwdriver and leaned against the wall near the back by the restrooms, keeping an eye on the entrance.

If Bristol's little spankee didn't show, that would be her problem.

All Waverly could do was try.

This was that try.

She checked her watch—9:55—then stepped into the ladies' room. There was a window cracked open a couple of inches. She raised it as far as it would go and stuck her head out. The drop to the ground wasn't far. The window was over-painted and wouldn't go all the way up, but it raised enough for her to slither her body out if it came to it. She could escape this way if Bristol showed up to trap her.

Back in the bar, the spankee still hadn't shown up.

Waverly downed what was left of the screwdriver, ordered another, and receded into the back corner.

Ten o'clock.

That's what it was now.

Game time.

THE FRONT DOOR OPENED AND a blond walked in, a blond in a red dress. She looked around as if expecting to meet someone. It was the spankee, alone, without Bristol. Waverly didn't move. The woman looked at her watch, didn't see anyone approaching, then took a seat at the only empty barstool, at the very end of the bar. As she ordered a drink, Waverly crossed the floor, stepped outside and looked up and down the street. If Bristol was hiding out there somewhere, he had hidden himself well. There were a few unsavory types here and there, but they looked like ordinary lowlifes, not guns for hire.

She headed back inside, stepped next to the woman, and said, "I'm glad you came."

The woman studied her.

"You're the one who wrote the note?"

"Yes. Where's Bristol?"

"He's back at the hotel."

"Did he follow you?"

"No."

"Are you sure?"

"I don't think he did."

"Did you check, while you were walking?"

"No—"

"How'd you get away?"

"He thinks I'm in the lobby bar having a drink." She took a swallow of alcohol. "Tell me who you are and what's going on. I don't have much time."

"Tom Bristol's a murderer," Waverly said. "He dangles women off the tops of buildings and then drops them. They always have a red dress, just like the one you're wearing right now. Let me ask you something. Is that something you bought yourself, or did he buy it for you?"

SUDDENLY THE FRONT DOOR OPENED and a man's figure appeared.

It wasn't Bristol.

It was a man in a black T-shirt.

He was strong but not like a gorilla, more in a taut way. It was too dark to tell if he had a scar on his face. Waverly grabbed the woman's hand and said, "I think one of us was followed. I know a way out the back. Hurry!"

102

DAY THREE
JULY 23, 1952
WEDNESDAY NIGHT

NIGHT CREPT OUT OF THE east and smothered Denver in a deep darkness. River sat on top of the middle boxcar staring east into the city lights. Next to him was a knife. Next to the knife was a bottle of Old Milwaukee with only a few sips left. Next to the bottle was a three-battery flashlight. Next to the flashlight was a Colt .45, not his old one—that was still out in the field somewhere with empty chambers—but his new one, the one just like it that he purchased this afternoon.

The chambers were full.

He checked twice.

He had racked his brain all day, going over every inch of his past, trying to detect the slightest clue as to who had hired him all these years, and consequently currently had Vaughn Spencer under employment.

He'd come up empty.

In hindsight, he'd been a fool to let such an arrangement creep into his life. He should have resisted the money. He should have just lived a normal life.

Spencer would come for him.

Hopefully that would be tonight.

River would be here.

Come on.

Kill me.

I'm waiting for you.

The specter of tearing through the terrain on the motorcycle toward January's hogtied body—only to find her gone—kept ricocheting around in River's brain. Spencer must have been pissed beyond belief to go to the trouble of fetching the woman after he already had what he'd come for.

Where'd he take her?

He took her to the same place as Alexa Blank, clearly, but where was that?

River had spent all afternoon going from one hotel to the next, big and small, luxurious and flea-bagged, knowing that Spencer would now have a more secret place but hoping against hope that he might have taken a comfortable room when he first got into town, which was most likely in the last few days. No one had a registration for Vaughn Spencer, not at any point in the last month.

No one recalled a man with a scar down his face or a tattoo on his forearm.

So where was he?

Was he down in the old abandoned warehouse district?

Did he break into a vacant house that had a For Sale sign in the front yard?

Did he kill a farmer out in the sticks?

Did the person who hired him rent a house for him?

SOMETHING FLEW OVER RIVER'S HEAD, swooping within feet. It was too dark for birds. It had to be a bat. He checked the skyline and saw nothing, not for some time. Then there it was, a dark silhouette darting back and forth in a rapid, jagged flight.

River found a piece of gravel the size of a marble and waited. When it came close, he tossed it up. The bat darted for it, thinking it was a bug, then diverted just before it hit and knocked itself out.

River nodded with respect.

Good reflexes.

HIS EYES WERE GETTING HEAVY. It had been a long, long day. His thoughts drifted back to January and finding her gone. Nothing in his life had been as empty as getting to where she was and then not having her there.

He needed motion.

Sitting here wasn't getting her found.

Come on, Spencer.

Hurry up.

Get your ass over here and kill me.

He heard a noise, something moving in the shadows, barely perceptible but definitely something.

A dog?

Spencer?

He held his breath.

No sounds came.

He listened harder.

No sounds came.

He shoved the flashlight in a back pocket and tucked the gun in his belt. Then with the knife in his left hand, he silently climbed down the ladder on the pitch-black backside of the boxcar.

103

DAY THREE
JULY 23, 1952
WEDNESDAY AFTERNOON

WILDE FOUND OUT SOMETHING INTERESTING from one of the waitresses at the Down Towner where Alexa Blank worked, namely that Alexa had suddenly left halfway through her shift on Tuesday with a Tarzan-like man who had long black hair. Before she left, she said, "If I die, he's the one who killed me," or words to that effect. She hadn't been seen or heard from since.

There was only one man in town who fit that description.

He was a guy who frequented the Bokaray.

Wilde had seen him there on several occasions.

They'd never talked, not once.

They didn't like each other.

They didn't look at each other.

They didn't acknowledge each other's existence.

Each was too much of a competitor of the other, especially when it came to the ladies. They were like two lions in the same cage, that much Wilde knew. Other than that, he knew nothing about the man, not his name, not where he lived, not a thing.

He hopped in Blondie and headed for the Bokaray.

The front door was locked, but the back one was open.

He headed in and shouted "Anyone home?"

"Back here."

The words were feminine and faint, from somewhere back near the restrooms. Wilde headed that way. The mysterious black door at the end of the hall was ajar. Inside, a woman sat behind a desk working on papers. Wilde knew her by sight as one of the co-owners of the place but didn't know her name.

"You're the drummer," she said.

"Bryson Wilde."

"Bryson Wilde, ladies' man," she said. "I'm Mia Lace. There, we've finally been formally introduced. Have a seat."

Wilde complied, tapped out two cigarettes, lit them up and handed her one.

"Thanks," she said.

He nodded.

"That woman you brought up on stage, she's got quite the voice."

"She does."

"She could be a star."

"I agree," he said. "The reason I'm here, though, is because I need to get in touch with that guy with the long hair who hangs out here, the Tarzan guy."

"Dayton River."

"Is that his name?"

She blew smoke and nodded.

"You two don't like each other," she said.

Wilde wrinkled his forehead.

"What makes you say that?"

She smiled.

"What do you want him for?"

"It's personal. Where does he live?"

"You look like you're going to kill him."

"That's not my plan."

"Are you sure?"

He shrugged.

"He might have something that doesn't belong to him."

"Something of yours?"

"No."

"What, then?"

"A woman."

"A woman?"

"Right, a woman."

"He has a woman who doesn't belong to him?"

"He might. I don't know yet, one way or the other."

"Your girlfriend?"

"No."

"Are you sure?"

"I'm sure."

"What's her name?"

"Alexa Blank," Wilde said. "She's a waitress."

"I never heard of her," Lace said.

"No reason you would have," Wilde said. "So where does Tarzan live?"

The woman studied him.

Then she told him.

Wilde stood up.

"Thanks," he said.

"Do you want some advice?"

"No."

"Too bad, because here it is," Lace said. "If you screw with him, you better be prepared, because he'll rip your head off and piss in the hole."

"My head doesn't come off that easy."

Lace blew smoke.

"You might be surprised."

TWENTY MINUTES LATER, WILDE SKIDDED Blondie to a stop in dusty gravel at the far end of the BNSF railroad yard. He pulled his gun out of the glove box, stepped out, and shouted, "Tarzan, you got company."

No one answered.

Nothing moved.

There were several boxcars converted to living quarters and some kind of tent canopy stretched between them. At the north end of it all was a car, a battered car that looked like it had been hit a hundred times by a freight train.

Wilde felt the hood.

It was cold.

"Tarzan, come out, come out, wherever you are."

The noise of colliding couplers and straining steel came from up the tracks. Other than that, though, silence ruled the world.

Alexa Blank was here somewhere.

It was the perfect place.

Wilde cocked the trigger and headed for the closest boxcar with a pounding heart.

104

DAY THREE
JULY 23, 1952
WEDNESDAY NIGHT

THE BATHROOM WINDOW DUMPED WAVERLY and the spankee into a dark alley behind the Flamingo, which they took east toward traffic. Halfway there, Waverly grabbed the blond by the arm, yanked her to a stop, and said, "Follow me." She headed up a dark fire escape at the back side of a building. At the first landing, she looked back.

The blond wasn't following.

She was standing there, looking up.

"Come on," Waverly said.

She continued up.

The next time she looked back, the blond was in tow, a floor behind.

They got to the roof and walked across to the front of the building. Larimer Street sprawled out, four stories down.

"Why are we up here?"

"There was a guy who came into the bar," she said. "I want to get a better look at him. I think he broke into my apartment. I'm pretty sure Bristol hired him."

"Why?"

"Because I'm on to him about being the murderer and he knows it." A beat then, "What's your name?"

"Jaden."

"Nice to meet you. I'm Waverly."

HIDING BEHIND THE PARAPET AS much as possible while still keeping an eye on the street outside the Flamingo, Waverly gave Jaden the gruesome facts, the most important being the murder of Kava Every, the young associate Bristol had had a secret relationship with, the second most important being the murder of Charley-Anna Black-ridge in Denver this past weekend.

Jaden hadn't known anything about either one.

She wasn't impressed.

"Bristol wouldn't do anything like that."

"He did and he will again," Waverly said. "You're next or, if not, next at least on the list."

"He'd never hurt me."

"Take a good look down, because this is the exact kind of place he's going to bring you sooner or later. You'll even be wearing the same dress you are now."

"I don't think so."

"Let me ask you something. Why are you two in Denver?"

"He has business here."

"What kind of business?"

"I don't know," she said. "I don't particularly care, either."

"Well, let me tell you what it is," Waverly said. "Either he came here to put a stop to me, that's one possibility. The other possibility is that after he killed the woman here this past weekend, something unraveled. Maybe he found out there was a witness or something like that. He's here to fix whatever it is that's coming unraveled." A beat, then "If I can prove it, will you do me a favor and get yourself somewhere safe? Or, better yet, help me bring him down?"

Jaden exhaled.

"How could you possibly prove it?"

"He met with a lawyer this afternoon," Waverly said. "Someone named Gina Sophia."

"I know that."

"She took notes," Waverly said.

"And?"

"Those notes are the proof."

"You have no idea what she wrote."

"Not yet, but I'm going to find out."

"How?"

"Break in to her office."

"Break in?"

Waverly nodded.

Jaden shook her head in disbelief.

"You're nuts. You can go to jail for that."

"I'm breaking in and you're coming with me," Waverly said. "You're going to see them with your own two eyes. You're going to know that I didn't fabricate them. Then you're going to save your life."

105

RIVER STEPPED SILENTLY OFF THE boxcar ladder and onto the ground, then stood there with a pounding heart, listening. Distant city sounds wove faintly through the pitch-black night; but other than that, the world was still. He took a careful step, then another, until he was around the edge of the boxcar.

There he stopped.

He didn't move a muscle.

He waited.

Spencer was out there.

River could feel him.

He needed to take the man alive. He needed to find out if January was still alive.

Another sound came.

It was farther away than the first one.

River listened harder.

No sounds came, not in the next few seconds or the next minute. He turned on the flashlight, scouted around, and spotted some type of animal scrounging around off in the distance.

That's all it was.

It wasn't Spencer.

It was just some stupid old animal.

He grabbed an Old Milwaukee from the fridge, wedged the top off with a bottle opener, and took a long swallow.

January.

January.

January.

Was she still alive?

Where?

SUDDENLY HE HAD A SICK thought. When he drove the motorcycle out into the terrain this afternoon and found her gone, what if he hadn't looked in the right place? What if he had veered a little to the right or the left, or hadn't gone far enough? What if Spencer hadn't taken her at all? What if she was still out there, hogtied, alone in the night?

A chill ran up his spine and straight into his brain.

He was positive—at least almost positive—that he'd looked in the right place. He had to admit, though, that he wasn't a hundred percent sure.

Damn it.

He needed to know; not in the morning, right now.

If by some miracle she actually was still out there, he couldn't let her stay in that position for even one more second than absolutely necessary.

He fired up the Indian, flicked on the headlight and spun the rear tire.

UNFORTUNATELY, HE'D DRIVEN HIS CAR back into town this afternoon, meaning it no longer marked the spot where he'd first pulled over and got tangled up with Spencer. It no longer marked the spot where Spencer pulled January out of his trunk and carried her into the terrain.

Now, River could only guess.

Plus it was night.

He kept going anyway, deeper and deeper into the country.

Night bugs were in the air.

They splattered into his face, not a lot but enough to keep him guessing. He kept his eyes squinted.

He suddenly realized how lucky he'd been.

If January was in fact still out there and River had simply missed her, and then if River got killed tonight waiting for Spencer to show up, January would have rotted to a slow death and it would have been River's fault.

He needed to grow some brains.

He wasn't thinking things through.

He was letting his emotions get the best of him.

He needed to stop that stupid shit and stop it now.

He needed to focus.

He needed to play things out.

HE GOT TO WHERE HE thought he should be and weaved left and right as he slowed, sweeping the headlight back and forth. It looked like the right place but he wasn't sure. He pulled off the road, turned off the engine and killed the lights.

Out of the bike's bag, he pulled the flashlight but left the knife and gun where they were.

Stars filled the sky.

They provided almost no light.

What he needed was a moon, but that was way down on the horizon.

He flicked on the flashlight.

Then he headed out into the terrain.

Twenty steps later, he came back and turned on the bike's taillight.

It would be an anchor without draining too much of the battery. It would let him gauge how far he'd gone.

He headed as straight away from the road as he could, sweeping the flashlight from side to side, trying to memorize the patterns of the rabbit brush and yucca and rocks.

Off in the distance a coyote howled.

He got a hundred steps in.

Then he took a second hundred.

He turned and looked at the taillight to find it wasn't much more than a red speck. He guessed he was about the right distance in but had to admit he could easily be off by fifty steps, a hundred even.

SUDDENLY A SHARP PAIN CAME from the bottom of his foot.

He toppled.

The flashlight dropped and went out.

River pulled his shoe off.

With it came a thick, two-inch cactus needle.

He pulled it out of the shoe, made sure there were no broken ones lurking around and put his shoe back on. The pain was still there, although not quite as sharp.

His foot was already swelling.

The terrain was darker than death.

He felt around until he found the flashlight and flicked the button, to no avail.

It was ruined.

He couldn't see two feet.

He had no option except to get back to the bike and bring it out into the terrain. That would give him a 99 percent chance of ending up with a flat.

How would he get back to the city?

Screw it.

He'd worry about it later.

Right now what he needed to do was just get the damn bike out here and find January.

He turned to find the taillight and get his bearings.

He didn't see it.

It wasn't there.

It was gone.

All he had in every direction was darkness.

106

DAY THREE
JULY 23, 1952
WEDNESDAY NIGHT

WILDE STOPPED PACING LONG ENOUGH to light a new cigarette from his old one, then continued his back-and-forth trek from one wall of London's living room to the other. London watched him from the couch, saying nothing. On the coffee table in front of her was a telephone. Next to it was a fake map. It was two minutes to eleven. If the universe worked the way it was supposed to, the phone would ring before Wilde finished his smoke.

Today had been a bust.

Crockett Bluetone was nowhere to be found. Wilde stopped by the man's office a dozen times. Each time, he was out and no one knew where he was; at least that's what everyone said, including the redhead receptionist, who Wilde believed. He wasn't at his house, either. That meant the original map was somewhere out in the universe and the game had to be played tonight without it.

Equally bad, Tarzan hadn't shown up at his lair all day.

Wilde searched the boxcars and every adjacent inch of space and found no signs of Alexa Blank, current or past. No one had been held prisoner there in recent history, either that or all traces had been meticulously erased.

Wilde looked at his watch.

Eleven o'clock on the nose.

The phone rang.

He looked at London.

Her forehead was tight and her eyes were dark.

He picked the receiver up and sandwiched it between his ear and London's.

"HELLO," SHE SAID.

"Do you have the map?"

The voice was a man's, the same one as before.

"Yes."

"You're going to get one chance and only one chance to do this right," he said. "It's important that you understand that. It's important that you do exactly as I say, not an ounce more and not an ounce less. Do you understand?"

She exhaled.

"Yes."

"Good," he said. "Are you alone?"

She hesitated.

"Yes."

"Did you call the police?"

"No."

"Think carefully about that answer," he said. "Because if you called them, I'll know it. I'll see them following you. If that happens, the devil comes to pay a visit to your little friend—her first, then you later. Do you understand?"

"Yes."

"I hope so, I really do." A beat, then "Here's what you're going to do. After we hang up, go to your bedroom and look under the pillow. You'll find two keys there. One key fits a padlock where your little friend is being kept. The other fits a handcuff that has her fastened to something. Put those keys in your pocket. Don't put them in your purse. Do you understand?"

"Yes."

"Okay, good," he said. "Take the map and put it in your purse. Does your purse have a zipper?"

"Yes."

"Be sure it's zipped tight," he said.

"Okay."

"There's a cab parked outside your house right now with the lights out. Go to the window and make sure it's there."

She did.

It was there.

Her heart raced.

"It's there," she said.

"Here's what you're going to do," he said. "When we hang up, you go get into the back of that cab. Here's the important part. Don't say a word to the driver. He's been instructed that if you say anything, even one word, he's to pull over to the side of the road and let you out. If that happens, we get back to the devil part of the equation. Do you understand?"

"Yes."

"Good, not one word, remember that," he said. "He's going to drive. At a point during that drive, he's going to say, *Get ready.* When he says that, you roll down the back window on the passenger side of the car. Do you understand?"

"Yes."

"At some point after he says *Get ready,* he's going to say, *Now.* When he does that, you throw the purse out the window. Don't look at it and don't look back. The driver will keep driving for a while and will eventually drop you off at a phone booth. He'll drive away. You stay right there at that phone booth. If I determine that the map is genuine and not a fake, I'll call you there and tell you where your little friend is. You can go get her and you two can live happily ever after."

"How do I know you'll call?"

"You don't. Now go get in the cab."

The line went dead.

107

WHILE THE SEEDIER POCKETS OF town still kicked with life, the financial district was quiet and motionless. The lights were out, the doors were locked, and the bus stops were empty. Waverly and Jaden made their way to the alley side of the building that housed Jackson & Reacher, then broke a window and took a position down the way behind a dumpster to see if anyone came to investigate. After two minutes of silence, they climbed in.

Now the trick was to find Gina Sophia's office.

They didn't have a flashlight.

Flipping a light switch would be too dangerous.

"Do you have a lighter?" Waverly asked.

"No."

"Why not?"

"I don't smoke."

"Yeah, but you break into buildings. Come prepared."

"You're the one breaking in," Jaden said. "I'm just following you."

"That's fine, but next time follow me with a lighter in your pocket."

"I'll make a note."

"You do that."

The law firm was divided into individual offices, each with a door, each door with a glass window and a venetian blind, and each glass window stenciled with a name. Enough ambient light filtered in to read those names when Waverly got her nose right up to them.

Gina Sophia's office turned out to be an interior one with no outside windows.

The women entered, closed the door and turned on the lights.

THE PLACE WAS A MESS.

Papers and files were everywhere, stacked on every conceivable square inch of desk, filing cabinet and chair—even over in the corner on the floor.

"It looks like a bomb went off in here," Jaden said.

Waverly didn't disagree.

"Bristol came today," she said, "so he should be on the top somewhere." A beat, then "Try to keep things as they are as much as you can. I don't want her to know we were here."

"They're going to know from the broken window."

"They'll know someone broke in but they won't know that this office was the target," Waverly said. "We'll go into a couple of different offices and mess them up before we leave."

"Sneaky."

"Thank you."

"I'm not sure I meant that as a compliment."

FILES LABELED *THOMAS BRISTOL* DIDN'T materialize, not on this stack or that one or the other one or on the floor or in a drawer or in the filing cabinet.

"This is useless," Jaden said.

"Keep looking."

"We already looked everywhere. She must not have taken any notes. Either that or she took them home."

"I doubt she'd do that. Keep looking. They're here somewhere. I can smell them."

They searched longer.

Ten minutes went by.

Then fifteen.

"We've been here more than half an hour," Jaden said. "Let's get out of here while we still can."

"Keep looking."

"Someone's going to notice that window and call the cops."

"There's no reason for anyone to be back there."

"You don't know that."

"Just keep looking."

"No. I'm serious. We need to get out of here."

Waverly exhaled.

"Go if you want, I don't care."

The woman headed for the door and put her hand on the knob. She turned and said, "Good luck."

"Bye."

Waverly kept searching.

The door didn't open.

She looked up.

Jaden was shaking her head as if doubting her sanity, then she came back in and said, "Maybe Bristol met with two lawyers. Maybe Gina Sophia was only one of them. Maybe the file is in someone else's office."

Waverly considered it.

It made sense.

It also meant going through another twenty or thirty offices. Most of them wouldn't be interior ones like this one. They'd have windows to the outside. Flipping on the lights wouldn't be an option. They have to get flashlights and come back.

"Five more minutes," she said. "If we don't find it by then, we'll go."

"Good." A beat, then "Did you hear that?"

Waverly focused.

She heard nothing.

"Hear what?"

"Quiet," Jaden said. "Be quiet."

She flicked off the light.

They stood there in darkness, breathing quietly and listening.

A MINUTE WENT BY, FOLLOWED BY another.

They heard nothing more.

Waverly quietly opened the office door and looked down the hallway. Everything was dark. There were no signs of cleaning people, cops, or anyone else.

"False alarm," she said.

"I don't know—"

Waverly flicked on the light and closed the door. "Five more minutes," she said. "If we don't find them by then, we're out of here."

A minute later a file caught her eye.

It was labeled John Stamp. The name was familiar but Waverly couldn't place it. Then she remembered. He was a private investigator, reportedly the only good one in town other than a guy named Bryson Wilde.

What was he doing with an attorney?

Was he being sued by someone for breaking into their house?

Waverly opened the file.

Inside was a single piece of paper.

> 7/23/52
> Meeting with Tom Bristol.
>   To do: Hire a PI to investigate the murder of Charley-Anna Blackridge. Got dropped off a building last weekend. Find out if there were witnesses. Find out what the police know. PI should keep Bristol's name out of it. Keep this case strictly confidential.
>   Retainer received.
>   Pay PI well. Get him on the case immediately. Pay more than hourly rate to ensure loyalty and confidence.

Waverly passed the paper to Jaden and said, "Read it." She waited for the woman to comply and then said, "There's your proof. Bristol must have gotten wind that there was a witness. He hired Gina Sophia to hire a PI to find out who that witness is. Once he finds out, that witness will end up having an accident, a fatal accident. Doing the investigation this way keeps Bristol's name out of it. The attorney is bound by law to keep his file confidential, even if she suspects later that Bristol hired her in hindsight to locate and kill a witness to one of his prior murders. You got to hand it to the guy, he's a smart fellow."

Waverly looked into Jaden's eyes.

The woman was processing it.

It didn't take long.

Her eyes narrowed.

"So what do we do now?"

Waverly tapped her foot.

"I don't know, but I'll tell you one thing, I'll bet he's done the same thing with some of his other murders. I'll bet he's hired other lawyers to hire PIs to get information."

"We need to find out what the PI is finding out," Jaden said. "What's his name again?"

"John Stamp."

"Do you know him?"

"Not personally," she said. "I know him by reputation."

"Which is what?"

"Which is, he has phone numbers, lots and lots of phone numbers, people low, people high, people in between, lots and lots of phone numbers. Put enough money in his hand to spread around and he'll find out anything you want to know."

Jaden tilted her head.

"So how do we get inside his world?"

108

DAY THREE
JULY 23, 1952
WEDNESDAY NIGHT

RIVER PICKED HIS WAY THROUGH the pitch-black terrain in the direction of the road, knowing he was probably veering off to the right or left but going in a straight enough line to hit it sooner or later. The land rose slightly upward, barely perceptible except for slightly heavier legs as he walked. Thirty steps later, his head must have crested a rise because the Indian's taillight came into view.

He exhaled.

Good.

Good.

Good.

No, not good, great.

He got there as fast as he could, fired it up, and pointed the front tire into the terrain, slowly, weaving around yucca and boulders. The prairie cactuses were nestled in the undergrowth and impossible to see. The only way he could deal with them was by luck.

The stars were silent, but the engine was consuming.

It sputtered and coughed.

It didn't like the slow speed.

River shifted into neutral and revved it up with enough RPMs to smooth it out.

How far had he come?

With no marker on the road, it was impossible to tell.

The front end of the bike felt mushy.

Was the tire losing air?

Did it have a cactus thorn in it?

The headlight lit up the top of it up very well but from River's angle it was impossible to tell if the rubber was compromised. He didn't see a thorn. That didn't mean anything, though.

He kept going.

The bike got more and more difficult to steer.

He brought it to a stop, got off and felt the tire.

Damn it.

Damn it.

Damn it to hell.

It was soft.

Whatever air was left in it wouldn't be there for long.

He got back on and headed farther into the terrain. Within moments, the rubber was flat and unwieldy. River kept the handlebars in an iron grip to keep the bike upright.

AS BEST HE COULD TELL, he was about where he should be. Any farther and he'd be overshooting. He stopped, swept the headlight around and shouted, "January!"

She didn't answer.

"January!"

No answer.

He looked back toward the road, or at least in the direction he thought the road was. He memorized the direction in connection with the position of the moon. Getting disoriented wouldn't be good.

He killed the engine.

The silence of the night was complete, uncut by even a wisp of wind or the batting of an insect's wings.

"January!"

No answer.

"Make a sound if you're out here. Anything."

No sounds came.

He listened harder, holding his breath, stilling the passage of air in and out of his lungs.

No sounds came.

He'd probably veered to the right or the left, but which? He fired up the engine, turned the front end to the right and paralleled the road.

January didn't appear.

Then something bad happened.

The tire broke away from the rim, shredded or cut or whatever. Whatever the reason, it didn't matter. The rubber was off. Only the rim was left. As hard as it had been to control the front end with a flat, it was ten times worse with just the rim. The metal dug into the dirt.

Turning was hard.

He kept going.

Suddenly the front end stuck and the bike tipped to the left. River braced his foot down but not quick enough to get leverage.

He lost control.

The bike went down.

The headlight shattered.

The world went black except for a red glow at the rear end. River got the bike upright and turned the headlight switch on and off. It did no good. He felt the light and found jagged glass.

It was shattered.

A strange smell wove through the air.

What was it?

Gas?

Yes, that was it, gas.

What happened?

Did the gas line get pulled loose?

River got oriented with the moon and continued parallel to the road.

He could see nothing except stars.

The smell of gas got worse.

It must be getting on the engine or exhaust and burning.

Suddenly the engine died.

River cranked it over.

It wouldn't start.

Damn it.

He tried again.

It wouldn't start.

He tried again.

Same.

A rock twisted his foot. River worked it out of the earth to find it was the size of a basketball. He raised it over his head with both arms and smashed it down onto the guts of the bike with every ounce of strength he had.

The sound was terrible.

The taillight went out.

There.

They were even.

HE LOOKED AT THE SLIVER OF moon, got oriented to the road, and headed that way at a quick walk. Thirty steps later, he stumbled on something.

It was January.

109

DAY THREE

JULY 23, 1952

WEDNESDAY NIGHT

WHEN THE LINE DIED, THUNDER pounded through Wilde's veins. "This is a problem," he said. "I don't know who was on the other end of that line, but I do know one thing: it wasn't who I thought it was."

"You mean that Tarzan guy?"

He nodded.

"Dayton River," Wilde said. "It wasn't him. I can't believe it wasn't him. How come it wasn't him?"

"Maybe it was that other guy, Mitchum."

Mitchum.

Robert Mitchum.

The name hadn't been in Wilde's brain for some time. Hearing it out loud made his shoulders tighten.

"Maybe," he said. "Either way, I have a bad feeling about this whole thing."

"So what do we do? The cab's waiting—"

"I know."

He grabbed a pack of matches from his pocket and ripped one off. London snatched them from his hand. "We don't have time for that."

"I have to think."

"We don't have time to think."

He knew that.

He knew that only too well.

"If we follow directions, he's going to kill her anyway," he said.

London made a face.

She wasn't convinced.

"How do you know?"

"I don't know, I just do." A beat, then "She's seen his face, that's how I know. He's better off if she's dead."

"He only wants the map."

"Right, but he wants it without complications."

"So what do we do?"

"I have to catch his ass."

London took a step back.

"No."

"It's our only chance," he said.

She didn't agree.

"No, it's too dangerous."

"We don't have a choice."

"No. Even if it works, he might not say where she is. She'll end up rotting to death."

Wilde grabbed London's hand and pulled her outside to the cab.

They hopped in the back.

The driver was a strong male in his early thirties. He stared directly at Wilde and narrowed his eyes.

"Drive," Wilde said.

"GET OUT," THE DRIVER SAID. "Both of you."

"Drive," Wilde said.

"It was only supposed to be the woman. My instructions are to abort."

"You have new instructions now."

"No."

"Get going, now," Wilde said.

"Screw you. Get out of the cab and do it now."

Wilde hardened his face.

"I'm going to count to three—"

"Don't make it difficult," Wilde said.

"One—"

"Drive!"

"Two—"

"Did you hear me?"

"Three."

Wilde pulled his knife and made it visible.

"I have nothing against you, but don't force me—"

The man's arm moved with lightning speed. His hand grabbed Wilde's wrist and squeezed it with a python force. Wilde wedged loose, stabbed the man in the upper thigh before he even knew what he was doing, and pulled back.

The man grabbed his wound.

"You bitch!"

"Drive!"

"You stabbed me, you little bitch."

"That's right, and I'll do it again. I'm not screwing around here."

The man winced.

Then he shifted into first, said "Your funeral, asshole," and took off.

THE NIGHT SHOT BY.

"Where's she supposed to throw the purse out?"

Silence.

"I said—"

"Okay, okay. Clarkson and 12th."

"Cut over to Delaware."

"But—"

"Just do it."

The man complied.

At 10th, Wilde said, "Stop here."

The man pulled over.

Wilde got out, leaned in the open door, and said, "Circle back around and follow your instructions. If you screw up, I'll hunt you to the ends of the earth. That's a promise."

He slammed the door.

The cab jerked away.

London stared out the back window all the way to 11th, where the taillights disappeared around the corner.

WILDE MADE HIS WAY THROUGH the shadows to as close to the throw-out point as he could, then wedged his body into the thicker shadows of a ragged hedge. If the man was in the vicinity, Wilde didn't see him.

He waited.

The gun was tucked in his belt.

The knife was in his left hand.

He couldn't use it to kill the man. London might be right in that Alexa might be stashed away where she couldn't be found. That would be a bad way to go, trapped and abandoned. Wilde might be able to find her. Once he had the guy identified, he'd have a good chance of backtracking. Still, you never know. If he couldn't, it would be too horrible to think about.

THERE WAS STILL TIME TO back out—just leave the guy alone and hope he releases Alexa like he said he would. There was at least some possibility he was telling the truth. If that was the case, everything Wilde was doing at this exact second was the exact wrong thing. Alexa might end up dead *because* of him, not in spite of him.

What to do?

What to do?

What to do?

Suddenly, headlights came up the street.

The passenger window was open.

London was next to it.

Her hair was blowing.

Her face was tense.

A purse flew out and landed on the sidewalk.

The cab kept going.

London kept her face pointed forward as the taillights disappeared up the street. At any second, a figure would come out of the shadows and grab the purse.

What to do?

Shoot him in the leg or let him go?

Think!

Think!

Think!

He pulled the gun out and cocked the trigger. He was too far away for a clean shot. If he went for the guy's leg he'd be just as likely to get his face, either that or the air. He'd need to be within four or five steps to shoot.

A dark silhouette appeared on the opposite side of the street, walking briskly up the sidewalk.

It was a man.

He wore a black T-shirt.

Strong arms stuck out.

He looked briefly for cars, then around in all directions, and trotted across the street. He snatched up the purse without breaking stride and kept going.

Wilde waited for a few heartbeats.

The man didn't look over his shoulder.

Wilde waited another second.

Then another.

Then another.

Then another.

The silhouette increasingly receded into the night. When the distance was right, Wilde came out of the shadows and fell into step.

His chest pounded.

With the knife in his left hand and the gun in his right, he picked up the pace.

The distance started to close.

He kept his footsteps as quiet as death.

Now he was thirty steps behind.

Now twenty.

Now ten.

Suddenly the man turned.

His arm rose.

From the end of that arm, a small flash of orange flame pierced the darkness, here and gone just that fast, simultaneous with an ear-shattering explosive pop.

110

DAY FOUR
JULY 24, 1952
THURSDAY MORNING

THE ONLY WINDOWSHADE IN WAVERLY'S roach-in-the-wall hotel was a spring-loaded, pull-down deal with tattered edges. She woke up Thursday morning when the first rays of daybreak pushed around the borders of that piece of junk. She lay there, torn between getting more sleep and getting things done, before finally rubbing her eyes and swinging her legs over the side.

She took a hot shower that got her 70% awake.

Then she headed over to the White Spot to take care of the other 30% with coffee, ending up on a barstool at the end of the counter with a piping hot cup in her hands and a gal named Jane behind the counter who kept that cup topped off.

This insanely early, the diner was a graveyard. All the barstools were empty, plus most of the tables. Two seats down, on the counter in a glass cake holder, was a stack of donuts. The ones on top were concrete, but the ones underneath might actually be edible.

She resisted.

If they still tugged at her in five minutes, she'd get one.

Today would be critical.

She needed to find out what Bristol's investigator, John Stamp, was finding out, if anything. What was the best way to do that? Follow him around? Break into his office while he was out?

She shook it off.

The gal behind the counter, Jane, came over with the pot and topped off the cup. "I saw you eyeing those donuts," she said. "They're evil. They'll break your teeth and steal the soul of your firstborn. Personally, I'd go with pancakes. You want some?"

She smiled.

Yes.

She did.

Good idea.

"Thanks."

Time passed.

The city woke up.

The diner filled.

At ten minutes to eight, Waverly left a healthy tip on the counter, checked her purse to be sure she had plenty of change, then headed outside to find a phone booth.

At exactly eight, she called Su-Moon in Cleveland.

THE WOMAN ANSWERED BEFORE THE first ring stopped.

"Waverly, is that you?"

The words were laced with explosion. It sounded like she had just stepped off a roller coaster.

"Yeah, what's going on?"

"You're not going to believe it," Su-Moon said. "Bristol was here in town when the woman got dropped off the roof."

"Are you sure?"

"Positive. I can prove it, too."

"How do you know?"

"I'll explain when I see you. I'm heading to Denver."

"When?"

"Now."

"Now?"

"Yeah, now. On the first flight I can catch. Tell me how to contact you when I get into town."

She did.

They'd connect at Waverly's hotel, fleabag that it was.

"See you soon."

"Okay," Waverly said. She almost hung up, then brought the receiver back to her mouth. "Su-Moon, are you still there?"

She was.

"How do you know Bristol was in town?"

"He stayed at the Renaissance. He signed the register."

"Was anyone with him?"

Silence.

"I don't know."

"Find out."

"Why?"

"The woman he's with here in Denver is someone named Jaden," Waverly said. "I'm just wondering if she was with him when he was there too."

A beat.

"No, I don't think so. I don't remember seeing a Jaden on the register."

"Do me a favor," Waverly said. "Go back and check. If there's no

Jaden there, at least find out if he paid the room rate for one occupant or two."

"Even if he paid for two, it wouldn't do us any good. There was no Jaden written on the register."

Waverly exhaled.

"Okay, forget it then."

111

DAY FOUR
JULY 24, 1952
THURSDAY MORNING

RIVER THOUGHT HE FELT A presence in the room Thursday morning and opened his eyes to find out if he was right or just having a trick of the night. He was right. The presence was January, sleeping peacefully next to him, naked, on her stomach with her arms up and her hands tucked under the pillow. The sheet draped over the lower half of her body. Her back and ribs and the sides of her stomach and the cusps of her breasts were exposed.

River studied her tattoos and the wonderful curvature of her body for a heartbeat, then rolled onto his back and closed his eyes.

Last night was still in his brain.

Finding January out there in the night still alive was by far, without a doubt, the best moment of River's life so far. With the first wiggle of her body that showed she was alive, a terrible weight lifted off River's shoulders. Everything in the world was suddenly right again, just like that.

He didn't want to bring her back home.

He wanted to get her a thousand miles away.

"Forget it," she said. "I hope he does come for me, or you, or us, or whatever sick plan is in his sick little brain. I really hope he does. In fact, I hope he does it tonight while I'm still mad enough to do what I'm going to do to him."

"Which is what?"

"Which is what he did to me."

River cocked his head.

The tone in her voice was absolute.

He could try to talk her out of it, but that's all it would be—a try.

"Fine, we'll go home," he said.

She looked into his eyes.

"You said *home*," she said.

"Right. So?"

"You didn't say *your place*."

"No, I said home."

COYOTES BARKED AND HOWLED UNDER the stars. The eerie sounds came from three or four different packs, all suddenly on the hunt at the same time.

January's bare feet were no match for the Colorado prairie.

River carried her all the way to the road without rest.

She was naked and even though River cured that by giving her his shirt, she was still naked underneath, not to mention imbedded with dirt. Her wrists and ankles were raw and chaffed, almost to the point of bleeding. River, now shirtless, was half naked.

They walked for an hour before the first car appeared.

It was a woman, fifty-something, a veterinarian, driving home to a nice warm bed after a night call. She took them all the way to River's place and wouldn't take a dime in return. Apparently there were still a few people like that left in the world.

They showered.

They melted their bodies together.

Then they passed out.

That was last night.

Now it was morning.

RIVER SLIPPED OUT OF BED without waking January and headed for the shower.

The water was hot.

The sound of the spray was heaven.

The fact that Spencer hadn't stopped to kill January didn't mean he wasn't going to. It only meant that he'd been too occupied with his new captive—Alexa Blank—to get distracted at that particular time and place in the universe. Spencer would get around to them first chance he had.

River knew that.

He also knew that might be as early as today.

It might even be in the next sixty seconds.

He got the soap off and turned the valves to the right until the spray stopped.

He listened for sounds.

There were none.

He heard no intruders.

January wasn't calling out for help.

Everything was normal.

River's blood suddenly raced.

Everything was too normal.

He stepped out of the shower.

Two towels hung next to him on a rack.

He didn't reach for them.

Instead he stood there, dripping onto the floor, listening for a stray sound with every ounce of energy he had.

112

DAY FOUR
JULY 24, 1952
THURSDAY MORNING

WILDE WOKE UP, NOT IN a bed. He was behind the steering wheel of Blondie, parked on the side of a street. The sky was lighter than midnight but not by much. A bona-fide dawn was still an hour away. He stretched and rubbed his eyes. The street was quiet, eerily so.

He stepped out.

His legs were heavy.

The thin Denver air was cool.

No one was around.

He walked over to the bushes, unzipped and took a long, heaven-sent piss. The bullet had missed him last night. It also forced him into a panic dive. By the time he got to his feet, the sprint was on. The other man was faster and that was that.

Wilde was stupid.

He was stupid beyond belief.

He should have made the cab driver tell him where he was going to drop London off. Was Wilde smart enough to ask that simple little question? No, he wasn't, because he was the stupidest man on the planet. So now there he was, having no idea where London was.

The other man knew, though.

He knew only too well.

Wilde hadn't planned for that contingency. He had planned to the point of capturing the guy, but not for failure.

That was stupid.

He had run over to Colfax, then east toward town until he was able to flag down a taxi. He took it to his house, got Blondie, dropped Alabama off at a hotel just in case the guy had been following London earlier in the day and had figured out who Wilde was, then started crisscrossing the city, hoping by blind luck to stumble across London.

That stumble didn't happen.

He checked her house.

She wasn't there.

He parked down the street and kept an eye on her front door. Midnight came and went, then one, then one-thirty, then longer. He must have fallen asleep at that point.

HE ZIPPED UP.

Back at Blondie, the gun and knife were sitting on the passenger seat. He grabbed the gun, tucked it in his waist, and headed for London's front door.

It was unlocked, just like they'd left it when they ran out last night, just like he left it after he checked the place last night.

Two doors down, a rough dog barked.

Wilde stepped inside.

The air was still and quiet.

"London?"

No one answered.

"London? You here?"

Silence.

The lower level was as before. He headed upstairs, not bothering to take the gun out of his belt. London's bedroom was vacant.

Wilde sat on the edge of the bed.

She was dead.

She was dead because he was stupid.

He flopped back and closed his eyes.

He thought he was tough.

He was wrong.

He was just a guy who did stupid things and got people killed.

He needed to get out of the PI business.

He needed to get out of Denver.

He needed to put all this behind him and hope to never get anyone else killed.

113

DAY FOUR
JULY 24, 1952
THURSDAY MORNING

JUST EAST OF THE FINANCIAL district, over on Grant Street, a number of former mansions had been converted into upscale offices over the years. One of those structures had a fancy wooden sign to the right of an oversized maple door that said JOHN STAMP, PRIVATE INVESTIGATOR.

Waverly headed for it down a fancy cobblestone walkway and put her hand on the doorknob.

She paused long enough to consider the sanity, or lack thereof, of what she was about to do.

Then she mumbled *Just do it* and stepped in.

That step brought her into a two-story foyer with a winding staircase that led to the second level. Beneath her feet was Mediterranean tile. The walls were paneled and the window coverings were an expensive weave. It was the Brown Palace on a private scale.

A stately drop-dead-gorgeous redhead with deep cleavage and curvy hips appeared from another room.

"Are you looking for John?"

Yes.

She was.

Five minutes later, she was in his upstairs office with the door closed.

THE MAN WAS A MOVIE star.

He tapped two cigarettes out of a pack, offered her one, then pushed hers back in when she declined. He lit up from a gold lighter and blew a perfect ring.

"What's your name?" he said.

Waverly leaned forward in her chair.

"Tom Bristol killed Charley-Anna Blackridge," she said. "You've been hired by him, through Gina Sophia, because Bristol found out somehow that there was a witness. After you find out who it is, that person is going to end up dead."

The corner of Stamp's mouth turned up ever so slightly.

"Let me guess," he said. "You're the one who's been nipping at Bristol's tail out in San Francisco."

The words took her by surprise.

She kept the expression off her face.

"Yes."

"You're ruining the man's life," he said. "Leave him alone."

"He's a killer."

Stamp leaned back in his chair, unimpressed.

"I generally don't share information about my clients with third parties," he said. "Here's a piece of fact, though. I've been hired to find out who killed Charley-Anna Blackridge. Once I figure that out—*and I will*—I'm giving the name and all the supporting evidence to Bristol. He's then going to give it to you."

"To *me*?"

He nodded.

"He wants you off his back," he said. "Getting you on the right track is his way of accomplishing that."

Waverly hardened her face.

"Charley-Anna isn't the only one he's killed," she said. "There was another woman out in San Francisco by the name of Kava Every. She was a young female architect in Bristol's firm. They were having a secret affair. There was another woman out in Cleveland, too. Her name was Bobbi Litton."

Stamp's face reacted, not much, but enough to show he hadn't been privy.

Waverly stood up and walked to the door.

Halfway through, she turned and said over her shoulder, "It looks like you don't know your client as well as you thought. If you proceed from this point on, you'll be an accomplice. I'll be sure you end up being held accountable as such."

Then she was gone.

114

DAY FOUR
JULY 24, 1952
THURSDAY MORNING

RIVER'S SENSE OF INTRUSION WAS well founded, because the dark silhouette of a man was approaching, fifty yards away on foot, closing hard with a purpose. He was strong and carried his body like a warrior. His posture was vaguely familiar.

River threw on clothes and had the gun in hand by the time the figure was close enough to recognize.

It was Robert Gapp.

He looked more like Robert Mitchum now than ever.

River motioned the man into the boxcar and closed the door.

They hugged.

The man focused on January, at first her face, then her tattoos, then her eyes. "You're too good for him," he said.

She smiled.

"It's the other way, actually."

"No, trust me, I have it right." Then to River, "We need to talk."

"I already figured that."

They stepped outside.

Gapp got right to the point.

"There's a dick named Bryson Wilde running around town trying to figure out who dropped that red dress off the roof this past weekend. I was buying her drinks and squeezing her ass right up until the minute she left."

"That was stupid."

"It would have been if I was the one who killed her," Gapp said. "That's not what happened, though. What happened is that you killed her and set me up to take the fall. You paid her to pick me up and be seen with me. Then you killed her."

Gapp stopped talking.

He let the words hang in silence.

River studied his face to see if he was joking.

He wasn't.

"That's bullshit," River said.

"Is it?"

"Yes, it is, total, one hundred percent, falling-down-dead-drunk bullshit. Why would I do anything like that?"

GAPP TIGHTENED HIS BROW.

"I'm still chewing on it, but once I get my brain convinced, I'm going to have to kill you. You know that. The only surprise in all this is that I'm giving you a warning."

River let the corner of his mouth turn up.

"You're going to kill me?"

"You forced me," Gapp said. "You'd do the same."

River picked up a piece of gravel and threw it at a pigeon down on the tracks.

He missed.

The bird and three more like it took to the sky.

He turned to Gapp.

"What we need to do is get this PI off your ass. We'll do it tonight. Meet me back here at nightfall."

115

DAY FOUR
JULY 24, 1952
THURSDAY MORNING

WILDE STAYED ALONE IN LONDON'S bed until dawn, neither sleeping nor awake, then headed over to Alabama's hotel and rapped on the door until her groggy face answered. Her hair was a mess, clearly the loser in the fight with the pillow.

She stretched.

"What time is it?"

Wilde stepped inside and shut the door.

"Time to get to work," he said.

"Did London ever show up?"

Wilde shook his head.

"No."

"That's not good. I got to pee and take a shower," she said.

"Do 'em both at the same time. The clock's ticking."

She headed for the bathroom and said over her shoulder, "There needs to be a law against having to wake up to you. I'm going to need coffee."

"Fine."

"I mean, as soon as I step out of the bathroom."

"What does that mean? You expect me to go fetch it while you're showering?"

She nodded.

"There you go."

AN HOUR LATER, THEY PULLED up to an abandoned warehouse in the old industrial area north of the BNSF rail yard. The building was brick, four stories, and boarded tight. Wilde worked at a window in the back until they got access, then led the way up the interior stairway to the roof.

The view was unlimited in all directions.

A crystal-blue sky hung above.

Puffy clouds were building up over the mountains, hinting of rain and maybe even a serious storm.

At the south edge of the roof, Wilde trained binoculars on Dayton River's boxcar setup, pulling the scene in good enough to make out someone's face if there was a face there to make out.

Right now there wasn't.

He handed them to Alabama.

She pointed them at the target and got them in focus.

"We good?" Wilde asked.

She nodded.

"We're good."

RIVER WASN'T THE ONE WHO'D shot at Wilde last night. However, he was the one who initially took Alexa Blank out of the diner during her shift. That meant River was connected to the man from last night. With any luck, that man would show his face at River's place today.

With even more luck, Alabama would see him.

She might recognize him.

If she didn't, she could at least memorize his face.

WILDE LOOKED AROUND.

The roof had a two-foot-high parapet at the perimeter on all sides. In the middle was a rusty heating unit.

"Stay low," he said. "Don't get spotted."

"Don't worry."

"I'm serious," he said. "Don't get spotted."

"I heard you."

"If you see him heading this way, even if it looks innocent like he's just out for a jog or something, get the hell out of here."

"I will."

"Don't let him trap you up here."

"You worry too much."

"I wish that was true. Are you sure you can do this?"

"Yes, stop pestering me."

Wilde looked at his watch.

"I'll be back at noon."

"Bring food and water."

He nodded.

"If the guy shows up, make your way over to the BNSF building," he said. "Call me at the office with their phone. If I don't answer, call a cab and get to the office. Wait for me there."

"Okay."

116

DAY FOUR

JULY 24, 1952

THURSDAY MORNING

FROM STAMP'S OFFICE, WAVERLY HEADED over to the Brown Palace and left a note for Jaden with the cigar-smoking peach at the reception desk: *Meet me at the corner of 16th and California as soon as you can safely break away.*

An hour came and went.

Then more time passed.

It was almost noon before the woman showed up. Waverly watched her from a distance for two minutes to see if Bristol was on her tail. Then she swept in and ushered the woman down an alley, around to the back.

"I went to Stamp's office this morning and told him that he was being used as a pawn to help Bristol find a witness," she said. "His response was that Bristol actually came into town to get information as to who the real killer was. He's going to feed that information to me to get me off his back."

Jaden nodded.

"That actually makes sense," she said.

Waverly leaned against the building.

"Have you ever been to Cleveland?"

Jaden wrinkled her face.

"No, why?"

"Are you sure?"

"I'm positive."

"What about Bristol? Has he ever been to Cleveland?"

Jaden shrugged.

"Not that I know of. He travels, though, that's part of his job. You know that."

Waverly exhaled, deciding.

Then she said, "I wasn't sure whether to tell you this or not, but I'm just going to do it. A woman named Bobbi Litton was killed in Cleveland in May of last year—same exact way, red dress, dropped off a roof, the whole nine yards. A friend of mine flew there to investigate. She hired a PI and he found that Bristol was in town at the time the woman was murdered."

Jaden wrinkled her face.

"How could he know that?"

"The hotel Bristol stayed at still had the registration book."

"Maybe it was another Bristol," Jaden said. "It's a common name."

Waverly shook her head.

"It was him," she said. "What I'm getting at is this. There are too many things coming together. You're in danger. What you need to do is disappear, right now, not ten seconds from now, right now. Don't go back to the hotel. Don't see Bristol again, don't talk to him, don't tell him you're leaving. Just vanish into the air."

JADEN PACED.

Her apprehension was palpable.

She wasn't faking.

"I'm going to find out if he was in Cleveland like you say he was. If he was, I'll do it—I'll vanish—but first I need to know for sure."

"I already know for sure," Waverly said.

"Maybe someone signed in as him," Jaden said. "Maybe someone else was setting him up."

Waverly frowned.

"Who?"

"I don't know."

"Why?"

Jaden shrugged.

"All you have is a handwritten name," she said. "You don't have that name attached to a face. We don't even know yet if the handwriting is his." A beat then, "Here's what I'll do. I'll get something with his handwriting on it. I'll probe around too. I'll bring up Cleveland in an innocuous way. I'll say my sister lives there or something. I'll ask him if he's ever been there. If he says yes, I'll ask him when. If he says last May, then you're right. I'll find an excuse to get away from him and run like hell."

"What if he says no?"

Jaden shrugged.

"Bristol has a meeting with his attorney at four o'clock," she said. "I'll find an excuse to not go with him. Meet me back here at four."

"Okay, but be careful." A beat, then "Does he have any enemies? Someone who would want to frame him for murder or bring him down?"

Jaden receded in thought.

"There's only one thing I know of," she said. "A couple of years ago, before I knew him, he was bidding on a project for a ferry terminal in Hong Kong. Something went wrong on that project. Something out of the ordinary."

"He has that file at his houseboat, hidden under a dresser."
"He does?"
Waverly nodded.
"See if you can find out what went wrong."
"Okay."
"Concentrate on Cleveland, though. That's the most important thing."
Jaden nodded.
"Four o'clock."

117

DAY FOUR
JULY 24, 1952
THURSDAY MORNING

MID-MORNING, RIVER NOTICED SOMETHING in his peripheral vision, way off in the distance, on top of one of those abandoned buildings over in the old warehouse district. It was a motion up on the roof.

He didn't stare at it.

Instead he headed inside, got behind the window covering, and pulled the area in with a pair of binoculars. The parapet came into view, distinguishable from the side of the building, but nothing moved. It hadn't been his imagination. He stayed with the scene, expecting Vaughn Spencer's face to pop up.

A minute passed.

Then a head appeared.

The face belonged to a woman.

She looked familiar.

Where had he seen her before?

Was she working with Spencer?

She brought binoculars up to her eyes and shifted them around until she got her bearings on the boxcar. River dropped back, stepped outside and stretched. Then he picked up a rock and threw it at a pigeon. January came out of the adjacent boxcar zipping her pants.

"I need that asshole to come for us," she said. "Sitting around and waiting for him is driving me nuts."

"Don't turn your head," River said. "To the north there's an old industrial area. A woman's up there on one of the roofs watching us with binoculars."

January started to turn.

"Don't look," River said.

She obeyed.

"Who is it?"

"I don't know, but I'm going to find out."

"How?"

"Sneak up from behind."

"I'm coming with you."

River considered it.

"One of us needs to stay here," he said. "If we both leave, she might too."

"You stay here," she said. "You're the target. Let me go get her."

River studied her.

"Are you up for it, after last night?"

She nodded.

"I'm fine."

River frowned.

"It's too risky," he said. "Spencer might be there."

"Did you see him?"

"No."

JANUARY PUT HER ARMS AROUND River's neck, brought her mouth up to his ear, and nibbled on it. "I'll take the car and head the opposite way," she said. "After I'm good and gone and out of sight, I'll swing around to the back and park way off where she won't see or hear anything. Then I'll close in by foot. You stay here and keep her focused on the prize."

River ran his fingers down her back.

It was risky.

Still, there was no way everything was going to come to a resolution without risk.

"Okay, but be careful," he said.

They stepped back inside.

January slipped River's gun into her jeans and draped the T-shirt over it.

"When you get her, signal me from the roof," River said. "I'll head over on foot. Bring her down to the ground level but stay in the building. Once I get there, you can tell me where the car is. I'll go get it and bring it over. Then we'll get her in the trunk."

January kissed him.

"Deal," she said.

118

DAY FOUR

JULY 24, 1952

THURSDAY MORNING

WILDE'S OFFICE WAS DARK AND undisturbed when he got there. No one had broken in. He kick-started the coffee machine, dangled a cigarette in his lips, and called Secret St. Rain at her hotel.

She actually answered.

"You dropped off the face of the earth," he said.

"Sorry."

"Where have you been?"

"It's complicated."

"We need to talk."

A tone must have been in his voice, because she said, "About what?"

"About you not really being Secret St. Rain," he said. "About you being Emmanuelle LeFavre."

A pause.

"How'd you find out?"

"It doesn't matter," he said. "What matters is that you lied to me. What I want to know now is how many more lies were piled on top of that one."

Silence.

"Tell me none," he said.

"I can't do that. I'm sorry, Bryson, I really am. I didn't mean for things to get like this."

The line went dead.

TWO MINUTES LATER, THE DOOR opened.

London stuck her head in, saw Wilde was alone, and ran to him. She wrapped her arms around his body and laid her head on his chest. Her blood trembled. Her breath was quick. She wore the same clothes as last night.

"I thought you were dead," she said.

"What happened?"

"Nothing, that's the problem. The taxi guy dropped me off at the phone booth but the call never came," she said. "I waited an hour. Then a car stopped on the opposite side of the street. I ran. I didn't wait to find out what was about to happen."

Wilde rubbed her back.

"It's okay."

"I was too scared to go home," she said. "I went to your house. You never showed up. I figured you were dead."

Wilde shook his head.

"I almost was. He took a shot but not a good one. I drove all over the damn city looking for you," he said. "Then I waited outside your house."

She exhaled.

"Do you think he killed Alexa?"

"I'm positive he did, unless he was smart enough to figure out the map was a fake," he said. Hearing the words out loud elevated his thoughts to a new level. "That's what we need to do. We need to tell him it was a fake."

"How?"

"I don't know. I don't know anything anymore." A beat, then "Dayton River has some kind of connection to this guy. Alabama has River's place staked out. If the guy shows up, maybe we can communicate with him—tell him he's got a fake."

London pulled back and looked into Wilde's eyes.

"Why don't we just tell River to give the guy the message?"

Wilde considered it.

He'd been hoping to ambush the guy.

The problem now was time.

Time was critical.

He lit a pack of matches on fire and watched the flames.

"Even if we get the message to him, he'll think it's a trick. He'll probably think we're just trying to draw him out."

"We'll get the real one back from Bluetone," she said. "Then we'll tell him what the problem was. The story's the truth and he's got to recognize it. It's too convoluted to make up."

"Maybe, maybe not."

Wilde paced.

"The other option is to wait and hope he shows up," he said. "I'm tired of him being the one in control."

119

DAY FOUR
JULY 24, 1952
THURSDAY MORNING

WAVERLY CALLED THE CHICAGO INVESTIGATOR, Drew Blackwater, to see if he'd found out anything about Bristol or the tattoo guy who broke into Waverly's apartment. It turned out that he had.

"The guy you described with the scar and tattoo—the one I thought sounded vaguely familiar—he's been around town before," he said.

"Really?"

"Really."

"You got a name?"

"Not yet," Blackwater said. "What I have is a bartender who remembers him. That's all."

"Did you check the hotels?"

"Yes, for him and Bristol. Nada on both of them."

"Can you keep digging?

"I can, but the bill's racking up."

"I'm good for it, I promise."

Silence.

"Where can I contact you?"

"You can't."

"Then call me in a couple of hours."

"Thanks." She almost hung up but pulled the phone back and said, "Drew, you still there?"

He was.

"When did that bartender see the tattoo guy?"

"He wasn't certain, but it was a ways back," he said. "More than a year."

"Two years?"

"Possibly."

"August of '50?"

"Possibly."

"So he's the one."

"We don't know that."

"Well, he certainly could be the one."

"I'll give you that much," he said. "Maybe he works for this Bristol guy."

"Maybe."

"Can I give you a piece of advice?"

"No."

He laughed.

"Good, because here it comes. Let it go. That's my advice, let it go."

"Some day."

"If you don't, it will kill you," he said. "Either from the inside or the outside, but one or the other for sure."

"I'll call you later today. Have something for me."

WAVERLY'S STOMACH GROWLED AND SHE ended up at a ratty diner with a plate full of meatloaf and mashed potatoes in front of her and a glass of milk at the side.

She needed to check in with the boss man, Shelby Tilt, but couldn't.

If he had any idea how deep she was, he'd pull her off faster than he'd yank her panties down if she ever gave him half a chance.

His cigar-stained face was best left in the dark for right now.

Clouds were building up outside.

Their bellies were black.

A storm was coming.

WHEN SHE GOT BACK TO her hotel, Su-Moon was sitting on the sidewalk, leaning against the building with her knees hugged up.

"Big news," Su-Moon said. "I just called my investigator back in Cleveland to see if he had anything else for me. It turns out that Bristol wasn't just in town the exact same day as when that woman—Bobbi Litton—got dropped off a roof, but there was a piece of paper in her purse that said:

"Tom.B.

"Monday, 1:00

"Euclid and 9th

"Tom B has to stand for Tom Bristol. Do you understand what I'm saying? He actually knew the woman. He was in town to meet her about something."

"How did the PI find that out?"

"He has connections down at the police department," Su-Moon said. "He called and asked if the name Bristol ever came up in the Bobbi Litton investigation. It didn't specifically, but they had this mysterious Tom B. note that never made any sense."

Waverly wrinkled her brow.

"The blond with Bristol, Jaden, had an interesting theory," she said. "She said someone might be setting Bristol up. If that's true, maybe he planted the note in the woman's purse. Jaden's running it down this afternoon. I'm going to meet her at four."

Su-Moon looked at the sky.

296 · R.J. JAGGER

"I thought it was supposed to be sunny in Denver," she said. "I can get this back in San Francisco." A beat, then "If someone was going to set Bristol up, don't you think they would have used his name instead of Tom B.?"

True.

Very true.

"I want to run it down anyway," Waverly said.

"We already know the answer. Bristol's the one."

"I need to be a hundred percent certain," Waverly said. "I don't want any second thoughts creeping into my life after I do what I'm going to do."

"Which is what?"

"Which is something serious."

Waverly must have had a tone in her voice, because Su-Moon backed off a half step and studied her.

"You're going to kill him?"

"Let's put it this way," she said. "If he stays on the streets, someone else is just going to end up dead."

Su-Moon shook her head.

"Let the police handle it."

"With what evidence?"

"What do you mean, with what evidence? With all of it."

"All of it is basically nothing," Waverly said. "There isn't enough at any one place."

120

DAY FOUR
JULY 24, 1952
THURSDAY MORNING

RIVER EXERCISED OUTSIDE WITH HIS shirt off, occasionally pulling in the industrial area with his peripheral vision to verify that the woman with the binoculars was still in place. January ought to be getting close. In hindsight, River should never have let her go. She was armed but the other woman might be too.

He worked through the pain of one final set of seventy-five pushups, then wiped his brow with the back of his hand and headed inside.

Thunder rolled through his veins.

He pulled the roof in with the binoculars.

The woman wasn't visible.

She was in her down position.

He kept the scene in sight, ready to dart to the side at the first sign of a head popping up.

"Whoever you are, you're going down."

Suddenly there was movement. Two figures were fighting, standing chest to chest and pounding each other in the face.

They dropped.

Seconds passed.

River ran outside and took the ladder to the top of the boxcar, hoping to get a line of sight over the parapet. It didn't work. Whatever was happening was out of view.

Come on.

Come on.

Come on.

Then a partial silhouette of a figure appeared, not frantic, not fighting, but visibly shaking. Then the figure stood upright and turned around.

It was January.

She looked directly at the boxcars and waved her arms.

That was it.

That was the signal.

River dropped the binoculars and ran that way, cutting across abandoned tracks and knee-high weeds, trying to not step on anything that would jack-up his foot.

WHEN HE GOT TO THE building, January was waiting for him at street level. Her face was a mess, her hair was disheveled, her shirt was ripped, her arm was scraped.

"Where's the woman?"

"She's up on the roof," January said. "She's dead."

"Dead?"

"Yeah, dead. We ended up in a fight. It was her fault. She's the one who started it." A beat then, "So what do we do now, just leave her there, or dump her somewhere?"

River weighed it both ways.

"We'll dump her. Go get the car, I'll bring her down."

UP ON THE ROOF, RIVER recognized the body. It was that woman who worked with Bryson Wilde. He picked her up, flung her over his shoulder, and carried her down to street level. January was already there, waiting for him with the car.

River looked around.

No one was in sight.

He dumped the body in the trunk and slammed the lid.

Then they got the hell out of there.

121

DAY FOUR
JULY 24, 1952
THURSDAY MORNING

WILDE COULDN'T THINK. THE SOUND of Secret hanging up was a noise in his head he couldn't quiet. Whatever relationship they had was either over or dangerously close to it. He didn't want it to be, but if it was, he wanted to at least know for sure one way or the other.

"I have to make a run," he told London.

"To where?"

"To see a woman."

"With everything that's going on?"

"Yes." He grabbed his hat and tilted it over his left eye. "Come with me. You can wait in the car. You'll be safer there than here."

"Okay."

Ten minutes later, he rapped on Secret's hotel door, expecting the usual, namely no answer. This time was different. This time the door opened.

"I thought we had something," Wilde said.

She turned.

"Come in."

He followed, shutting the door.

"I know you're a model," he said. "I know you're big-time."

"Look, Bryson—"

"Tell me what's going on," he said. "Tell me if I fell in love with the wrong woman."

"You didn't fall in love with anyone, Bryson."

"I'll be the judge of that."

He waited.

She studied his eyes.

Her face softened.

"I'm not who you think I am," she said.

"I already know that."

"No, I'm not talking about my name, I'm talking about inside, in my heart."

"What's that supposed to mean? I don't get it—"

"What I mean is that I did something," she said. "Something that was wrong."

"I don't care," he said. "I do something wrong every day."

"I don't mean like that," she said. "I mean something serious."

He frowned.

"Tell me."

She walked to the window and looked out, keeping her face away.

"It was in August of 1950, about two years ago," she said. "It happened in Chicago. I was there on a photo shoot. My manager was with me. His name is Sam Lenay. He was in trouble. I did something to help him. At the time I did it, I didn't realize exactly what I was doing."

"Did what?"

"I played a role," she said.

Wilde lit a cigarette, took a deep drag and blew smoke.

"You're confusing the hell out of me," he said. "I don't have a clue what you're talking about."

"I seduced someone," she said. "I did it for Sam, to get him out of trouble."

"I don't care who you slept with."

"It's not about sleeping with someone, Wilde. It's about doing something that makes them end up dead."

Wilde stopped a puff halfway through.

He pulled the cigarette from his lips.

"What are you saying? Are you saying that you killed someone?"

She exhaled.

"Yes," she said. "More than one."

THE PIECES DIDN'T FIT.

He didn't care.

He wasn't interested in the pieces anymore.

He turned her around, took her in his arms, and pulled her tight.

"I don't know who you are and I don't care what you did," he said. "I do know one thing though. I know that I don't want to lose you before I even really have you."

122

DAY FOUR
JULY 24, 1952
THURSDAY AFTERNOON

SU-MOON STEPPED BACK, ALMOST AS if pushed in the chest by Waverly's words, and said, "I can't believe you're even talking about killing someone. If that's your goal, count me out. I'm all for doing whatever it takes to get this guy off the streets—I think I've already proved that—but I'm not going to turn myself into one of his kind to do it. You shouldn't either. I can't believe we're even having this conversation."

Waverly lowered her eyes to the ground.

Then she looked up.

"I had a sister," she said. "Her name was Carmen Key. In August of 1950, she was murdered. Someone dressed her up in a red dress and dropped her off a roof. It happened in Chicago."

"I had no idea."

"No way you would," Waverly said. "The police got nowhere. I hired a private investigator, a man named Drew Blackwater, who didn't get much further than the police, but did get something. He found out that a woman named Emmanuelle LeFavre was in the vicinity at the time it happened. Emmanuelle in turn remembered seeing Carmen with a man that evening. They were entering the alley that ran alongside the building. She got a glimpse of the man. It wasn't a good one, but it was at least something."

"Okay."

"I flew to Chicago and met with her," Waverly said. "She felt my pain. She agreed to help me in any way she could. The police didn't know about her. She didn't want to get involved with them. She thought they weren't confidential enough. She thought that if the guy found out there was a witness, he'd be able to get that person's name."

"Through a bribe?"

Waverly nodded.

"A bribe, a leak, whatever," she said. "I agreed to keep her identity secret and not tell the police about her. She spent two weeks combing the city on foot, hoping to run into the guy by blind luck. Their paths never crossed."

"Too bad."

"RIGHT, TOO BAD," WAVERLY SAID. "She was a model from New York. She returned home. Meanwhile, my investigator, Drew Blackwater, kept pressing forward. He came up with a second piece of information. He found out that another woman—a lady by the name of Brittany Pratt—had been killed in an identical manner exactly one year before Carmen, meaning August 1949."

"In Chicago?"

"No, in New York," Waverly said.

"Where Emmanuelle lived."

"Right," she said. "I flew there, hired a local private investigator, and stayed with Emmanuelle for three weeks, trying to get a lead on that prior murder."

"Because the same guy did both."

"Exactly," Waverly said. "That turned out to be a waste of time. In the end, we got nothing, no witnesses, no leads, no motives, no nothing."

"Damn."

"The hardest part about it was that I knew that there was something there somewhere to be found. We just never found it."

"So what'd you do?"

"Well, I figured if there were two, maybe there were three," she said. "My Chicago investigator—Blackwater—actually came up with another victim, a woman named Geneva Robertson who was murdered in Las Angeles in March of 1950. Again, the woman was dropped off a roof wearing a red dress."

"So August wasn't set in stone."

"No, now we had two in August and one in March," Waverly said. "I did the same as before, flew to Los Angeles, hired a local investigator, the whole bit. Emmanuelle met me there."

"That's quite a friend."

"That's putting it mildly," Waverly said. "She paid all the bills, too. She had the money, from her modeling. I had hardly anything. She paid for the plane tickets, the hotels, the investigator fees, everything. In the end, though, it was a giant waste of time. We didn't get anything useful."

"Damn."

WAVERLY GRABBED SU-MOON'S HAND. "COME on, let's walk," she said. They headed for 16th Street, where the buzz was. "Last weekend, we had a similar murder in Denver. My boss, Shelby Tilt, saw it as a big story, not because it was a murder, but because he was personally aware of a similar murder that had happened out in San Francisco when he worked there," she said.

"Meaning Kava Every."

"That was the first I'd heard about a fourth victim, fifth actually, if you count the one in Denver," Waverly said.

"Did you tell Tilt about everything you already knew?"

"No."

"Why not?"

"Because I knew from the start of all this that I might have to personally kill the guy if there wasn't enough information to take to the police," Waverly said.

"So you've had revenge in mind from the start."

"Yes, if by revenge you mean justice," Waverly said. "My goal is to ruin this guy's life and get him off the streets. If that can be done through the cops, then great. That's my route of choice. If it has to be done through alternative means, though, then I'm prepared to do that as well."

Su-Moon let the corner of her mouth turn up.

"Don't let me get on your bad side."

Waverly frowned.

"You know, from the beginning I've really had no second thoughts about killing the guy if it came to that," she said. "Now that I'm getting close, I'm not so sure I'm up for it."

"What we need to do is figure out a way to trap him," Su-Moon said.

"How?"

"I don't know. There must be a way, though, if we think hard enough."

THEY WALKED IN SILENCE.

"Why didn't Emmanuelle meet you in San Francisco? Is she dropping out?"

"No, she's playing a role."

"What does that mean?"

"It means we had two murders to cover at the same time," Waverly said. "I went to San Francisco, Emmanuelle came to Denver."

"She's here?"

"Yes."

"What's she doing?"

"She hired a dick named Bryson Wilde to investigate the murder here," Waverly said.

"Why would he take the case?" Su-Moon said.

"Money."

"I know, money; what I'm saying is, why wouldn't he scratch his head and say, *What's your interest in all of this? What do you care about who killed someone?*"

"Okay, I see what you mean," Waverly said. "She made up a cover."

The words hung.

"Which is what?"

"Which is she pretended like she saw it from a distance, pretty much like what actually happened to her in Chicago. She's hoping that the investigator will crack it. If that happens, her plan is to view the guy from a distance, without him knowing it, and see if he's the same guy she saw in Chicago."

Silence.

"If she saw him back in Chicago, maybe he saw her too."

Waverly nodded.

"That's possible. So?"

"So, what if he sees her by some random happening while he's out walking around?" Su-Moon said. "What if that happens and she doesn't know it happened?"

THE CITY WAS FULL OF life.

Cars moved.

People moved.

Everything made its own special little noise.

Su-Moon stopped, then looked into Waverly's eyes. "Have you ever considered that maybe Emmanuelle is the killer?"

Waverly laughed.

"Good one," she said. "How do we trap Bristol? That's what I want to know."

Su-Moon grabbed Waverly's elbow.

"I'm serious," she said. "She was in the vicinity when Carmen got killed. After you found out about her, she got you to promise not to tell the police about her."

Waverly started to open her mouth.

Su-Moon cut her off.

"Hear me out," she said. "Another murder happened in New York, where she was—again. She paid all the bills for all the investigations, including the investigators themselves. Maybe that was her way of being sure they didn't find anything, or if they did, they only told her about it and not you."

Waverly wasn't impressed.

"We need to trap Bristol," she said. "That's what we need to focus on."

Su-Moon frowned.

"Maybe she's been tagging along not to help you but to be sure you don't get anywhere," Su-Moon said.

"Stop it."

"I'm just saying—"

"And I'm saying I heard you," Waverly said. "So stop saying. Enough's enough. Emmanuelle didn't kill anyone. She couldn't hurt a fly."

123

DAY FOUR
JULY 24, 1952
THURSDAY AFTERNOON

FIFTEEN MILES WEST OF DENVER, where the flatlands collide with the Rockies, a frothing whitewater river snakes out of the mountains into Clear Creek Canyon. Next to the river is a twisty, dangerous road. With a dead body in the trunk, River took that road west between vertical rock walls, deeper and deeper into the mountains.

Ten miles into it, he turned right on 119.

Eight miles later, an abandoned road appeared on the left. The mouth was barely recognizable as something other than overgrown vegetation.

The guts of the road disappeared over a jagged ridge into thick lodgepole pines.

River headed down it.

He hadn't been this way in years.

Five miles down that road was a long-abandoned gold mine, filled with thirty or more dangerous vertical shafts that disappeared straight down into the belly of the world.

River used to come here as a kid.

He and Butch Bannister would dare each other to jump over the shafts. Some were narrow and easy. Others were a whole different world.

River pulled next to one of the wider shafts and stepped out of the car.

The thin mountain air was ten degrees cooler than Denver, maybe fifteen.

With the clouds and the wind, it was almost cold.

He opened the trunk and pulled the body out, tipping it over the lip and letting it drop to the ground with a thud. He grabbed the feet and dragged it toward the hole, stopping two yards short.

He looked at January.

"I'll bet she's not the first to be dropped down here," he said. "I'll bet she lands on ten more just like her."

"Be careful. Don't get too close."

"Don't worry," he said. "I used to play here as a kid."

He got behind the body and pushed it with his foot, closer and closer to the opening, then in.

The body banged against the sides on the way down.

It was a familiar sound.

River had dropped five hundred rocks down the shafts.

The sound was always the same.

In spite of the chill, his brow was moist. He wiped it with the back of his hand and looked around.

The world was silent.

Not a sound came from anywhere.

"She's in China," he said. "There's one thing we don't have to worry about, and that's anyone ever finding her."

JANUARY WRAPPED HER ARMS AROUND him.

"I'm sorry we had to do this."

River shrugged.

"It was her fault," he said. "She was the one who got all fancy with the binoculars. She's the one who fought back when she shouldn't have. Screw her. She got what she deserved."

January picked up a rock and threw it in the shaft.

"What'd you do here as a kid?"

"What do you mean?"

"You said you used to come and play here as a kid. What did you do?"

"We jumped over the shafts."

January smiled.

"No way."

"Yeah, I'm serious," River said.

"Show me."

"Show you?"

"Yes."

He tilted his head.

"And what's my reward, if I do?"

"Whatever you want."

"Be careful, because there won't be any take-backs."

"Stop stalling and show me."

River looked around. There were a good dozen shafts in sight, all smaller than the one in front of him, which was somewhere in the neighborhood of three good-sized steps, ten or eleven feet.

"This one will do," he said.

"Go for it."

He walked back, judged the distance until it burned into his brain, then sprinted for it with everything he had. At the very last inch of ground, he planted a foot and then catapulted his body high and twisting, not in a way to land on his feet, only in a way to clear the mark.

He landed on the other side with a thud and rolled.

He got up, brushed the dirt off his pants, and walked toward January with a grin.

"I never did that one before," he said. "It always scared me too much as a kid."

"Looks like you're growing up."

"Anything I want," he said. "That was the bet."

"That's right."

"Get in the back seat of that car."

"Yes, sir."

124

DAY FOUR
JULY 24, 1952
THURSDAY AFTERNOON

THE CLOUDS THICKENED AND DROPPED lower. Ordinarily they had the same effect on Wilde as sunshine did, except in the opposite direction. Right now he could care less about them. Things were good between him and Emmanuelle. They were on solid ground again. They had a future.

London was waiting for him in Blondie.

"You look like you just got laid," she said.

Wilde lit a cigarette.

"No one can tell that just by looking at another person's face."

"I wasn't looking at your face."

She cast her eyes down.

He followed them.

His fly was open.

He zipped up, cranked over the engine, and squeezed into traffic. They went to the office to see if Alabama had taken a taxi over from her post at River's.

She hadn't.

The place was empty.

Nor had she been there; everything was the same.

Wilde scratched his head.

"Okay, here's the deal. You stay here. Keep the door locked. There's a gun in the top drawer of the desk. If anyone forces their way in, shoot first and ask questions later."

He headed for the door.

"Where are you going?"

"To see Alabama first," he said. "If the guy showed up at River's, we'll try to track him. If he hasn't shown up, I'll have to decide whether to go to River and give him the message that the map's a fake."

"We still don't have the real one."

"We'll get it by tonight."

"How?"

"I don't know," he said. "One thing at a time."

"Crockett has it."

"I know."

"I'll get it from him while you're gone," London said.

"No, just stay here. I already have enough to worry about."

"I just can't sit here," she said. "I won't."

Wilde recognized the look in her eyes. He got the gun from the drawer and handed it to her.

"Where do I carry it?"

Good question.

Her purse was gone.

Wilde grabbed a paper bag out of the cupboard.

The gun went inside.

TWENTY MINUTES LATER, HE WAS on the roof of the abandoned warehouse with a white paper bag in his left hand. Inside that bag was a grilled cheese sandwich, a pack of peanut butter crackers, and a chocolate bar. In his other hand was a bottle of RC.

Alabama wasn't there.

"Alabama."

No answer.

He checked behind the vent just to be sure she hadn't fallen asleep back there.

She hadn't.

She wasn't there.

He headed back into the building to see if she was taking a leak somewhere.

"'Bama!"

No answer.

She must have headed over to the BNSF office.

Wilde headed back to the roof to have a quick peek at River's place. As he got closer to the parapet, he spotted the binoculars sitting on the ledge.

That was strange.

Then he saw something even stranger.

Alabama's purse was over by the heating unit.

He opened it up and rummaged through. It was hers, all right. She must be around somewhere.

"Alabama!"

Silence.

He leaned over the parapet and checked the ground to see if she'd fallen off.

She wasn't down there.

HE CHECKED EVERYWHERE.

She wasn't there, not on the roof, not inside the building, not even in the area around it.

Wilde went back to the roof and pulled in River's place with the binoculars.

It was empty.

The doors were shut.

His car was gone.

125

DAY FOUR
JULY 24, 1952
THURSDAY AFTERNOON

BRISTOL'S LITTLE BLOND SQUEEZE JADEN didn't show up for the four o'clock meeting in the alley. Waverly paced and checked her watch every five seconds. Where was the woman? Was she just late, or not coming at all? Ten after the hour came and went. At a quarter after, Waverly left.

On her way out, she encountered Jaden coming from the opposite direction.

They headed to the back of the building.

"Sorry I'm late," Jaden said. "I zigzagged around. I wanted to be absolutely sure no one was following me."

Her words were laced with stress.

"What's wrong?"

"Bristol's the killer," she said. "There's no question in my mind."

"Did he confess it?"

"No," Jaden said. "But when I started to bring up Cleveland, he said he'd never been there. It wasn't so much what he said but the way he said it. The more I talked about it, the more agitated he got."

"So he was hiding it."

"More than hiding it, trying to deflect it," Jaden said. "I might have pressed it too far. By the time I was done, I had the feeling that he knew that I knew something. He knew that I was probing him. When he looked at me, it was like an alligator looking at a frog."

"It's time to run."

"That's what I'm doing," Jaden said. "I'm doing it right now, as we speak. I'm never going back."

Waverly exhaled.

"Good."

"I'm going to take a cab to the airport and just fly somewhere."

"Where?"

She shrugged.

"I don't know. Not San Francisco, that's for sure."

"That's a good plan."

THEY WALKED OUT OF THE alley, hugged goodbye at 16th Street, and headed in opposite directions.

This was good.

If nothing else positive came of everything that had taken place, at least Jaden wouldn't be the next statistic.

Suddenly someone tapped Waverly on the shoulder.

It was Jaden.

"You're still going after him, aren't you?"

Waverly nodded.

"Yes."

"I should help."

"No, you shouldn't."

"Yes, I should. Don't get me wrong, I'm scared, but I owe you something for saving my life."

Waverly retreated in thought.

"I need a way to trap him," she said. "Do you have any bright ideas?"

126

DAY FOUR
JULY 24, 1952
THURSDAY AFTERNOON

WILDE WOULDN'T BE EASY TO kill. River knew that and knew it well. What he needed was a plan where Wilde would never see it coming, never have a chance to react, and in fact wouldn't even know it happened. He'd be alive one second and dead the next.

Something that fast meant a bullet to the brain.

It also meant River couldn't miss.

He'd have to be close.

As he drove back to Denver with January at his side, the mountain topography was every bit as spectacular as he remembered. He really needed to get up here more.

January put her hand on his knee.

"You're thinking about something," she said.

He was.

He was indeed.

"I have to do something tonight," he said.

"What?"

"Something that you're not going to be involved in."

"What if I want to be?"

He shook his head.

"Sorry, not this time."

"That's not fair."

He tossed his hair and looked at her sideways, then gave her a peck on the lips. "Tomorrow we're leaving Denver."

"To where?"

"I don't know yet," he said. "I have some money stashed away. It's more than enough to give us time to think."

"Think about what?"

"About getting normal," he said.

She laughed.

"Normal is boring."

"I'm not talking about totally normal," he said. "Just enough that we don't have to keep looking over our shoulder all the time."

THE ROCKY MOUNTAIN SCENERY ROLLED by, seriously riveting. When they got to the outskirts of Denver, River didn't go home. Instead, he turned south on Santa Fe.

"Where we going?"

"A graveyard."

"Are you serious?"

Yes.

He was.

"Why, who's there?"

"No one, yet."

"What's that mean?"

"It means it won't officially be a graveyard until tonight," he said.

She ran her fingers through his hair.

"You couldn't get normal if your life depended on it."

He smiled.

"You're probably right."

"There ain't no *probably* about it."

127

FROM THE WAREHOUSE, WILDE CHECKED the BNSF office to see
if Alabama had shown up there, which she hadn't. When he got back
to the office, she wasn't there either. He paced next to the windows
with a cigarette for all of one minute before the door opened.

London stepped in.

Her face was beautiful but serious.

She put a piece of paper on his desk.

"That's the original map," she said.

Wilde picked it up.

Compared to the two he'd seen previously, this one really did look
authentic. It had dirt smudges on it, reddish in color, not indigenous
to Colorado.

"How'd you get it away from Bluetone?"

The woman lowered her eyes.

"I'm going to tell you something and you're going to hate me," she
said. "I had it all along."

The words slowly sunk in.

"Are you telling me you had this last night when we were busy giving
the guy a fake?"

Her eyes met his briefly then darted away.

"Yes."

Wilde pounded his fist on the desk.

"That little trick may have cost Alexa Blank her life."

"I know," she said. "That's why it's here now."

Wilde looked at her in disbelief.

"Is this really the original?"

"Yes," she said. "No more tricks."

Wilde studied it again.

"It's time for you to leave," he said.

"Wilde—"

"I'll handle it from here."

"But—"

"Go! Do it now before I say something I'd rather not."

She gave him a short look, then walked out the door and closed it gently behind her. Wilde set a pack of matches on fire and lit a cigarette from the flames. From the window he watched London disappear down the street.

128

DAY FOUR

JULY 24, 1952

THURSDAY AFTERNOON

JADEN COULDN'T THINK OF A way to trap Bristol but did come up with an alternate thought. "What if he admits the murder?"

"You mean to you?"

"Yeah, say that, for starters."

"That's no good," Waverly said. "That's not evidence. Even if you told the police about it, they'd just assume there was some kind of lovers' quarrel at work. And even if they did believe it enough to sniff around a little bit, they wouldn't find enough corroborating evidence in the end. Meanwhile, while they were looking, Bristol would know about it. He'd disappear or lay a bribe or something."

Jaden didn't disagree.

"You said if we couldn't trap him, you'd kill him if you could be certain he was the killer," Jaden said. "Did you mean that?"

Waverly hesitated.

Good question.

"Yes," she said.

"Okay, then think about this," Jaden said. "The sky's filling up with clouds. It's going to rain tonight."

Waverly looked up.

That was true.

"I don't get where you're going."

"Here's where I'm going," Jaden said. "I'll rent a car. I'll drive Bristol to some remote place tonight after dark. When we get there, I'll tell him that I'm on to him but I don't care. I'll tell him I want to stay with him no matter what he did in his past. I'll tell him that I want him to share it with me, though."

Waverly shook her head.

"Even if he does, like I said, it's not evidence."

"Wait, let me finish," Jaden said. "What Bristol won't know is that you'll be there listening."

"How?"

"You and me will agree on the place beforehand," Jaden said. "I don't know Denver hardly at all, so I'll let you choose the place. You get there before we do and hide in the dark. After we get there, I'll roll a window halfway down, ostensibly to get some fresh air. Then I'll get Bristol talking. You creep up silently and listen in. Bring a gun. If Bristol confesses, you'll have your proof. You can shoot him."

Waverly receded in thought.

Then she looked at Jaden.

"Do you really think you can get him there, to a secluded place?"

Jaden nodded.

"He'll go for two reasons," she said. "One, he loves to make love in the car, especially in the rain. We've done it twenty times. Two, and more importantly, I'll tell him I want to talk to him someplace private. He'll go out of curiosity as to whether I know about his past or not. He'll see it as a chance to probe me. He'll also see it as a chance to kill me if he figures I know too much."

Waverly frowned.

"It's risky."

"So is crossing the street," Jaden said.

"They're not exactly the same."

She smiled, nervously.

"Maybe not, but what other option is there?" Silence, then she said, "Do you have a gun?"

"No."

"Then we need to buy one. We're going to need some cleaning products too, in case you end up shooting him while he's still in the car. I'm going to have to return it at some point. I think we should have a shovel, too. There's less likely to be a problem down the road if there's no body."

"You're serious about all this."

"I am," Jaden said. "All I ask is that you try not to let me die."

"I'll give it my best shot."

They shook hands.

129

DAY FOUR
JULY 24, 1952
THURSDAY AFTERNOON

WILDE WENT BACK TO THE warehouse and found no Alabama, not on the roof or anywhere else. He pulled River's place in with the binoculars to find it equally lifeless. He was pretty sure what had happened. If he was right, River would die a million deaths and not one of them would be pretty.

An hour came and went.

The sky got meaner.

The clouds turned into storm clouds, not spitting yet but building up a hellacious arsenal.

Wilde didn't move.

The map was in his shirt pocket. He didn't take it out, he didn't look at it, he didn't care about it.

Suddenly something happened.

A figure moved quickly toward the boxcars.

It wasn't River.

It was a man with a scar on his face and a tattoo on his forearm. Wilde's chest pounded. This had to be the man from last night. Wilde raced through the guts of the building down to ground level and headed directly across the tracks and weeds and gravel toward his target. He made no effort to conceal himself.

The man saw him.

Wilde expected him to take cover and pull a gun.

That's not what happened.

The man stood there in the open and waited.

Wilde stopped two steps away.

"You're a bad shot," he said.

The man smiled.

"It happens."

Wilde hardened his face.

"I want the woman."

"Alexa?"

"Yes, Alexa. Where is she?"

"She's dead," the man said. "Don't look surprised. It's your fault. You broke the rules."

"The map you got is a fake," he said. "I have the original."

"Bullshit."

Wilde pulled it out of his pocket and tossed it on the ground.

"I want the woman."

The man bent down, slowly, keeping his face pointed at Wilde. He picked up the map and opened it. Then he looked at Wilde. "If this is a trick, I'll kill you and everyone you ever met."

"It's not a trick," Wilde said.

The man shrugged.

"I lied when I said she was dead. She's actually alive. You can have her. It's only fair."

WILDE EXPECTED THE MAN TO lead him off to the south to a car. Instead, he headed across the tracks to the north. Wilde fell into step.

"I'm Vaughn Spencer," the man said.

"Why would you tell me your name?"

"You're Bryson Wilde."

"How do you know that?"

"I have my ways."

"If the woman's dead, I'm going to kill you," Wilde said.

"You're going to try," Spencer said.

"There was no word 'try' in what I just said."

Spencer smiled.

"You got some balls, Wilde, I'll give you that."

THEY WALKED PAST THE WAREHOUSE Wilde had just come from and into a similar one a half block down. "Don't tell me you have her in there," Wilde said.

"Either that or I'm taking you in there to kill you," Spencer said.

Wilde didn't break stride.

The building was windowless.

In the back, a steel door was chained shut. Spencer pulled a key out of his pocket, got a padlock off, and pushed through the opening.

"River killed your little assistant," he said.

Wilde stopped.

"What'd you just say?"

"You heard me," he said. "He spotted her up there on the roof and sent his little tattoo shit of a girlfriend up there. The woman killed her. They threw her in the trunk of a car, to dump her would be my guess. I saw the whole thing."

Wilde pictured it.

He could hear the thump of Alabama's body dropping into the trunk. He could see the back end of the car dipping.

"How do I know you didn't kill her?" he asked. "How do I know you didn't see her over here, figure she was after you, and kill her yourself?"

Spencer grinned.

"Now that's something I hadn't thought of," he said. "You're right. You don't know. Maybe it happened just like that, for all you know. It's a bitch, isn't it?" He held out the key and dropped it into Wilde's hand. "The woman's up on the top floor."

He turned to leave.

He stopped and said over his shoulder, "Be sure she understands that she's not to go to the police. You too, for that matter. If that happens, I'll know. I always know."

He walked away.

Wilde pulled his gun.

"Hey, Spencer."

The man stopped and turned.

Wilde raised the barrel and pointed it at Spencer's chest.

"Why'd you tell me about Alabama? Just to watch me squirm?"

Spencer shook his head.

"My job is to kill River," he said. "Now I don't have to because you're going to do it. Have a nice life."

He turned and walked away.

"Hey, Spencer," Wilde shouted.

The man stopped again.

He turned.

"Why didn't you kill Alexa? You thought you had the real map—"

"That was going to happen this afternoon, right after I killed River," he said. "I was going to plant Alexa at River's place and make it look like he did it."

He turned and walked.

"What about London?" Wilde said.

Spencer stopped.

He tilted his head as if in thought.

"Tell her it's her lucky day. She's off the hook," he said. "You too, for that matter. Anything else?"

"No."

WILDE HEADED INTO THE BUILDING. It was windowless and the only light was the little bit that trickled through the door. That was enough to get him oriented to the stairway.

He headed over and felt his way up.

At the second floor, the light from the first floor disappeared altogether.

He continued up.

"Alexa Blank. Are you in here?"

There was no response.

He shouted louder.

"Alexa? Are you here?"

A muffled sound came from an upper floor, barely audible but recognizable as a voice, a female voice.

Wilde increased his speed.

"Alexa!"

"I'm up here!"

"I'm coming. I'm a friend—"

"Help me!"

"I'm coming. Just hold on."

"Please! Help me—"

130

DAY FOUR

JULY 24, 1952

THURSDAY NIGHT

THURSDAY NIGHT AFTER DARK, THE heavens let loose with a storm to end all storms. Mean heavy rain pummeled the earth with a monstrous rage. Lightning raked across the sky, one bolt after another, pushing explosive cracks of thunder across the world. Waverly took what cover she could with her back against a scraggly pinion pine, the same as she had for the past hour. She was at the upper turnout on the Lookout Mountain switchbacks west of Denver. Normally the million lights of the city played to the senses and brought the lovers here. Tonight not a single flicker cut through the weather. All the lovers were somewhere else, somewhere saner.

Tucked in her belt was a Smith & Wesson.

She put her hand under her T-shirt and ran her fingers over the handle.

The grip was rough, slip-resistant.

Su-Moon's words rang in her ears.

"Don't do this. If you do it, you can't undo it. It's forever."

That's what the woman said before she headed for the airport. That and "I don't want any part of this. I'll never tell anyone, you don't have to worry about that, but I won't be a part of it. You better be damn sure you have the right person, too. If you ask me, you should be taking a good hard look at Emmanuelle."

She got in the car.

It merged into traffic and disappeared.

That was late this afternoon.

Now it was 9:40 P.M.

If all went as planned, Jaden and Bristol would be showing up in the next twenty minutes.

Waverly pulled the gun all the way out, pointed it at the rocky cliff behind her, and pulled the trigger. A blast of yellow fire shot out of the barrel and the weapon kicked back, almost out of her hand.

Okay, good.

It worked.

She tucked it back in her waist.

The barrel was warm.

It felt good.

EMMANUELLE.

Emmanuelle.

Emmanuelle.

Could she really be the killer?

Was she really keeping tabs on Waverly instead of helping her? The more Waverly thought about it, the more it quivered up her spine. If she was going to kill Bristol, she needed to be absolutely sure he admitted to the killings and that the admission was unambiguous.

Suddenly lights snaked up the mountain from below.

Waverly wedged back into the rocks.

A car pulled into the turnoff, its front bumper against the boulders that had been placed there to keep cars from running off the edge.

The headlights went out.

The engine turned off.

Waverly stayed where she was.

No one got out of the car.

It was too dark to see who was inside.

She pulled the gun out of her waistband.

Then she crouched down and made her way slowly toward the back end of the vehicle, ending up on the passenger side, next to the tire. Suddenly the window rolled halfway down.

Waverly heard a woman talking.

The voice belonged to Jaden.

This was it.

Her chest tightened.

Her lungs hyperventilated.

She crept forward until she was next to the passenger door, staying down in case a bolt of lighting struck too close.

A man said, "Hold on a minute, I have to take a piss."

The voice belonged to Bristol.

The driver's door opened.

The vehicle rocked slightly as the man got out.

The door shut.

Waverly didn't move a muscle.

Bristol wouldn't go far, one or two steps away from the car at most. He'd piss, he'd get back in, and that would be it. Waverly concentrated on keeping down and not moving even an iota.

Suddenly the side of her head exploded in pain.

Lights flashed inside her skull.

Her legs gave out and she crumbled to the ground.

Gravel grabbed her cheek and bit in.

Then rough hands grabbed her, yanked her up, and threw her into the back seat. Before she could get her bearings, Bristol was in the front seat, twisted around, pointing a gun into her face.

"Surprise," he said.

His face was contorted, almost insane.

Waverly looked at Jaden.

The woman's face was cold.

It showed no compassion.

"I don't understand," Waverly said.

"It looks like I'm really not your friend after all," Jaden said. "It looks like you've been set up."

"No!"

Bristol swung his arm back and smacked Waverly on the side of the head.

"I gave you every chance to back off," he said. "You worked yourself into this corner. You don't have anyone to blame but your own stupid self."

WAVERLY FOUGHT THROUGH THE PAIN.

Think!

Think!

Think!

She reached into her back pocket with as little motion as she could and pulled out a knife. She unfolded it. Bristol was too far away.

Jaden was right in front of her, though.

Waverly grabbed the woman's hair, yanked her head back, and put the blade to her throat. Then she hardened her face and looked into Bristol's maniac eyes.

"Put the gun down!"

He smiled.

"You won't kill her."

"Yes, I will."

"Show me."

Jaden squirmed.

Waverly pulled harder on her hair and sank the blade deeper against her skin.

"I'll do it, I swear to God."

"Go ahead," Bristol said. "You'll save me the trouble."

"You're bluffing."

"Kill her," he said. "Do it." He brought the barrel of the gun up over the seat and pointed it at Waverly's face. She was trapped. There was no way she could get her hand out from around Jaden's neck and over to him. He'd be able to pull the trigger five times. "I'm going to count to three," he said.

"One."

Waverly couldn't move.

"Two."

She couldn't breathe.

She couldn't think.

She couldn't do anything.

"Three!"

The gun fired.

131

DAY FOUR

JULY 24, 1952

THURSDAY NIGHT

WILDE TOOK REFUGE FROM A violent storm under River's boxcar, waiting for the man to return. The rail yard was darker than death. A few city lights could be seen through the weather, but only as washed-out shells.

Wilde's heart was hard.

Alabama was dead.

River was the one who did it, him and his twisted little sidekick. Now it was time for them to pay the price. Screw the police, screw the courtrooms, screw the hundred little chances they would have to squirm their way out.

Wilde would never regret doing it.

He already knew that.

The only thing left to do at this point was to do it.

Headlights suddenly cut through the weather. Wilde crawled out and hugged the opposite side of the boxcar, then scurried around the vehicle from behind as it came to a stop.

He opened the back door, darted in and shoved the barrel into the back of River's head.

"You killed Alabama," he said.

"No, I didn't."

Wilde pointed the gun at the roof and pulled the trigger. The explosion was like a thousand lightning bolts striking the car. He smashed River's head with the barrel.

"You killed Alabama," he said.

January started to say something, but River said, "Shut up!" Then to Wilde, "Alabama's fine. We have her, that's true, but she's unharmed."

"Bullshit."

"That's the truth," River said.

"Where is she?"

"She's in a shed up in the mountains."

"Take me to her."

"Sure, let's go."

River shifted into first.

The vehicle pulled forward.

THEY HEADED WEST TO GOLDEN and then into Clear Creek Canyon. Wilde knew the area well. He used to kayak the river back when he was a kid.

"If she's dead, you're both dying," Wilde said.

"Fair enough."

"It won't be quick. I'm going to start with your kneecaps."

River chuckled as if amused by something.

"What's so funny?"

"Your timing is pretty good," he said. "Me and Gapp were going to kill you tonight."

"Why?"

"Why do you think? You've been snooping around that Charley-Anna Blackridge murder too much."

"Meaning you were afraid I was going to find out you were responsible sooner or later," Wilde said.

The storm pummeled down.

Vertical canyon walls were to their right, not more than a few feet off the edge of the road. To their left was a drop into the river.

"Actually, no," River said. "I didn't kill the woman. I suspect Gapp did, but I'm not sure. He was in the club with her that night."

"Gapp? Who's Gapp?"

"Gapp is Robert Gapp, Robert Mitchum's double."

Robert Mitchum.

Robert Mitchum.

Robert Mitchum.

"If you didn't do it and he did, then what do you care if I'm snooping around?"

River shrugged.

"Yeah, sure, I'll tell you, why not? We have to have a deal, though, right here, right now. You get your little assistant back safe and sound. Then you go your way and we go ours. You drop the investigation. You leave me and January alone. We leave you alone."

Wilde shook his head.

"No deals."

"That's the deal," River said. "Like it or not, that's the deal. If you don't take it, you can kill us. But I guarantee you that will be the death knell for your little friend. You won't find her in a million years. She'll rot to death. Hell of a way to go, don't you think?"

Wilde pictured it.

He said nothing.

"I kill people," River said. "That's my job. That's what I get paid to do. I came up with a plan several years ago that at least for the female victims, they'd all be killed the same way, namely put in a red dress and dropped off a roof."

"Why?"

"Because it was an MO," River said. "It was a signature. It would be looked at as the work of one person. I brought Gapp in as an accomplice several years ago and set up a system. One of us would do the abduction when the other one was someplace public with an ironclad alibi. Then the other one would do the dropping, when the first one was someplace public with an ironclad alibi. Beautiful, huh?"

"Yeah, real pretty."

"We spotted your little assistant on the roof with her binoculars," River said. "We took her so we could bait you into a trap and kill you. Now that's not necessary because we're going to agree to give her up and you're going to agree to lay off. Then again, maybe I'm lying. Maybe she's already dead and I'm drawing you up into the mountains to kill you, even as we speak." He chuckled. "Got you thinking, don't I?"

"Shut up. Don't say another word. You hear me?"

"Sure, no problem."

THEY DROVE IN SILENCE.

When the canyon ended, River turned right on 119, deeper into the mountains. Other than eerie snapshots of vague images brought to life by lightning bolts, the world was pitch-black.

Miles passed.

Then River slowed, almost to a crawl.

He kept that speed for more than two or three hundred yards and then said, "Bingo. There it is."

He turned left onto an abandoned road that was hardly there.

"What is this?"

"It's an ancient mining road," River said. "There was quite an operation up here back in the day. I used to come up here and play when I was a kid."

"How'd you get here?"

"Motorbike," he said. "I've been riding since I was eight. Where we're going is a few miles up. Have you ever been up here?"

"No."

"You're going to like it."

"She better be there," Wilde said.

"She is, don't worry."

Fifteen minutes later, River brought the vehicle to a stop and killed the engine.

"We're here." He turned to January and said, "You wait here."

"No," Wilde said. "You come with us."

They got out.

River got a flashlight and rope out of the trunk.

"What's the rope for?"

"I lied to you about the shed," River said. "She's down a shaft. We lowered her down on a rope. She's fine, but she's about twenty feet down. We'll need to pull her up."

Wilde pressed the barrel into River's back.

"Let's go."

THEY WALKED, SLOWLY, ONE FOOT at a time, with River sweeping the flashlight back and forth. There were lots of vertical shafts.

"Watch your step," River said.

The weather hammered down.

River flickered the light on a shaft about fifteen steps away. "That's the one. That's where she is."

Wilde's eyes followed the beam.

It was then that the side of his head exploded.

River's knuckles broke the skin wide open and made direct contact with Wilde's skull. Then the man's python hands were around Wilde's neck, viciously twisting it and forcing him to the ground.

The gun went off.

January screamed.

River turned and Wilde punched him.

Two bloody minutes later, Wilde was standing over River, training the gun down on the man's head. January was two steps away, holding a bleeding shoulder.

SUDDENLY WILDE HEARD A VOICE.

It was coming from the shaft to his left, not the one River had pointed out before.

"Don't move!"

He headed over and shined the light in.

Alabama was on a wooden beam, thirty feet down.

There was no rope around her chest or anywhere in sight.

"Are you okay?"

"Help me, Wilde! I'm losing it!"

Wilde walked over to River.

"You're going to go down and put a rope around her," he said.

"You're crazy," he said. "She's not even alive. She's dead."

Wilde fired the gun into the air.

"I'm not playing."

HE AND JANUARY LOWERED RIVER down on a rope to the beam.

"Do it!" Wilde shouted down.

River hesitated, then unwrapped the rope from around his chest and secured it around Alabama's. Wilde and January pulled her up.

She put Wilde into a bear hug.

FROM THE SHAFT, WILDE HEARD muffled words.

They came from River.

"Pull me out. Hurry up."

Wilde walked over and shined the flashlight down.

The beam wasn't very big.

"It was just an accident that Alabama landed on that," Wilde said. "You didn't even know it was there."

"I thought she was dead."

"No, you didn't," Wilde said. "You were burying her alive."

"That's not true. Pull me out. We had a deal."

"That's right," Wilde said. "The deal was you go your way and I'll go mine. So go your way. I'm not stopping you."

SUDDENLY ALABAMA WAS NEXT TO him.

"Wilde, you can't leave him there."

"He tried to kill you."

"I don't care. Don't do it."

He exhaled, deciding.

Suddenly a shape darted at them.

Wilde saw it in his peripheral vision.

It was January charging with stiff arms, intent on pushing Wilde or Alabama or both of them into the shaft.

He grabbed Alabama's waist and swung her to the ground.

The shape went over them.

Wilde grabbed January's ankle with his right hand.

Her momentum propelled her forward and her torso disappeared into the shaft. She pushed wildly against the shaft wall, screaming.

Wilde dragged her out.

She rolled away from the hole and curled up in a ball.

WILDE GRABBED THE ROPE, DROPPED it down to River, and said, "Tie it around your chest."

River didn't answer.

Wilde leaned over and shined the light down.

River was gone.

It wasn't clear if he'd lost his footing or whether a rock had fallen on him from January's commotion or something else had happened altogether. The only thing that was clear was that he was gone.

132

DAY SIX
JULY 26, 1952
SATURDAY NIGHT

WILDE LIKED THE NAME "SECRET" better than "Emmanuelle," so that's what he called her. Saturday night he took her to the Bokaray. She wore a short black dress and white panties. In her left hand was a glass of wine. In Wilde's was a double shot of whiskey, his third.

They had a table in the corner.

The dance floor was sardine-tight.

The band was good.

Perfume and cigarettes permeated the air.

Secret leaned close.

"I'm going to tell you something, but you have to promise not to repeat it," she said.

He shrugged.

"Whatever."

"It's sort of a completion of what I started to tell you the other day," she said. "It's about me and my agent, Sam Lenay."

"Right, him."

"River got his hooks into Lenay. To this day, I still don't know how, but he did. Lenay brought me into it to get a job done. My job was to seduce a woman named Carmen Key."

"Waverly's sister?"

She nodded.

"She was going to be in a bar that night," Secret said. "My job was to seduce her and get her to the roof of a certain building, supposedly to make out."

Wilde raised an eyebrow.

"Are you a lesbian?"

"No."

"Was she?"

"Yes," Secret said. "I did what I was told, to help Lenay. I got the woman to the roof, then slipped away." She took a drink of wine. "The next day, I found out she got put in a red dress and dropped off the roof. I didn't know that was going to happen. All I knew is that I was supposed to get her up onto the roof."

"Did you know someone would be up there waiting for her?"

"Not specifically, but I guess I assumed it. The dead woman's sister, Waverly, ended up coming to town. I made it my mission to help her, but I never told her my role in it. To this day she thinks that I was only a witness."

Wilde considered it.

"That's fair," he said. "You didn't know you were doing anything wrong when you did it. After it happened, you couldn't undo it. About the best you could do at that point was help her. What about Lenay? Certainly he knew who was behind it—"

"He claims he didn't," Secret said. "He was being blackmailed, but he didn't know by who."

"Blackmailed for what?"

"He'd never tell me," Secret said.

"WAVERLY ALMOST KILLED BRISTOL."

Wilde cocked his head.

"She couldn't kill anyone. She doesn't have what it takes."

"I'm glad you think so," Secret said. "She got suckered into a trap. At the last minute, right before Bristol was going to shoot her, Jaden shot him. She did it with Waverly's gun."

"Are you serious?"

"You can't tell anyone," she said.

"I won't."

"It happened in a rental car," she said. "They cleaned it up as good as new and turned it back in."

Wilde lit a smoke.

"So I guess that means they took Bristol's body out first."

"That's true. They buried him up in the mountains."

"Where?"

"I don't know and I don't want to know," Secret said.

"That's pretty intense."

"Jaden knew a lot of stuff about Bristol," Secret said. "His firm was bidding for a Hong Kong project. He was strong-armed. He was told to withdraw his bid or else a woman he was seeing would be killed."

"Strong-armed by who?"

"My guess is River," she said. "River working for one of the other bidders. Anyway, Bristol was a stubborn man. He didn't do it. Then it went down. His girl—a woman named Kava Every—was killed. She was dropped off a roof in a red dress."

"That's River."

"River or Gapp," Secret said. "Anyway, it wasn't until then that Bristol took it seriously. He withdrew the bid before anyone else got killed."

"So Waverly almost killed an innocent man."

"Not entirely," Secret said. "Bristol killed a woman in Cleveland, a woman named Bobbi Litton. He did it for Jaden. He did it the red-dress way, to make it look like a copycat."

"Damn."

"Right, damn," Secret said. "Anyway, Jaden was indebted to him. When Waverly started closing in on Bristol, Jaden was his spy. She drew Waverly into a trap. The only thing that went wrong is that

Bristol turned on Jaden at the last second. If he hadn't done that, he'd still be alive today."

"Interesting."

"Jaden told all this to Waverly after the fact. That's how I know: she told me."

WILDE DOWNED HIS DRINK AND set the empty glass on the table.

"I'm going to get a refill," he said. "You want another wine?"

She nodded.

"That'd be nice."

He got up, then leaned down and got his lips close to her ear.

"While I'm gone, I want you to think about whether you have any more secrets to tell me. I want everything on the table."

She smiled.

"Sure."

She watched him disappear into the crowd. Then a memory grabbed her, a memory exactly one week old, a memory so vivid and clear that it was as if she was really there.

—–—

The night was cool.

She was in Denver to visit with Waverly. They'd been to the El Ray Club and had more alcohol in their guts than was healthy.

The night was over.

They were walking down the street.

"I got to pee," Waverly said. "Wait here."

She ducked into an alley.

"Are you really going to do that?"

"Just hold on. I'll only be a minute."

"I can't believe you sometimes."

It was then that Secret needed a cigarette and needed it now. She checked her purse. It was empty. Waverly didn't smoke.

Cars were parked on the street, one after another.

Traffic was thin to nonexistent.

No one was around.

Secret started checking out the dashboards of the cars on the off chance someone had left a pack sitting around. The fourth car down, she spotted a pack. The door was locked but the window was rolled down a ways. It was tight, but she got her arm in. Then she brought her body all the way against the car to get an extension. The pack was at the end of her fingertips. She couldn't get it. She pulled her arm out, frustrated, then spotted a rock. She broke the window, reached in and grabbed the pack.

Then she heard a voice.

"Hey, that's my car!"

She turned.

The words came from a woman.

The woman was alone.

She was drunk.

"I'm just borrowing a smoke," Secret said. "I'm sorry. I'll pay for the window. I shouldn't have done that."

"Damn right you shouldn't have done that."

The woman charged.

Fists flew.

Then a head slammed into the curb.

It was the head of the other woman.

She lay there, sprawled out, not moving.

Waverly ran over.

"What the hell's going on?"

"She wouldn't stop, I tried to stop—"

Waverly kneeled down and checked the woman. She felt no pulse. She detected no movement of her chest. She brought her face close to the woman's mouth and detected no movement of air.

Then she stood up and said, "She's dead."

They stood there for a few heartbeats, frozen, then ducked into the alley.

No cars came.

No people came.

They dragged the body into the alley, back far, way into the deepest shadows.

"Here's what we'll do," Waverly said. "I have a red dress at home. I'm going to go get it. You stay here. Then we're going to take her to the roof and drop her off."

"Why?"

"Because then you didn't kill her," she said. "The guy who killed my sister killed her."

THEY GOT THE BODY TO the roof, made sure the woman was dead, changed her into the red dress and dropped her off. They disposed of her clothes in a dumpster three blocks away.

"There's a PI in town by the name of Bryson Wilde," Waverly said. "Tomorrow, what you need to do is hire him. Pretend you're a witness to the murder. Pretend that the guy who did the killing may have seen you. Pretend that you're in danger. Pretend that you want Wilde to find out who the killer is."

"Why? I don't get it."

"Because Wilde will have a pipeline into what the police are finding out," Waverly said. "If they start getting close, Wilde will know it, then we'll know it."

Secret exhaled.

"Okay."

———

WILDE EMERGED FROM THE CROWD, set a fresh glass of wine in front of Secret and slid in next to her.

"So, are there any more secrets I should know about?"

She looked like she was in thought.

Then she grabbed Wilde's hand, brought it under the table and set it on her leg above the knee.

"That's for you to find out," she said.

He inched his hand up.

"It looks like I have no alternative but to do a little exploring."

She opened her legs, just a touch.

"It looks that way."

ACKNOWLEDGMENTS

Thanks to all the fantastic people who played a part in making this happen. Special appreciation goes out to Tonia Allen, Carol Fieger, Dawn Seth, Kenneth Sheridan, Martha Stoddard, and Shannon Trout, as well as the wonderful people at Pegasus, and of course the extraordinary Noah Lukeman.